AUNT RACHEL'S FUR

AUNT RACHEL'S FUR

RAYMOND FEDERMAN

TRANSACTED FROM THE FRENCH BY
FEDERMAN AND
PATRICIA PRIVAT-STANDLEY

FC2
Normal/Tallahassee

Published by FC2 with support provided by Florida State University, the
Unit for Contemporary Literature of the Department of English at Illinois
State University, the Program for Writers of the Department of English at
the University of Illinois at Chicago, the Illinois Arts Council, the Florida
Arts Council of the Florida Division of Cultural Affairs, and the National
Endowment for the Arts.

Address all inquiries to: Fiction Collective Two, Florida State University,
c/o English Department, Tallahassee, FL 32306-1580

ISBN: Paper, 1-57366-093-0

Library of Congress Cataloging-in-Publication Data

Federman, Raymond.
  **Aunt Rachel's fur: novel improvised in sad laughter / by Raymond
Federman; transacted from the French by Patricia Privat-Standley
in collaboration with the author.-- 1st ed.**
    p. cm.
  ISBN 1-57366-093-0
  I. Privat-Standley, Patricia. II. Title.
  PS3556.E25 A95 2000
  813'.54--dc21
                              00-012026

Cover Design: Polly Kanevsky
Book Design: Adam Jones and Tara Reeser

Produced and printed in the
United States of America
Printed on recycled paper with soy ink

NATIONAL
ENDOWMENT
FOR THE ARTS

This program is
partially supported
by a grant from the
Illinois Arts Council

AUNT RACHEL'S FUR

RAYMOND FEDERMAN

a novel
improvised
in sad laughter

TRANSACTED

FROM THE FRENCH BY

FEDERMAN AND

PATRICIA PRIVAT-STANDLEY

Pour Patricia
qui a tout de suite pigé

**It comes to me in a flash
that something bad
is going to happen.**

Louis-Ferdinand Céline

**All that is written
is fictive.**

Stéphane Mallarmé

**What's the point of writing
your life if you can't
improve it a bit?**

Moinous

Tiens	Hey
si ce soir	why don't
j'écrivais un roman	I improvise a novel
en triste	tonight
fourire	in sad laughter
pour la postérité	for posterity
fichtre	damn
la belle idée	what a great idea
je me sens sûr de moi	I feel sure of myself
j'y vas	there I go
et	and
à	posterity
la	can
postérité	go
j'y dis merde et remerde	fuck
et reremerde	itself
drôlement feintée	posterity
la postérité	you've been had
qui attendait mon roman	if you waited for my novel
ah mais…	ah but…

[*merci raymond*]

OH YOU WANT TO KNOW WHY...

Oh so you want to know why I came back to this country, this stinking country, why after ten years, tennears over there, in Amerrr-ica, I decided to come back here...

Oh no, not for a vacation...

Tourism ... you must be kidding, not me, I hate monuments, they depress me, and here in La Belle France all their monuments, all their statues smell of the dead, how morbid...

No I didn't come back for that, and certainly not to see the family, well what's left of it, ah my family, what a bunch of bastards, cheaters, thieves, radins, all of them, aunts uncles cousins, wallowing in guilt and envy, everyone envious of the other, but I suppose it's like that with all families...

Used to be a large family, eight brothers and sisters on my mother's side, nine on my father's side, but on that side only three cousins left, the rest, all of them, remade into lampshades, but on mother's side, they all survived...

Except my...

No, I can assure you, it's not to say hello, coucou me voilà, here I am, still alive, that I came back to France after ten years over there, ten fucking years of stumbling from one misfortune to another...

Okay, so I could say I came back because I love Paris, ah Paree, the place in the world where humanity has reached the highest intellectual level, therefore it's here that one finds the highest form of suffering, in Paris one suffers from not suffering enough, but that's not the reason why I came back...

You have to understand, things were not going very well for me over there in America, you can say that again, not at all, no steady job, no place of my own, broke all the time, depressed, lonely, sad, homesick, lost in the great disenchantment of American reality, lost in the Walt Disney illusion...

Lonely, ah yes, lonely too, no real friends, nobody, and then one day, inevitably, kicked out from that crummy furnished room in the Bronx full of cockroaches, talk to me about American modernity, there wasn't even a fucking toilet in the room, it was down the corridor, and did it stink in there, eight bucks a week I was paying for that hole in the wall, that sad pathetic hole in the wall, in the Bronx...

Yes, thrown out of my apartment because I couldn't pay the rent, what could I do, always broke, no education, no profession, so all I could get were miserable temporary jobs, you think it's fun to be a dishwasher in filthy grease joints, I tell you, the shit that fell on me from all sides, yeah, talk to me about shit, I've seen it in all colors, all forms, shapes, textures, hard, soft, smelly, dégoulinante, parfumée, wait till you hear the rest of this story, you'll see the shit, and on top of that, the chick I was shacking up with dumped me, like I was a piece of shit, a burnt-out lightbulb...

We had a fight, about money, Susan was rich, that's her name, but American women who have money you cannot imagine how stingy they can be, and Susan she was loaded, she had inherited a million dollars, yes one million from an old aunt in Boston, can you believe that, I'm not exaggerating, one fucking million bucks, I was dumbfounded when she told me, I would have married her immediately if she'd let me, with all that dough we could have been so happy Susan and I...

Ah Susan, that's really her name, but me I always called her Sucette, you know Sucette, like a lollipop, because she always gave me fantastic blow jobs, I don't know where she learned, but I tell you, for a rich puritan American, a Wasp from Boston, Sucette when it came to sucking, wow...

What a fight we had, I had borrowed 50 bucks from her to pay my rent in the Bronx, but instead of paying the rent I lost the money in a poker game in Brooklyn, some dumb assholes I met in a bar, so I tried to borrow another 50 from Susan, and that's when we had that fight, she told me I was irresponsible, I'd never learn, you should have seen her face, when Susan gets angry, she's even more beautiful, more sexy, she told me I was irresponsible, that I had no sense of human relations, thatthaaat thaat thaat iiiiiaieaiiii, she was so angry she started stammering, she who always speaks so clearly, so correctly, wow was she beautiful, Susan, maybe a bit grassouillette, you know a bit too rounded, especially around the ass, but sexy like hell, with boobs like grapefruits, nice and firm, me I like them nice and firm, the skin, soft and milky, and eyes, big blue eyes which changed color whenever her moods changed, she has oceans of all colors in her eyes, sometimes calm, other times stormy, ah Susan, Susan, did she love to screw, yes, it's too bad, in a way we loved each other...

Okay, you see what a lousy situation I was in, really piss poor, alright, so I was writing, working on a novel, my first novel, and normally, I've been told, a guy is supposed to suffer when he writes a novel, and when it comes to suffering I own all the records...

My novel ... you want to know what it's about...

Alright, quickly, more or less the story of my life up to ... up to now, well, a version of my life, you know what I mean, it's hard to stick to the facts when the fever of recitation grabs you, one version among many possible others, somewhat distorted, exaggerated, accelerated, embellished, and greatly romanticized, what the hell, what's the point of writing your life if you can't improve it a bit, one can only tell the truth, I mean the real truth, with detours and lies, it's an old dictum, and besides, the only way a life can pass for literature is through exaggerations...

So, I was writing a novel, my first one, I was at it already two years when I decided to pack it in and get the fuck out of that stinking country...

Wow, was I fed up with America...

So, you want me to tell you more about the novel, okay just a few words, since you insist, it's the story of a guy who locks himself in a room for one year with boxes of noodles, 365 boxes to be exact, one per day, he calculates, to write a novel about a guy who locks himself in a room for one year with 365 boxes of noodles to write the story of his life, does that make sense to you...

Yes noodles, pasta ... you see the guy doesn't have much money, that's why he chooses noodles to write his novel, noodles are cheap and they keep forever, as you can see it's a story of survival, the guy swears not to come out of the room before he finishes his novel, and since he has very little dough, he decides that he will survive only on noodles, in his case it's okay because the guy loves noodles, like me, I adore noodles, give me a good portion of baked macaroni sprinkled with Parmesan cheese on top and I can last forever...

Well, enough of that, I'll tell you more about **A Time of Noodles** later...

Yes, that's the title of the book the guy is writing, **A Time of Noodles,** but now I want to tell you why I was fed up with America and why I dropped the damn place to come back to my ... my mother country...

You see what really bugged me over there was the reality of America, reality, my ass, you want me to tell you something, nobody gives a damn about reality, and you know why, because reality is always a disenchantment, la réalité c'est du bluff, I think it's Rimbaud who said that, reality is fake, or maybe it's somebody else, another mad poet, doesn't matter ... what makes reality fascinating at times, it's the imaginary catastrophe that hides behind it, especially behind the American reality, I could tell you a few things about the catastrophe of American reality, I know what I'm talking about...

Here let me tell you more about America and my misfortunes over there, ah the **U.S.A.** what a disaster, and for me, ten years of disaster, ten years of dégringolade, you want to know why I came back to Paris, I came back to see if I could start a new life, a quiet normal regular life, finish my novel, about the guy with the noodles, have it published by a good maison d'édition, and after that ... after that, we'll see, maybe find myself a cute sexy gonzesse who will make me happy, a nice girl, less stingy than Susan, but I must tell you, it was not an easy decision to come back to this ... ce fumier de pays, that's because of what happened here during ... during my childhood...

Ah my childhood, what a hole, what an abyss of misery, did I eat shit when I was a kid, you wouldn't believe it, wait till you hear...

I was so fed up with America, the great American dream, more like a nightmare, a nightmare of misery, violence, loneliness, bigotry, racism, greed, and everywhere, everywhere failures who still believe in the American dream, drunks, winos, jobless homeless bums who sleep on the sidewalk in cardboard boxes or wrapped in newspapers, bag ladies who push their little buggies from one garbage can to another, dope addicts with eyes like oysters, and everywhere cowards, assholes, religious fanatics, crooked politicians, hillbillies who speak the language as if they had marmalade in their mouth, and what's more, car salesmen, ah yeah the car salesmen, thousands, millions of car salesmen who sweet talk you while trying to put one over on you, they all look the same, they all dress the same, they're like clones of each other, have you ever tried to buy a car in America, it's a total rip-off, pure unadulterated swindling, those miserable car salesmen what a bunch of crooks, and that's not all, that's not all...

Wait, you don't think that's all I have to say about America, about this **Amer Eldorado** ... America the land of misrepresentation...

They always tell you in America that the products you buy have been improved, on every box, every bottle you buy for cooking, cleaning, make yourself look better, smell better, feel better, crap better, on all the boxes, bottles, and packages it says in large letters, **IM-PROVED**, do you realize what that means, it means that the products you bought before must have all been shit since they had to be improved, does that make sense to you, do you get the logic of American business, that means that the soap, the toilet paper, the toothpaste, the shaving cream, everything you bought before this so-called improvement was an inferior product since it needed improvement, as it is said on the boxes and the bottles and those fucking plastic bags you have to fight with to open them, on all of these it says, in large letters, **IMPROVED**, it's unbelievable, that means that a bunch of fucking bastards, those who fabricate these products, try to have the rest of the population believe this kind of bullshit, and it's the same thing for what they call the **FAMILY SIZE...**

The family size ... oh you don't know what it is, you don't have la taille famille ici en France, you guys are really retarded ... well the family size, it's a box or a tube or a container which is bigger than the normal size and in which, supposedly, there is more stuff, more merchandise, but of course that's not true, it's another one of those stick-it-up-your-ass misrepresentations from the big businesses, for instance, you buy a tube of toothpaste, regular size, let's say you pay a buck 79, and out of curiosity, to inform yourself, or just for the fun of it, to pass the time, you decide to count the number of squeezes in the tube you bought, the regular-size tube, a squeeze is the amount of toothpaste you normally put on your toothbrush when you brush your teeth, that's obvious, doesn't matter if you brush in the morning, in the evening, or after each meal, basically a squeeze is a squeeze, for the sake of our discussion, let's say that all squeezes are more or less equal, I'm inventing a bit here for the commodity of the story, let's say then that you count 60 squeezes from your regular size tube, 60 seems like a good round number for an ordinary tube, this way if you brush your teeth regularly, morning and evening, as your dentist recommends, then your regular tube will last you exactly one month, but you, you're not very rich, you want to economize, so the next time you buy toothpaste you get the family size, which costs $2.29, therefore, 50 cents more, in America, by the way, all the prices always end with a 9, that's another one of their tricks, to make you believe that's it's cheaper, that you pay less than if it were a dollar 80 or 2 dollars 30, I call that the penny deception, what can you do with that penny, that lousy little penny they give you back, that useless penny that you stick in a box or in a drawer somewhere and is lost forever...

Bon je continue, so you just bought yourself a family-size tube of toothpaste, personally I prefer Colgate, excited because you think you saved, you go home and start counting the number of squeezes in this family size tube, on which it says, in large letters, not only **IMPROVED** but **TWICE AS MUCH TOOTHPASTE AS IN REGULAR-SIZE TUBES**, however, to your surprise, your disarray, when you have finished counting, at most there is perhaps half a dozen more squeezes in this larger family size, therefore, once more, you've been had, the tube seemed bigger, larger, it even felt bigger in your hand when you squeezed it, felt like ... like a cock in erection, but in fact it was an illusion, the motherfuckers they put air into the tube, yes lots of empty air instead of toothpaste, and that's true of all brands, always the same whether it's Colgate, Polident, Pepsodent, Close-up, Aquafresh, Crest, Smeardent, Merdedent, whatever the name, always more air than merchandise...

So now you see how capitalism uses merchandise to deceive you, to make you suffer, to torture you, to ... to ... well you know what I mean...

What ... oh you want another coffee, okay, me too ... garçon ... allo garçon, encore deux cafés s'il-vous-plaît ... Hey can I bum a cigarette...

That's okay, I like Gauloises ... you got a match...

Okay, I was telling you how in America they always get you with their improved products and their family size, I told you, it's the land of misrepresentation, and also the land of repetition and duplication...

They say America is a melting-pot where anyone can become whatever he wants to be, bullshit, me, I'll tell you what it is, not a melting-pot, but a stewing pot, a huge marmite in which the exploited, the oppressed, the dispossessed, the displaced are slowly being cooked for the benefit of those who exploit, oppress, dispossess, displace them, the second third and fourth class citizens, the Afros, the Chicanos, the Red Skins, the Good-for-Nothings, the Underprivileged, The Rabble, oh you want more, I got more, here, I'll give you a whole list, in neat columns, of what the Americans call each other in the stewing pot...

The Stewing Pot...

Spades	Gooks	Fairies
Spooks	Hebes	Fruits
Spics	Kikes	Queens
Schwartzes	Yids	Fags
Coons	Youpins	Lesbos
Chinks	Black Beauties	Goyem
Colored	Bleeding Hearts	Four-eyes
Niggers	Freaks	Daigos
Commies	Yentas	Sheenies
Commi Crappola	Atheists	Punks
Chosen People	Weirdos	Yankees

Jigs	Dumb Pollacks	Pussy Eaters
Jungle Bunnies	Dingbats	Frogs
Pinkos	Dumb Bells	Frenchies
Pansies	Meatheads	Krauts
Red Skins	Micks	Bums

And there is more, much more, the Americans, what an amazing collection of ethnic eponyms, you should hear that extraordinary language, that's the beauty of the English language, its richness, its inventiveness, that much must be said for it, maybe when they tell you in America anybody can become a millionaire, maybe they mean a millionaire of words...

Words, that's about all I got from America, a million useless words, which I can barely pronounce...

You want to know where I learned all these words...

Watching TV, working in factories, in the army, in the streets of New York City, in the black ghettos, that's where you learn how the Americans refer to each other, especially the upperclass when they refer to the slobs, the depressed, the oppressed, the exploited, the minorities, the canaille, the rabble, the poor, the underprivileged...

Of course, there are rich guys over there, what do you think, in America you find gold in the streets, that's what I was told before I went there, you should see the privileged bastards afflicted with money and me-meism, guys loaded with dough who drive huge fancy deluxe cars with fur seats and wheels made of gold, no I'm not kidding, Cadillacs, Lincolns, Chryslers, Mercedes, BMWs, Rolls Royces, Infinitis, Acuras, oh and I almost forgot the Porsches and the Lexuses, the people who drive these cars are called celebrities, haha, celebrities without talent of course, wallowing in money, perversion, deprivation, exploitation, envy, you know what I mean, that's what they're called these sans-talent who spend their time on the talk-shows, and let's not forget the multi-multi-millionaire athletes who brag of fucking four or five women a day, every day before going to play their games of football, basketball, baseball, yeah, talk to me about baseball, one should rather say **baiseballe**...

You may not know this, but there is a basketball player who recently bragged that he fucked twenty thousand women in his life, I am not exaggerating, and the guy is not even dead yet, he's only thirty-four or thirty-five years old, do you realize what that means, twenty thousand broads, you, if you counted how many you fucked in your life you would arrive at what, half a dozen, a dozen, maybe two dozen, if you exaggerated a bit, if you said fifty, nobody would believe you, but twenty thousand, that my friend is beyond human comprehension, it's bestial, you have to be an animal to fuck like that, you have to be really obsessed with sex, I know only one other guy who could screw like that, who bragged to have fucked that many women, Georges Simenon, yes, Simenon, I've been told, was one of the great fuckers of our century, and he was not even an American writer...

In America, money and sperm, that's what flows everywhere, from coast to coast, and all these rich cats, ces richards qui mijotent les affaires, they get fat, puffy, pot-bellied, senile, they fart and burp in public, they fornicate in groups, they even masturbate in public...

No, it's true, in public, I've seen some of these millionaires beating their meat in public, in Las Vegas you see them all the time, once I saw a guy, he was shooting craps, he was losing, and I mean losing big, suddenly, right there in front of the crap table surrounded by a mob of losers, he opened his fly, right there, in front of everybody, took out his cock, grabbed it with both hands, rubbed it, squeezed it, worked it over, and before you know it the guy came in his hands, he rubbed the sperm in the palm of his hands, he put a thousand bucks on the line, and another thousand on crap-eleven, grabbed the dice, and you won't believe this, the masturbator rolled seventeen passes in a row, yes, that's right, seventeen, I was there, I saw, I counted, I don't remember how much he won, but the rest of us losers, we were completely dumbfounded, baba, especially me since all I could afford to play that day was one buck on the line, the minimum at that table...

What ... me, masturbate in public, who do you take me for, I've got too much self-respect, doesn't mean I don't like it, but in public, how can you enjoy yourself, isn't masturbation a form of self-enjoyment, I mean something you do alone, in private, in front of the mirror, for your own pleasure, without sharing the pleasure with anyone else...

Well, you wanted me to tell you about America, now you know, I should have been warned before going there, to seek fame and fortune, that the American dream was phoney, a joke, for the birds ... makes you feel like pissing on Independence Day...

America, for the birds, pour les oiseaux, I'll tell you what America is, it's like a Hollywood movie, an illusion, a block-buster delusion, and like all the Hollywood movies, it self-destructs with its own mediocrity and banality...

You know something, America was invented by Walt Disney, it's a giant cartoon for adults with the mentality of a four year old...

Just read Baudrillard, you'll see what I mean, yes Baudrillard explains it all, the French love to explain everything, especially America to the Americans, as if they had invented it, the French always claim they've invented everything, electricity, atomic power, jet propulsion, telephones, vaccines, steam propulsion, capotes Anglaises, French fries, French toasts, the French they brainwash each other into believing that they have invented everything...

When I was a kid in grammar school, the teachers always told us, nous les Français nous avons tout inventé, everything, even toilet paper, and the teachers started with the Eiffel Tower, explaining that only a Frenchman could have invented something that great, that big, that tall, personally I think the Eiffel Tower is a monstrosity, a huge phallic symbol that makes Paris look like it has a permanent erection...

No, listen, on second thought, don't waste your time with Baudrillard, that pseudo-prophet didn't understand a damn thing about America, and you know why, because he hasn't lived there, I mean lived there in the guts of America, he just looked at it, from above, from a distance through his lunettes cacadémiques...

To understand America you have to have lived deep in it, as I did, ten fucking years, me I saw the real America, in all its beauty and in all its horror, Baudrillard he didn't work in a factory in Detroit, like I did, on the line, at Chrysler, Baudrillard he didn't live in the black ghettos of Detroit and New York, like I did, when I wanted to be a jazz musician...

Oh you didn't know I played jazz, yes the tenor sax, I'll have to tell you about that too...

No Baudrillard he didn't spend three fucking years in the fucking army with the racist hillbillies of North Carolina, no Baudrillard never worked, like I did, as a dishwasher in the grease joints of New York City...

So now you understand why I couldn't take it anymore, so here I am in Paris, six weeks already, in a shitty filthy flea-bag of a hotel in Montparnasse, Rue Delambre to be exact...

Yes, Rue Delambre where the prostitutes do their business ... hey, how come you know that, don't tell me you too frequent that street...

Not far from here, in fact very close to where Jean-Paul Sartre lives, and the other night I saw him Sartre à la Coupole, he was there with Simone, you know, Simone la Beauvoir, and Boris Vian was there too, wow did they look drunk the three of them...

I am serious, I saw them, you cannot imagine comme il est moche Sartre, and Simone, not very sexy, Boris Vian, sort of good-looking, but Sartre, he may be a smart guy, but ugly, ugly as hell, and cross-eyed, qu'est-ce qu'il louche ce poisson rouge strabique, as Céline once described le seigneur tartre...

Merde, you see how I digress all the time, here I'm again in a detour, this time a detour out of time, a literary detour in the middle of the story of my life, okay I'll leap-frog Sartre and his buddies, and hoplà me revoilà dans mon histoire...

So here I am in Paris, six weeks already, and yesterday I get a telegram from Susan, from America...

Susan she always communicates by telegrams, and me telegrams scare the hell out of me because it never fails, a telegram always brings bad news, always tells you that somebody died, or somebody failed and was rejected, or you failed and were rejected, or else that you owe somebody money, telegrams never tell you that something good happened, like winning a million dollars at the lottery, no, telegrams are made to circulate sadness...

In any case, the telegram from Susan announces that she is arriving in three days with TWA, that I should meet her at the airport because she'll have lots of luggage, she says she's sorry, she's not mad at me anymore, it was a long telegram, must have cost her a fortune, especially from America, she says she still loves me, adores me, please forgive me Darling Moinous...

That's what she calls me all the time, Moinous, Darling Moinous, it's not bad as a name, she invented it because, she says, it gives her a sense of togetherness with me, you know, me us, what can I do...

Susan knows a bit of French, she speaks it with a delicious accent, an American accent of course, she makes adorable mistakes, especially with le masculin et le féminin...

So in her telegram she tells me when she is arriving, and implores me to come and meet her, and you'll see Darling Moinous everything will be fine, just like before, we'll start brand new, we'll get a little apartment together, we won't fight any more, I'll take care of you, I'll cook for you, I'll do your laundry, I can't wait to see you and hold you in my arms to love you, caress you...

Well well, that's all I need, no it's not tenderness and caresses, or clean underwear, or even gourmet cooking that I need at this point, though a good juicy hamburger with French fries right now would be delicious, yes what I need now is bread, dough, cash, pognon, flouze, dollars...

You see, I have a problem, a serious financial problem on top of all my other problems, let me explain...

Thanks, I'll take another smoke ... two weeks after I arrived in Paris, I met this girl, a British girl, cute as hell, petite, maybe a bit too skinny for my taste, but absolutely gorgeous, très Britishe, she works for a travel agency, anyway, I can't say it's love, but man what good old-fashioned British fucking we do together...

What's wrong ... well last week she tells me she missed her period and she panics, she needs five-hundred bucks immediately to get rid of the thing, some doctor she found in the Province, where the hell does she think I'm going to find that kind of dough, five-hundred bucks, and now here comes Susan with her tenderness and her cooking...

Borrow from Susan ... now really, who do you take me for, I told you I have self-respect, and besides Susan she would kill me if I told her...

But that's not all, I got other problems besides Susan and my British girl, I'm broke, and I cannot find a fucking job, nothing, absolutely nothing in sight, I'll take anything, the few bucks I had with me when I came, gone, finished, evaporated, okay mon Anglaise loaned me a few francs the other day, but now she says no more, especially with the thing she claims she's got to get rid of ... the thing ... you would think with my knowledge of English, in spite of the accent, I could find a decent job, maybe with an American firm, but no, nothing, I haven't had a decent meal in more than three days, ah La Belle France, for the birds too...

Oh, Monsieur reacts, Monsieur doesn't like when I say things like that about La Belle France, you say it's not that bad here, much better than over there, here le patrimoine et le patriotisme ça compte, you know what, you can take your patrimoine and patriotisme and stick them up your ass, I'll tell you a few things about this rotten country, I'll tell you what happened here, back then, during the war, what these salopards de Français did to us, yes to us...

Don't look at me like that, this bitch, this whore, yes that's what La Belle France is, a prostitute that couldn't wait to get fucked in the ass by Hitler while my family was being remade into bars of soap, oh I'll tell you more about that...

Here, maybe you don't know this, but at the Olympic Games of 1936 in Berlin when the French athletes paraded before Hitler, they all gave him the Sieg Heil salute, only the Americans and the British didn't, good for them, I know because I saw a documentary on TV about the '36 Olympics, I saw the whole parade, it's on film, well the French athletes when they marched in front of Hitler and his cohorts standing up there on the platform, not only did they give the Sieg Heil, but they stretched their arms higher and further than all the other athletes to show how they couldn't wait to get fucked in the ass by Hitler, no I am not inventing this, it's on film, it's inscribed in history, impossible to erase that unless one destroys the film, you see why I say la France is also a rotten country, for the birds, but we'll talk about that too, for now let me tell you about my immediate problems...

My immediate problems ... you want a list, money of course, but also Susan who is going to break my balls with her tenderness, my little English cutie from Manchester who tells me I knocked her up, how do I know it's me, and on top of that my family, or what's left of them, you'll see, I'll tell you the whole thing, but especially I'll tell you about my aunt Rachel, the only one of all the aunts who was nice and decent with me, ah Tante Rachel, wait till you hear her story, what an incredible story her life...

My aunt Rachel and me we were like ... well, you'll see ... but the rest of the family, all a bunch of bastards, des radins, des ordures, des pourris, des fauchetons, des salopards ... no, I really didn't want to see them again, but what could I do, finally necessity, hunger pushed me to go see them...

So, last Sunday, exactly five weeks after I got here, totally broke, not a centime in my pocket, nothing to eat for days, and my British girl refusing to loan me any more dough, I said to myself, fuck it, I can't take it any more, I'm going to go see them, what else could I do, look, a free meal is a free meal, even with uncles aunts and cousins you detest, one cannot be too...

And who knows, I told myself, maybe I can squeeze a few francs out of them, after all it's them, that bunch of salauds who took everything from me before I left for America, everything we had, after they abandoned us...

Not that I am a beggar, a parasite like le Neveu de Rameau, oh no, me I always managed to get along one way or another since the day I was orphaned, when I was twelve, but still, I decided to go see them, the aunts and uncles, on my mother's side, hoping that, yes hoping what...

How dumb can a guy be, why go and rummage in the ruins of one's past, why dive into the filth of what one was before becoming what one wanted to be, even if one never succeeds in becoming what one wants to be, you see what I mean, what I am trying to say...

No, forget it, all this makes me so fucking angry, sick to my stomach, anyway, I was saying, six weeks already in Paris, and yesterday I get this telegram from beautiful Susan...

OH YOU WANT ME TO TELL YOU
MORE ABOUT SUSAN...

You want me to tell you about Susan, ok, here we go, Susan like I told you before, she's the broad, la gonzesse quoi, I was shacking up with in New York, you know, before I took off to come back here, we had a huge fight, I told you that, we'd been living together for more than two years in her swanky apartment on Westend Avenue, near Riverside Drive, it was small but well furnished and super cozy...

Oh my apartment in the Bronx, the one I told you about yesterday, that stinking furnished room for which Susan supposedly loaned me some dough, it doesn't exist, I just invented it so that the story I'm telling you could go on, and also to give the story a touch of naturalism, do you really think I'm telling the truth here, how dumb can you be, it's fiction what I'm talking here, just a story I'm making up as I go, I'm improvising, so if I tell you that I had an apartment in the Bronx you don't have to believe it, just accept the fact that maybe there was such a flat in the Bronx where I once lived and that's that, don't start bugging me with the question of credibility, I don't believe in credibility, it handicaps me, you see for me the simple fact of saying that I was living with Susan in her apartment becomes instantly the truth...

You make a face, I know what I'm talking about, truth, you want to know what truth is, it's only what one says and not necessarily what one does, in real life words are always true and actions false...

Yes, I know that some people, especially the anti-logo-cen-tristes, will tell you it's the contrary, that actions are true and words false, but they're full of shit, I know what I'm talking about, and don't ask how I know, or where I got it, probably from Namredef, me I always steal things from him...

Namredef, that's the name of the guy who locks himself in a room with the noodles, you know, in the novel I'm writing, the noodler, Namredef that's his name...

Anyway, to go back to the question of truth in fiction, just accept the fact that when I say I was living with Susan in her apartment, I'm just settling, or rather sinking into the truth of my story, that's all...

Hey, you know, this little restaurant isn't bad, the food is great here, and they give large portions, how about another bottle of wine, don't you think it's really good, only if you want of course, you're picking up the tab, right...

Okay I go on with the story, what a fantastic pad she had Susan, not luxurious but comfy, cozy, lovely, nice, really nice, with live plants everywhere, even in the bathroom, when I went in there to crap or shower the plants tickled me like little fingers, and wow did she have books, shelves full from floor to ceiling, in English of course all the books, Susan didn't speak a word of French...

Oh yesterday I said she spoke French, well I made a mistake, listen, you're starting to get on my nerves with your objections, ok so sometimes I contradict myself, big deal, don't you understand, all that stuff I'm telling you is pure invention, improvisation, don't tell me you believe that what I'm telling you is really the story of my life, one would have to be completely mad to tell that story straight...

My life, ah, a big hole full of shit, that's what it is, a huge hole full of garbage, full of unrepeatable dirty jokes not suited for the kind of literature that's being sold to the general public, certainly not, you see, what I'm telling here it's a story, maybe a bit scatological, what the hell, just a story...

Alright, I'll admit that from time to time I borrow from my life, but that's normal when you create fiction, or what my neurasthenic buddy Serge Doubrovsky calls auto-fiction, all novelists do that, they all plagiarize their own lives, it's a well-known fact, look let me put it this way, there's not a novelist who doesn't plagiarize his life or somebody else's life, so stop being such a pain in the ass with your objections and interjections and let me go on with Susan, but first I have to ask you a question, a simple question, and I want you to give me an honest answer, your answer will determine whether or not I will continue...

What do you think of what I'm telling you right now, I mean the way I am telling you this story...

What ... what kind of crap is that, me doing célino-beatnik stuff, you must be kidding, if you think I sound like Céline that really shows you don't understand a fucking thing of what I'm telling you, nothing, especially not my technique...

35

Céline it's something else, Céline it's ... it's like underground spoken writing, yeah like le métro, Céline he writes subway-style, he said it himself, don't you remember, he explained it in his **Entretiens avec le Professeur Y**, my stuff, he said, is all-nerves-magic-rails-ties-three-dots-subway-style that continually remembers writing, so you see, he pretended to speak but in fact he was writing, he wrote writing that pretended to be like speaking, only writing, whereas me, if you prefer, I fabricate speech, only speech, my writing is all spoken, pop-surface-speech that remembers nothing because it invents itself on the spot, word by word, and let me tell you, it's not vicious speech like his, not at all racist, and certainly not anti-Semitic like his stuff, no way, Céline was full of meanness, anger, full of hatred, full of scorn, Céline, he was a nervous sonofabitch, a hater to the backbone, compared to him, me I'm calm, relaxed, gentle even, there you have the real difference...

As I said, Céline he traveled by subway in his books, like a maniac, full speed ahead in his words, and along the way he assaulted everybody, his mouth was like a big asshole crapping out words full of shit, he defecated his enraged wordshit in everybody's face, his mouth was like an anus...

Me I go on foot, je suis un flâneur de la littérature, a pedestrian of fiction, I stroll gingerly in words, from one word to the next, I word-word, and if sometimes my blood is boiling and I start screaming because of all the stupid zombies I encountered in my life that doesn't mean I've lost hope for humanity, even if humanity is in terrible shape these days...

Now you're probably going to tell me I don't seem to know much about humanity, you may be right, I could probably tell you more about the lousy spongy potatoes

36

I shoved in during the great war than about humanity, oh did I shove them in, those miserable potatoes, when I was on the farm, wait till you hear...

Still I have to admit, in spite of all the crap he shoved in my face with his *Bagatelles* and his *Cadavres* anti-Jews, I still have respect for Céline, I admire his writing, yes me dirty little surviving Jew, qu'est-ce-qu'il a pu me flanquer dans la gueule this old anti-Semitic grouch, but that doesn't matter anymore, soon there won't be anybody left except the surviving victims to remember that this great writer of our century was a dirty bastard, a swine, and that he was our contemporary with his ignominious neurotic pathetic existence...

Oh you didn't know I'm a Yid, un Youpin, a dirty Brudny Żyd, as the Pollacks call us, just look at my schnaze, here look, touch it, don't be afraid, you see this nose, it's a topological monument to the memory of those who were erased from history...

Look at it, look at this great big crooked Jewish nose...

You say my nose is like any other nose, big, small, crooked, hooked, that means nothing, doesn't make any difference, you're very kind my friend, very liberal when it comes to noses, you say I look more like a Frenchman than a Youpin, do you want me to drop my pants and show you my circumcised cock, believe me my dear friend, this nose made me suffer in my life, a big Jewish nose is like a little tragedy in the center of your face...

Well then, forget my nose, and let's go back to Susan, and also forget the question I asked, and **La Question Juive** as Jean-Paul Sartre used to say when referring to us, Sartre avec ses yeux de poisson lubrique dans son bocal existentialiste pas très casher...

Susan, did she have books, novels mostly, love stories, adventure stories, detective stories, spy stories, philosophical novels, even unreadable avant-garde novels, and at night, when Susan fell asleep after we'd made mad passionate love, I spent the rest of the night next to her in bed, my head propped on two fluffy down pillows, reading a novel picked at random from Susan's shelves, no kidding, that's how I discovered literature, at night, haphazardly, while Susan was dreaming next to me, and sometimes talking in her sleep, telling how much she loved me...

I discovered literature haphazardly, and that's how it should be, because you see, I believe that reading and writing have to be done au petit bonheur, chaotically if you prefer...

I didn't invent that either, it's Namredef, the noodle-eater, who said that, Namredef always comes up with stuff like that, things that seem profound but that are completely farfelu, of course you have to understand that I'm the one writing this novel, therefore I'm the one who is putting words in the noodler's mouth, so to speak, in a way one could say that the noodles are symbolic of language, understand, instead of putting them in his pen, like the cliché says, I put them in his mouth, but that's part of the creative process, the process that lets you transmit your thoughts and words to someone else, I call that process playgiarism, in French it would be called plajeu...

By the way, I assume you understand everything I'm telling you here, I mean when I speak English, otherwise...

Oh you studied English in school for ten years, hey that's great, and you even visited England several times, that's very good, but careful, me I don't speak British, I speak American...

Oh no, it's not the same, especially the kind of English I speak which I invent as I go along, but it's normal, since English is not my mother tongue I don't have to stick to the rules, I'm free to do anything I want with the English language, but don't confuse American with British, just put a hillbilly from Oklahoma or Kentucky in the same room with a cockney from Manchester or Liverpool and let them have a dialogue, well I can assure you these two guys will not understand a fucking word of what the other is saying...

Anyway, I was saying, playgiarism, that's my technique...

Mais non, how dumb can you be, playgiarizing doesn't mean faire du plat, it has nothing to do with trying to make out with a broad, it means to play the game of substitution of the self into the other, a game of substitution and appropriation...

You see, literature is always a form of playgiarism, everything in it is a game, it must be a game, otherwise life would be deadly, I mean the life of the writer, if a writer cannot borrow, or even steal words, he has no business being a writer...

Here let me explain, I pretend that the noodler is the one who is inventing the novel he's writing, but in fact I'm the one who puts words in his mouth, it's part of the game, and that's what playgiarism is, moving what's over here over there, it's that simple...

That's right, a kind of displacement, but in the process of displacing whatever you are displacing you make little changes, you give it your own personal touch, you make it yours, you give it your style...

All this may seem complicated, even stupid at first glance, it's not, but in order to understand what I'm talking about you need a good sense of humor, and also the willingness to abandon rational thought, otherwise you'll never understand la littérature-plajeu-en-fourire, you know, the kind of literature that makes you piss in your pants, my noodler he calls that laughterature, not bad eh, laughterature, impossible to translate that into French though, littérarire doesn't work...

Oh you don't think it's funny, you don't think laughterature is that clever, well let's skip it then, and let's talk some more about Susan...

So you want to know how old she is, my lovely Susan, ten years older than me, that's right, ten years, but don't start imagining that because I sleep with a woman ten years older than me I have the mommy complex, absolutely not, not me, pas de refoule-maman-originerf, as my friend Christian Prigent says, no way, even though I lost my mother when I was a kid, I told you didn't I, that I became an orphan at the age of twelve...

I suppose I'll have to go into that sad story too, how I became an orphan, but even as an orphan I don't have any hang-ups, my Oedipus complex vanished when my mother and father were dispatched...

What do you mean everybody has complexes...

Well maybe I have just a small one, a tiny inferiority complex because I haven't yet succeeded in life, but don't you worry, it's going to change, one of these days I'm going to be famous, it's bound to happen, I just know it, it's written above in the sky, as Jacques le Fataliste used to say to his master, just watch, one day my noodle novel is going to be published and cause a scandal, and I'll be interviewed and televised to death, yeah you just wait and see...

Ah ça t'en bouche un coin hein, damn right I've read Diderot, it's not because I am a displaced person that I don't know mes classiques, moi je l'ai cuisiné Diderot, as a matter of fact he's the one who taught me that in life we only listen to others so we can repeat what they have said, you like everybody else, you regurgitate any bullshit you hear even though you don't always get it, it just takes one time, and you remember it for the rest of your life, but you have to listen real good to be able to repeat what you heard, have you ever met a guy who's capable of inventing something by himself, so you see even if I always seem to talk bullshit at least I know where it comes from, in that sense I'm aware of my futile importance...

Even Susan used to say to me, you Darling Moinous, you'll become somebody one day, you'll be famous and maybe even rich too, but only when you'll be past forty, just be patient, mon chéri...

Ah Susan, what a terrific girl, you know I really loved her, and I still do ... I think ... that's why it bothers me to talk about her like this, I'm even starting to wonder if I shouldn't change her name in this story, so nobody can recognize her, because Susan really exists, I didn't invent her ... well, maybe later, if it becomes too bothersome I'll change her name, I'll call her something else...

Oh you don't think I should, you like that name, and you like my Susan too, don't tell me you're falling in love with her, but listen, imagine that one day Susan happens to read all this, after it's been published, and she doesn't like it, finds it too wild, too filthy, and she is embarrassed to be part of it, have you any idea of the deep shit I could be in, one never knows what to expect with these rich chicks, they have lawyers you know, to be frank, I'd prefer to call her something else, something not so common, and besides there are too many Susans in the world, don't you think...

You know what, I never really liked her name, it always gave me the impression of being too ... how shall I say, too pious, Susan, Suzanne, Susannah, see what I mean, too biblical, and listen to this, one time when Susan and I were in bed, our hands all over each other, about to make love, me so horny I just couldn't think straight, in the heat of passion I inadvertently whispered in dear Susan's ear, ah Judy Judy je t'adore...

What can I say, I like the name Judy a lot, so that night while Susan and I were going at it, well, Judy slipped out of my mouth, just like that, unconsciously, and of course Susan immediately wanted to know who Judy is...

She explodes, **Who's Judy**, and right away she starts imagining things, like I found myself another piece of ass to fuck on the side while I'm still with her, not at the same time of course, I mean the fucking, but you see how I goofed, Susan was so jealous and possessive like you wouldn't believe, she treated me like she owned me, like I was a piece of furniture in her apartment, like I belonged to her like the rest of her stuff, that's so typical of rich American broads like Susan who have everything they need, and more, they treat guys like objects, can you picture me as a chair or a stool in her pad, no way man, me, you want to know what I used to say when she treated me like an object, I used to say, darling, it's abject to take me for an object, how about that...

Okay, I have to admit, it was stupid to come out with the name Judy in the middle of our sweet cuntversation, what can I say, it just came out, and there I was bareass, looking like a jerk avec ma queue au garde-à-vous, my cock at attention, trying to explain to Susan that it was a mistake, a terrible mistake, that I don't know, je sais pas, queque thatthat, I started mumbling in Frenglish, you understand ma chérie, mon amour, don't you, it's just that, moi I like that name a lot and it just came out like that for no reason, je sais pas pourquoi, maybe, maybe I saw a movie or read a book in which there was a Judy, that must be it, that's what I'm trying to tell Susan, but of course she doesn't believe a word of what I'm saying, she insists, she wants to know the truth, and let me tell you I'm such a bad liar that even when I tell the truth it sounds like a lie, so I'm getting more and more nervous, squirming around in the bed like a worm while Susan keeps screaming at me louder and louder, she absolutely wants me to tell her who that Judy is, or else I can get dressed and get my ass out of her place...

Susan doesn't usually talk like this, but she is so pissed, so to calm her down, because you know Susan had already thrown me out of her place a couple of times before when she had one of her crises of jealousy, and that night it was raining cats and dogs on top of that, so I didn't want to end up sleeping on a bench in Central Park like the guy in the novel by Georges Michel, did you ever read it, it's called **Les Bancs**, great book, so I begin to invent a Judy, any Judy, it's the story of an old fart who collapses on a bench and who just can't get up, to make up a story about some girl called Judy I once met, a situation like this of a guy spending the rest of his life on a bench that stays with you for the rest of your life, after all, there're loads of Judys in America, millions of them...

So while caressing her, I tell Susan that once upon a time, long before I met you, I insist on this so she doesn't get more jealous, long ago, I met a girl, in Detroit, yes it was in Detroit, whose name was Judy, but I was only thinking of you, my love, when I whispered Judy in the heat of passion, maybe, I go on telling Susan, even though I should have kept my fucking mouth shut, yes maybe I got so aroused caressing your breasts, my darling, so excited that in the depth of my subconscious it felt a bit like your beautiful breasts, ma chérie, were as voluptuous by their hardness and whiteness to those of that Judy of Detroit, but it doesn't mean a thing, it doesn't mean I'm not faithful to you now and that I don't love you, it was simply by free association that I said that name Judy, but the more I was bullshitting her, the deeper I was sinking into the mud of my fabrications...

No, finally she didn't kick me out, she cooled off, and man did we fuck that night, I don't know if it was her jealousy that got her all worked up or what, it must have been, she was wild, you know sometimes jealousy can get lovers more excited, it often happens after a crisis of jealousy, wow did we come together that night, after that we were so exhausted, we slept in each other's arms like two angels, and Susan, well, she forgot all about Judy in her sleep, so let's forget her too, in fact I don't even remember why I told you this story...

Ah but you want to know more about Judy now, you get a kick out of listening to my filthy stories, petit saligaud, you little lecher, okay quickly, the story of my encounter with Judith of Detroit...

Judith, yes Judith, with a TH at the end, us frogs we have trouble pronouncing the TH when we speak English, avec les thé-haches we don't know how to squeeze the tip of our tongue between our teeth, like that, but we sure know a lot about faire des langues, the Americans call that French kissing, they like everything French the Americans, they are so dumb, for them French kisses or French fries or French toast it's all the same, they love everything French...

Oh you too you like the name Judith, but like me you cannot pronounce les thé-haches, doesn't surprise me, for us Frenchmen it's almost impossible, but doesn't matter because in America they always say Judy anyway, they always cut names short over there, they reduce names to little porno syllables, like Richard becomes Dick, Robert Bob, William Bill, Theodore Ted or Teddy, Charles becomes Chuck, Lucien Lou, Joseph Joe, James becomes Jim, same for girls, Elizabeth becomes Liz, Patricia becomes Pat, Gertrude Trude, Jennifer becomes Jennie, Susan becomes Sue, and so on, and worse still, you have Rusty for the redheads, Lefty for the left handed, Whitey for the guys who are blonde, and then all the ethnic stuff, Dagos for Italians, Krauts for Germans, Japs for the Japanese, Gooks for Koreans, Meatheads for Poles, Spades or Jungle Bunnies for Negroes, Kikes for Jews...

The French, ah the French, they call us Frenchies, or Frogs, that's what they call us, Frogs, but don't ask me why...

Do you think we look like frogs, do we look like we can croak like a crapaud...

Oh you may be right, of course, it never occurred to me that it's because us French we eat frog legs, that's it, that must be the reason why they call us Frogs, how come I never thought of that, can you believe it, ten years in America and I didn't even realize that, well you just taught me something, shows you how complicated America is...

Over there, they always reduce names to almost nothing, trivial monosyllabic nicknames, Pam Tim Chris Max Stan Tom Ray...

Ray, that one really burns me, makes me mad because my name is Rémond, but over there they never call me

Rémond, never, it's always Ray, Ray, I'm fed up with Ray, I hate when they do that to me, reduce me to a syllable...

See how I get all worked up, I can't even remember what I wanted to tell you, I always get lost in roundabouts, in fucking digressions, it's a bad habit, I really shouldn't go backward and forward like that, jumping from one story to another, I'd better watch out otherwise I'm going to get lost in my own fabulation, and I won't be able to tell you what I really want to tell you, the story of my aunt Rachel, what a story, wait till you hear, be patient my friend, Aunt Rachel will make her great entrance in time, just at the right moment...

Where was I, wait, don't start imagining that because I jump all over the place like that in my story I don't know where I'm going, even if I seem lost, you'll see, my goal will eventually become clear, even if everything seems mixed up, and it looks like I'm even more confused now than before, that doesn't mean I won't get out of this muddle, or what you French guys call embrouillamini...

Sure go ahead pour me another glass of wine, it's really good, c'est du Beaujolais, what year, '59, great year for Beaujolais...

Do you know that Voltaire loved Beaujolais, no I'm serious, it's le cacadémicien Michel Serres who told me that...

Of course I know Michel Serres, I know a lot of important people, just because I'm still an unknown and unpublished novelist it doesn't mean I don't know famous people...

Where did I meet him...

Somewhere in the past, or perhaps it was in the future, me I make no distinction between past present and future, it's all the same to me, so when I tell you I know someone like Michel Serres, I may not have met him yet, but I will eventually, for sure, so don't be surprised if I mention people I haven't met yet, that's how I function...

By the way, if I'm sharing that important fact with you about Voltaire and his love of Beaujolais it's because, who knows, that information might be useful to you some day, especially to impress those little nobodies wallowing in the delusions of grandeur who think they're somebody, who think they're upperclass simply because they have un quart d'idée dans le crâne, and a few pennies in their pocket, and pretend to be connoisseurs de vins, these nobodies who were born in Trifouillis-la-tirelire plutôt qu'à Sans-sous...

Shit, I'm doing it again, digressing all over the place, wait, wait, what was I saying, I always get lost in my saute-grenouillements, dammit, what was I talking about, remind me...

Oh yeah, Susan, right, you wanted to know more about her, how she looks, how old she is, how much dough she has, etcetera, etcetera, but in the middle of telling you about Susan, I deviated, I made a detour into Judy, and now you want to know more about Judy, okay...

Quickly then, how Judy and I had a great fuck in Detroit, she did it to me as much as I did it to her, a great reciprocal fuck, yes she wanted it as much as I did...

Did I tell you that I lived in Detroit for two years, when I first arrived in America after the war ... Detroit what a rotten filthy disgusting city, the worst...

Yes, I forgot to mention that I lived in the navel of America, le nombril de l'Amérique, Motown, Shitcity as the natives call it, I'll have to tell you more about that depressing place later, but for now, the story of how I landed in Judy's bed, it didn't last long you know, the fucking I mean, only two days, two days and two nights, but **wow** quel baisage monstre, unbelievable, forty-eight hours of fucking without a break...

She worked in a shoe store, sold shoes, and it so happened I needed a pair of new shoes, so I went into this store downtown, and while she was trying all kinds of shoes on my feet she knelt on the floor in front of me, her legs slightly spread apart displaying a piece of delicious white thigh above her stockings...

You understand, this was before the panty hose era, you know when women still wore stockings with garters, it was so much more sexy then, especially when they exposed their little secrets...

Anyway, whether or not she was exposing herself deliberately, I couldn't tell for sure, but man was it tempting to see her entre-cuisse like that, so exciting in fact I just couldn't resist, and suddenly I reached for her head and stroked her hair telling her how gorgeous it was, and she really had beautiful brown hair, kind of curly, long and shiny, the girl looked up at me, still holding a shoe in one hand and my foot in the other, no need to say I was expecting her to jump up and scream, even kick up a big fuss because I touched her, well only her hair, but none of that, no, instead she said, *Oh Sir, Sir you mustn't do that*, with such a lovely languorous tone of voice and with such a sensual provocative smile, I immediately felt a hard-on ready to burst out of my fly, and I think she noticed because her face became all flushed, and the shoe dropped out of her hand, but she stayed down on one knee still showing me her crotch and her gorgeous thighs...

Do you want me to continue, are you still interested, or shall I skip the rest...

Okay, but I'll skip the details, because what I want to tell you is what happened later that evening, so pay attention, because you're going to hear something really amazing now...

When the store closed, I was standing outside at the corner of the street, waiting for the chick, I must have looked kind of pathetic standing there in the middle of the crowd, waiting like a jerk, but when she saw me, she immediately understood that she was the one I was waiting for...

I should tell you, and maybe you won't believe it, I've always been very shy, no don't laugh, it's true, it's not because I talk a lot now that I'm not shy, especially in certain situations, and so in the shoe store I didn't have the guts when she said that lovely and suggestive, *Oh Sir, you mustn't do that*, as if she was pleading me to touch her some more, I didn't have the guts to ask her if by any chance she was free that evening, but as soon as I came out of the store, I told myself, dammit I'm going to wait for this girl, I think she wants some, so I waited for more than two hours, until the store closed, and when the chick saw me, she blushed, just a little, and asked what I was doing there, like she didn't know, the little cunt...

The shoes ... what about the shoes...

Oh you want to know if I bought them, no, no I didn't buy them, not even the pair that looked great on me, the Italian ones, black, all leather, no I didn't buy them because they were too expensive, and the little cutie understood right away that I wanted this pair of shoes real

49

bad but I couldn't afford it and, well I think she felt a little something for me, especially when she said with her lovely soft voice, maybe next time, maybe you'll come back when we have a sale, after Christmas we always have a sale, don't forget, come back...

What...

Of course she said that in English, how jerky can you be, quel branquignole, you're really something, stop interrupting me with your stupid questions, do you think that this poor little shoe salesgirl was going to start speaking French all of a sudden just because she noticed my sexy French accent, listen, everything I'm about to tell you happened in English, is that clear...

So she sees me standing there in the street, shivering a bit, I forgot to mention it was wintertime, just before Christmas, and man was it freezing cold, real bad that day, I'll never forget how cold it was that day, in Detroit it can get damn cold, and on top of that I didn't have a winter coat, just a lousy jacket, you know a blouson with a zipper, and not very warm, as always I was flat broke, in fact I really don't know why I went into that store, I certainly couldn't afford a new pair of shoes, maybe I went inside that store to warm up a bit, in any event the broad understood right away that it was because of her that I was standing there at the corner of the street freezing my ass off, my hands stuffed in my trouser pockets, the collar of my jacket turned up to my ears, can you visualize the scene, I must have looked like a bum, comme un vrai clochard...

Bon, let's leap-frog the whole conversation, rather banal, we had in the coffee shop where we went for a cup of coffee to warm up, and let's go directly to what happened an hour later when we got to her place, but first I have to tell you her pad wasn't as luxurious as Susan's, that's for sure, after all the girl wasn't a millionaire like Susan, just a shoe salesgirl, but her pad was so shabby and so messy, I'd never seen such a mess in my life, dirty laundry everywhere, lingerie, bras, soiled panties laying all over the floor, shoes piled up in every corner, cardboard boxes full of old clothes, well I'm not going to do an inventory for you, I'm just trying to give you an idea of how sloppy she was, it even gave me a bit of a shock when I came in, it was so messy, and it smelled funny too, it smelled like rancid piss, and you should have seen the toilet, disgusting, there were dirty dishes in the sink, the bed wasn't made, and the sheets didn't look too clean, to tell you the truth it kind of surprised me because in the store the girl looked rather neat and stylish, well put-together if you see what I mean, well made-up, long polished nails, nicely combed hair, but her place, wow, what a dump, and she didn't even apologize for the mess, well I wasn't here to do house cleaning, that's for sure, and besides I didn't get much time to contemplate the mess because as soon as the door closed, the chick grabs me, literally climbs all over me, shoves her viper tongue down my throat and wiggles it all over, then she begins to rub her pelvis against mine with such frenzy that I just stand there dumbfounded, not for long though, the broad sure does want some, and I feel mon thermomètre sexuel rise up to the ceiling, so without further ado, if I may be lyrical a moment, I undress her, I think I even tore her panties as I pulled them off, she does the same to me, and presto here we are the two of us full naked on top of the bed doing some incredible full-blast-porno-erotico-gymnastic never seen before, I don't know if I'm saying it right, but believe me it was something...

What a gorgeous body that little cunt had, I won't go into the details because of censorship, but let me tell you, she was gorgeous, sexy as hell, and what we did together was exquisitely vicious, that's the only way I can put it...

I stayed in her place for two days without going out, two whole days, and nights, oh I should have told you that ce grand baisage, this glorious fucking, happened during a weekend, that it was a Friday when I waited for the girl and that she didn't work that weekend, so I was able to stay with her from Friday until Monday morning, just fucking and eating, eating everything she had in her fridge, not that there was much, leftovers, stuff she had cooked at least a week before, half a chicken, two or three twisted hot dogs, some boiled potatoes, a piece of dry Wisconsin cheese that smelled and tasted like shit, stale white bread, two half rotten tomatoes, but did she have beer, we must have drunk at least thirty bottles in two days, cheap beer, I forget what kind, and we put away two bottles of bourbon, we gulped down everything between les séances de montage et surmontage, woow did we go at it, you cannot imagine the orgy we had during those two days, quelle bacchanale de jouissance suprasensa, sex sex and more sex, food and drinks, and the obligatory cigarettes after each orgasm, in those days I smoked Pall Malls, and she smoked Chesterfields...

We barely talked, no kidding, we didn't say more than a dozen words to each other, I told her my name, Rémond, she told me hers, Judy, and after that no questions, no chatting, no inquisition, no resistance, no blah blah, just pure simple unadulterated fucking, her on top of me, me on top of her, on the bed on the floor on the couch standing up against the fridge in the kitchen even in the bathroom on the sink in the shower, like animals, moi des descentes à la cave, elle des pompiers, but you know what, sometimes it feels damn good to make love just for the sake of it, without having to charm, to sweet-talk, without asking any questions, just like that, for the sake of it, for the sport of it, and above all without having to explain oneself, to tell who you are, and that was perfect for me because me I wasn't much of a talker in those days...

No I'm serious, believe me, you know it's not because I can't stop talking now that I don't know what silence is, I went through a long period of silence, almost five years, after I arrived in America, five years without talking, and it's not because I didn't speak English, actually I learned the language rather quickly, it's easy to learn because in English you don't have to respect the rules of grammar, you can say anything any old way without paying attention to the order of words, and it works every time, that's the beauty of the English language, its grammatical irrationality, anyway, I didn't talk for five years, except, of course, to say the words that one has to say every day in order to survive, you know what I mean, *yes, no, I-don't-know, thank-you, hello, hi, good-bye, maybe, how-much-is-it, where-is-the-john*, stupid stuff like that, but that's not talking, no, it's more like mumbling...

So you see, I spent five years in silence, my long babbling period I call it, I didn't have anything to say, and now I seem to have so much to say, well I'll tell you, at the time I didn't have a damn thought in my head, not that I have many of them now, who has thoughts anyway, do you, of course not, it's not easy to have an idea, I mean an original idea, tiens c'est Descartes who said that normally a thinking being has only one idea per year, and he probably meant by **thinking being** a philosopher, not just anybody, and that guy who has a little thought like a flash of light in his head, that guy spends the rest of the year cogitating that little idea, and that's what eventually gives him the impression of being, of existing, whereas those who don't have any thoughts up there in their heads, they have nothing to cogitate, those poor slobs, they don't even have the sensation of being, so for them, there is no ergo sum, and that's the way I was at that time, when I spent those two days fucking with Judy of Detroit, I was just a vibrant body overflowing with passion but without any thoughts or words in my head, I was a non-being with no cogito, but with a huge libido, that's for damn sure, and that's why we didn't speak much Judy and me, except for groans of jouissance, and a few shhs when we were making too much noise in the heat of action...

That's what I wanted to tell you about Judy, or to put it simply, with her fucking was strictly physical, like a sport, Olympic gymnastic, and you'll probably won't believe me, but it's quite possible that together we broke the world record of fucking during those two days, not that I want to brag, but I tell you, it's unbelievable the erotico-stuff we did together, too bad I didn't keep track of how many times I climbed her, but it certainly was a record...

Now you understand about Judy, at least once in my life, I made love for forty-eight hours straight without taking a break, except for a few minutes between the ups and downs to swallow a sandwich or drink a beer or smoke a cigarette, otherwise in and out, iiin and out, iiiin and out, up and down, ^v^v^ up and down ^^vv^^, two or three minutes rest to regain a little strength, to erect again, and bang bang in and out up and down, and, man, did the chick keep up, even better than me, at the end, it was her who was on top of me, encouraging me, pumping me up with her hands or her mouth...

Well, that's enough, I don't want to go too far, otherwise you'll get all excited and you won't be able to listen to me, look at you, you're blushing already, better go back to Susan...

Here take my handkerchief and wipe your face, you're sweating, hey you really got worked up my friend...

Oh by the way, I should mention that I never saw that Judy again, soon after that great encounter, I left Detroit...

Now, with Susan screwing was completely different, not a sport, on the contrary, more like an artistic performance, dancing if you want, classical ballet, we had to prepare ourselves, it was like a rehearsal, undress slowly, take a bath, make conversation, you know chit chat a bit, then touch each other gently, but no entre-chats, no arabesques, all this in slow motion, well synchronized, no groaning, no screaming, no brusque movements, and always in the dark, Susan always turned off the lights when we fucked, with Susan it was only sighs, and whispers with our eyes closed, and at the end dozing off gently, that gives you an idea of the kind of love life I had with Susan, and now she's arriving in a few days, that's all I need...

Sure I'm happy to know that I'm going to see beautiful Susan again, but what bad timing, what the hell am I going to do with my British girl, the one I met in the métro last week...

Oh, yesterday I told you I picked her up two weeks ago, it's possible, I made a mistake, do you think I pay attention to chronology in this story, I told you, chronology and credibility handicap me...

Oh, excuse me, it bugs you that I make such mistakes, you're saying that these temporal displacements don't stand up and that eventually it's going to mess up the whole story, you're such an old-fashioned listener, don't you know that the beauty of a story has nothing to do with the question of time, with the order in which you tell things, not at all, it's all about rhythm, tone, it's all about the way you tell the story, it's the telling that counts, not what you tell, anyway you're getting on my nerves with your obsession with time, fuck time...

So I don't respect the chronological order of things, big deal, yesterday I said two weeks ago, and now I'm saying last week, and who knows tomorrow I might say a month ago, and the day after tomorrow I'll say something else about what I did or didn't do in the past, or even about the stuff I'll do or won't do in the future, what the hell do you think time is, a straight line that goes in one direction only, something stiff always standing at the same fucking place, how stupid can you be, the past and the future are not frozen like scenery on a postcard, that's what most people don't understand, yesterday, today, tomorrow, next year, people imagine time as if it were some kind of place from which we come and go, have you any idea how boring it would be to live your life as if it was a little trip by train, knowing in advance where each stop would be, where the final destination would be, and what time you would arrive, how boring, there wouldn't be any surprises, and you know as well as I that surprises are essential and necessary in one's life, even if they're not very funny sometimes, otherwise life wouldn't be worth living, even life itself is a surprise, don't you sometimes wonder how the hell you came to be alive, I am sure even your old man must have been surprised when your mother told him, Darling I think this time we did it, I think I'm pregnant, too bad you couldn't see the look on your father's face, the look of surprise, and probably fear too...

For instance, take the surprise of Susan's telegram, I didn't expect her fucking telegram, but the fact that I got it makes my story more interesting, it gives it suspense, and it makes it progress, even if it stumbles along, but that Susan might arrive in three or four days or next month or even à la saint-glinglin doesn't solve my problems, it's not when she's going to come that bugs the shit out of me, it's the fact that she's actually coming, so that's why I give an approximation of time, maybe in the final version I will have to reorganize the whole thing a little better, otherwise nobody will want to publish my stuff, but for now, if I say that I met that British broad with the nice firm boobs two weeks ago, and then I say it was last week, that doesn't change anything, except that my lousy situation is getting more and more complicated, especially now that Susan is jumping into the mess, what a bummer...

Hey, wait a minute, I have an idea, maybe if I don't talk about my British girl, I mean if I don't say another word about her, nothing, maybe she'll disappear from the story...

What do you think, not a bad idea, see what I mean, if you don't talk about something it's like it doesn't exist, right, in fact according to certain contemporary thinkers who claim they know what they're talking about, everything in life exists only in language, in the logos, therefore it's simple, I won't say another word about my cute sexy British girlfriend, and you don't mention her either, agreed, and certainly not when Susan will be here in three days, or four, or next week, don't forget, mum's the word...

Okay, see you tomorrow...

———

THE STORYTELLER & THE LISTENER
TAKE A BREATHER...

YOU WANT ME TO TELL YOU
ABOUT THE FAMILY...

Oh you want me to tell you what happened when I went to see the family...

Yes, finally I went to see them, the aunts and uncles on my mother's side, that's the side I'm talking about...

My father's side, maybe I'll tell you later, or never, because on that side not too many left, most of them exterminated, erased, only two or three cousins left on that side, but on my mother's side, somehow they all managed to survive, except my mother...

It's they who fucked me over, those rich aunts and uncles who managed to save their own asses down in the zone libre while my parents and sisters were being reduced to ashes, did those bastards screw me, rob me, crap all over me, but what could I do, I couldn't take it anymore, not a sou left, I hadn't eaten in three days except for the loaf of bread I stole from a boulangerie, what would you have done, so I went to see them, not to beg, no, simply to show them I was still alive, that everything was great, and that after all I didn't do too badly in America these past ten years, well you know, that's what I told them, yeah I told them that everything was going marvelously for me over there, I studied literature at the University of New York, comparative literature, and for a while, I was a professor at a big university, but now I'm a writer, I write books, I gave up teaching to concentrate on my writing, they all looked dumbfounded when I told them I'm a writer...

Why, because when I was a kid they all thought I was mentally deficient, no, I'm serious, that's what they thought, maybe because when I was a little boy I never had anything to say, I was sort of a daydreamer, even my mother used to say, il est toujours dans la lune ce pauvre garçon, on top of that my nose was dripping all the time, and I was knock-kneed, quite frankly there wasn't much hope for me...

Anyway, I told them I was writing a novel about the family, a novel about what happened to us during the war, and that's why, I explained, I was back in Paris, to verify the facts, the important details, to dig into the past, of course I didn't tell them I was here to settle my accounts, and did I have a score to settle with them, no, I didn't tell them that, at first I even pretended to be happy to see them again...

I told them that my novel was also, more or less, about my life in America, but I didn't explain to them, as I did to you, the business of the noodles, they wouldn't have understood, not that they're stupid, my aunts and uncles, but I didn't feel like going into the noodles with them, and besides I don't think they would have given a hoot about my noodles...

But to prove to them that I was really a writer, I brought with me a copy of a magazine in which a couple of my poems were published, this way, I told myself, they'll be impressed to see my name in a magazine, even if they don't understand the poems...

Yes in English, the poems, I thought that should impress them even more that I could write in English, me the stupid little nothing nephew...

But you know what my uncle Léon said, wait till you hear about that sonofabitch, he's the worst of the family, he's the husband of my Aunt Marie, my mother's older sister, quel pourri, you know what he said, well Namredef that's a rather common name, could be somebody else by that name who wrote those poems...

He meant my name ... yes Namredef, that's my name, Rémond Namredef...

Oh, I'm sorry, I should have introduced myself, but can you believe this, the motherfucker didn't believe these were my poems, and that's not all he said, he went on saying that writing poetry is a waste of time because poets never make any money, for Léon that's all that counts, money money money, and then he made a dirty gesture and said, poets write poetry only to impress women...

I didn't answer, I know I should have told him to go screw himself, but instead I just stood there like a dumb ass with my magazine in my hand, but you know what, that's what Léon always does to me, he makes me feel like nothing, like a piece of shit...

Do you know what he always called me, Schimele-Bubke-Zinn, that means the son-of-the-piece-of-shit in Yiddish, he used to call my father, Schimele-Bubke, and so me I was always the son of that piece-of-shit...

Oh well, I went to see them anyway, look a free meal is a free meal, so last Sunday I went to Montrouge to show them that I was back in Paris, and still alive after ten years, ten years of disillusion in America, of course I didn't tell them about the disillusion, you know what they would have said, they would have said, you see, you see, we told you that you would starve over there, that's how they are, oh that doesn't mean they would have done a fucking thing to help me if I had stayed here, not them, those cheap bastards...

Still, I went, I remembered that every Sunday the whole family got together for lunch chez Tante Marie, it's an old tradition those Sunday reunions, yes I remembered that on Sundays the whole clique always got together to complain about their miserable life, how poor they were, how difficult it was to make a living, how their children were costing them a fortune, how scared they were that things would get worse with the economy, all this while pulling their hair and shoving the food down their throats...

They were not poor, on the contrary, they were all loaded, they all had businesses, crooked businesses, that's why they managed to escape deportation, they paid their way to survival, they paid with the money they were hiding under the mattresses of their beds, that's where they kept their money, under the mattresses, I knew that because once, when I was a kid, I saw my aunt Marie shove big bills under the mattress in her bedroom, I tell you, if I had had a chance last Sunday I would have grabbed a handful of those big bills, but they didn't leave me alone a moment, maybe they were suspicious, maybe they thought that I had come to take back what they had stolen from me, I'll tell you later what they stole from me...

They were all loaded with dough, but Léon and Marie were the richest, that's why Marie was like the matron of the family, especially after my grandmother died during the war, of a natural death, only those who had the means died of natural causes during the war, I mean in my family...

But last Sunday, only three of my aunts were there, Marie, Sarah, and Rachel, and also Léon, plus my cousin Marco, the son of Marie and Léon...

By the way, remind me to tell you about my cousin Marco, ah what a lout, what a salaud he was, you cannot imagine how miserable he made my life when we were kids, the dirty tricks he played on me, you see we lived in the same building in Montrouge, the building belonged to Léon and Marie, they owned property all over the place, yes that's where I spent my childhood in Montrouge, 4 Rue Louis Rolland, Marco was four years older than me, and he used to beat the crap out of me, and one time, he must have been about thirteen or fourteen then, and me nine or ten, this was before the war, he asked me to suck his dick, no I'm serious, he wanted me to give him a blow job, we were in the living room of their apartment, he was helping me with my homework because Marco had already learned algebra in school, but me I didn't understand all that algebra stuff too well, Marco was the chouchou, the darling of the whole family because he was the oldest of all the children, and everybody said he was the smartest, so he was showing me how to do my algebra and suddenly he asked me to suck his cock, just like that, I got scared, and I said no, I told him it was disgusting to ask his little cousin to do that, but he almost forced me, he grabbed my head with one hand, right there in the back of the neck, and he pushed it down toward his cock in erection which he had taken out of his pants, can you believe that, and when he pushed my head down, the tip of my nose touched his prick, it gave me the weirdest sensation, and you know, for a long time after that I kept rubbing my nose with my hand instinctively as if I wanted to erase that disgusting sensation, it became like a tic, and my mother used to say to me, will you stop rubbing your nose like that, it's going to turn all red and people will make fun of you, they'll think you're a drunk, was I ashamed...

No, I didn't suck his dick, I managed to escape his grip, and I told him that if he ever did that again I would tell his father, Marco was afraid of his father, so he never tried again, everyone in the family was afraid of Léon, he was such a loud-mouth, always screaming at everybody, he was really mean, and my cousin Marco, what a filthy jerk he was, so spoiled, and yet we always played together when we were kids, we went to the same school, and because his parents were rich and mine poor, Aunt Marie always gave me Marco's old clothes when they became too small or too worn out for him, pants, shirts, coats, even his underwear, his stained underwear, things like that, shoes too, Marco's shoes, they always hurt my feet because, you see, Marco's feet were a little smaller than mine, so my feet were always killing me when I wore his old shoes...

All my life my feet have been killing me, that's what my friend Moinous used to say to me all the time, and I would answer him, me too, all my life my feet have been killing me...

Who is Moinous, my best friend, didn't I tell you, my buddy, Moinous, Me Us, I call him, we are so close the two of us, interchangeable...

Marco also gave me his toys and his books, comics mostly, you know, **Tarzan, Mandrake le Magicien, Les Pieds-Nickelés, Tintin**, and all his Jules Verne, the one I liked the best was Michel Strogoff...

Do you know that novel, it's the one in which the soldiers of the Tzar burn Michel Strogoff's eyes with a sword, a sword they put in the fire, when I was a kid I always wanted to be like Michel Strogoff...

Anyway, that's how they are in my family, on my mother's side...

What ... oh you don't care what kind of stuff Marco and I used to read, it's not interesting you say, doesn't add anything to the story, okay...

You'd rather know where the other aunts and uncles who didn't come last Sunday were, I didn't ask, maybe they were already dead, but more likely they didn't come any more to these Sunday reunions because they had a fight with the others, in this family, the uncles and aunts argued and fought constantly like a bunch of vultures, always about money, they were so envious of each other, you have to understand, before the war, there were eight brothers and sisters on my mother's side, what a tribe, and of course plus the sisters-in-law, the brothers-in-law, and their kids, my cousins, who aren't kids anymore since they are more or less my age now, in any case, I was telling you that every Sunday, before I left for America, all of them used to show up at Aunt Marie's, because she was the oldest and also the richest, so now you understand why I knew where to go last Sunday...

Yes, eight brothers and sisters on my mother's side, two brothers, Maurice and Jean, and six sisters, Marie Fanny Lea Sarah Rachel, and my mother Marguerite, but I already told you, my mother is the only one who was exterminated during the war together with my father and my two sisters, but that's another story I've already told too many times, so I won't bother you with that Unforgivable Enormity, instead let's go back to my Aunt Marie in Montrouge, and I'll tell you what happened last Sunday...

Knowing that usually they ate the big Sunday lunch around one o'clock, I arrived just before noon, this way, I told myself, they'll have to ask me to stay, I wasn't in a very good mood that day, there was the problem with my British girl, you know, the thing, my novel wasn't going too good, it was sort of stalled, my noodles were in regress, and on top of that the lady manager of my crummy hotel was threatening that if I don't pay for the room, you're out mister, and she meant it...

No, you confuse everything, I had not received Susan's telegram yet when I went to see the family, it came later, you keep mixing everything up, it's not because I don't give a damn about chronology that you should do the same, what I'm telling you now happened before Susan's telegram, pay attention or you'll get lost in my recitation, what's the point of me telling you these nice stories if you keep confusing the whole thing...

What did you say ... oh you have to take a leak, okay but hurry up or I'll forget what I wanted to tell you, go ahead I'll wait for you here ... hey, don't beat your meat in there...

Tatataduumm tata ta taduumm those foolish things remind me of you humhum tata duumm tata dudumdum ... pardon me ... oh, the check, give it to the gentleman who is with me ... *tatataduum tata...*

You're back, how was it, that was a long leak, you know why you have to piss so much, you drink too much pinard, that's why you have to run to the toilet every five minutes...

Ok where were we, oh yes, I was talking about last Sunday's lunch chez Tante Marie...

You don't know Montrouge, it's not far from here, you take le métro to Porte d'Orléans and from there to Rue Louis Rolland it's only a ten minute walk...

I've got an idea, one of these days you and I should go to Montrouge, this way I can show you where I lived, in the apartment building that belongs to Marie and Léon, that's where I spent my childhood, Marie and Léon lived on the second floor, in a luxurious five-room apartment, us, we were on the third floor, in a tiny place, only one room and a minuscule narrow kitchen like a corridor without a window, a hole in the wall our apartment, and there were five of us living in there, my mother, my father, my two sisters and me, we weren't rich like Léon and Marie, they were the owners of the building, but you know what, even though we were poor we had to pay rent, oh were they cheap, I remember how Léon used to argue with my old man when he couldn't pay the rent, they were filthy rich Léon and Marie, but they acted poor all the time, like schnorrers...

Not a bad idea to show you where I suffered in my youth, this way you'll understand better why I had to get out of that fucking place...

No, we won't go in, are you crazy, I just want to show you the house and the street where I used to play when I was a kid, I really don't want to see them again, that asshole Léon and that snob cousin of mine, especially after that disastrous lunch last Sunday...

You want to hear the details...

Okay, so I arrived chez Marie just before noon, nothing had changed in their apartment, everything was still the same, you realize it had been ten years since the last time I was there, but I recognized everything, except that it all seemed smaller and older, I mean the rooms and the furniture, but then it's normal to feel like that when you come from America where everything is so big and so new, here in France everything is smaller and older, the furniture was the same, good old antique furniture, massive and solid, the same oriental rugs on the floor, and also the piano in the salon, before the war Marco took piano lessons, and he was going to become a doctor, but instead, because of what happened during the war, he became a tailor, like his father, so it goes...

In my family, on my mother's side especially, they were all either tailors or shopkeepers, except my father, he was nothing, he was a painter, did I tell you that he was an artist, a surrealist painter, that probably explains why we were so poor, my father was a starving artist, un artiste maudit aussi...

Anyway, let me finish the description of Aunt Marie's apartment, in the bedroom there was a huge wardrobe with a mirror on the door, a large bed where they used to hide their money under the mattress, I told you already how when I was a kid without her noticing me, I saw my Aunt Marie slip her hand under the mattress and shove in big hundred francs bills, their kitchen was very modern, and there was a salon in their apartment with a sofa with soft cushions, and leather armchairs on either side, in the dining room, besides the big square table and the chairs, there was a fireplace, yes they had a fireplace in their apartment, and next to it there were two big Chinese urns with dragons and Buddhas on them, before the war all the rich people had Chinese vases like these, it was the vogue, these Chinese vases indicated that you belonged to the upper-class, to the bourgeoisie, all that stuff must have cost a fortune, oh and also the floor, le parquet, it was beautifully waxed, so shiny and perfectly waxed you couldn't walk on it with your shoes, when you came into the apartment you had to slide along on cloth pads, imagine that, Léon and Marie they were cheap, but let me tell you they knew how to impress people with their possessions...

Our apartment upstairs, on the third floor, that hole in the wall, let me describe it, as I told you, it was just one lousy room divided by a big curtain, that was my mother's idea the curtain, this way we had a dining room on one side and a bedroom on the other, my mother and father slept behind the curtain, and sometimes I could hear them breathing heavily because I slept in the dining room, on the other side of the curtain, on a small cot near the window, my two sisters slept in the kitchen, dans un lit cage, you know the kind of cot you have to unfold every night, it wasn't very practical because when the cot was open it blocked the kitchen door, so when my father or me we needed to go take a leak in the kitchen sink, we had to step over my sisters' bed, and did they bitch, especially Sarah, my older sister, the two of you are disgusting she would scream while hiding her face behind her hands not to see us pissing in the sink, you have no manners, she would hold her nose and say, it stinks in here, can't you go downstairs...

What do you think, of course we didn't have a toilet in our apartment, Marie and Léon had a toilet in theirs, they had a bathroom, you have to remember that what I'm talking about now is before the war, before the war only rich people had toilets in their apartments, but us on the third floor we had to go either in the sink or in a chamber pot, yes, we had a chamber pot for my sisters and my mother because they couldn't go in the sink like my old man and me, and we also had a pail...

Oh you don't know what a pail is, un seau hygiénique, a slop pail, you must have been raised in a good bourgeois home, we had a pail, and every morning I had to go down three flights of stairs to empty that stinking pail in the outhouse at the far end of the courtyard in front of our building, ah did I hate doing that...

That pail was such a big part of my childhood, here let me tell you about it, did I complain every morning when I had to carry that pail full of our besoins downstairs to empty it, that filthy pail plein de caca et de pipi, did I moan and groan and bitch saying that it's always me who has to do the dirty work, yeah why can't Sarah carry the pail downstairs, she's older and stronger than me, why can't she empty the pail, that's what I said every morning when my father shouted at me because I had not yet emptied the pail, why can't Sarah do it, she's stronger than me, I kept repeating, and it's true my sister Sarah was stronger than me, she always kicked me and punched me when we fought, and she always won, how come she can't go empty that stupid pail, how come it's always me, but my father would say that it wasn't a job for girls, and when I kept on whining he just slapped me across the face screaming, get the hell out of here p'tit fainéant, so every morning I went down the three flights of stairs carrying my stinking pail...

No, my father he was not mean, but when I did something stupid or when I didn't do what I was supposed to, he didn't hesitate to swat me one, ah my father, man, did he have a rough life, maybe that's why he yelled all the time, I think he failed in everything he did, as a father, a husband, an artist, a man, I'll have to tell you more about him, but not now, now I want to finish the story of the pail of our needs, I'll come back to my father later, remind me...

No, let me tell you more about my father right now, the pail can wait, the other day I wrote a little something about my father, I suppose being back here got me thinking about him and what a failure he was, here let me read it to you, it's called **Ramona**...

My father's favorite song was Ramona. It goes like this, *Ramona je t'aimerai toute la vie, Ramona je t'aimerai* ... In French, because I only know the words in French. But I think that song also exists in English.

My father always listened to this song, that's why I know it only in French. *Ramona je t'aimerai toute la vie...*

My father, Papa, mein Tate, the dreamer, l'artiste manqué, le romantique tuberculeux, the Trotskyist, the gambler, le coureur de femmes, the Brudny Żyd, my tubercular father, who never achieved his vocation, my father while listening to Ramona on the scratched record playing on our old dusty phonograph with the big speaker and la petite manivelle, my father, Papa, mon père would dream.

La petite manivelle! That's funny. I don't even know how you call that in English, la petite manivelle, you know the thing you crank to rewind le phonograph. Sometimes toward the end of the record, remember, when the phonograph was running out of gas, when its motor was unwinding, then the voice of the singer would become so slow, so sad.

I never knew who was singing the Ramona my father loved so much to listen to all the time. It was a woman, a young woman, I think, with a beautiful deep sad voice. She died young. It's my father who told me that. She had tuberculosis. Like my father. That's all I know about her. I don't even know her name, or perhaps I knew it once but have forgotten it. But even me when I listened to Ramona with

73

Papa, I could feel tenderness, yes, that's what it was, tenderness toward her.

No, not passion, I was too young to know passion. Well maybe it's possible that I felt something like passion while listening to Ramona, but I didn't know what it really was then. Papa I am sure knew what passion was. Papa was a very passionate man. He loved women. Il était coureur de femmes. That's what all my uncles and aunts said about him. Un coureur de femmes. Un fainéant. Un rien-du-tout. A good-for-nothing. Papa.

In any case, even me, while listening to that singer sing I would feel tenderness for her and I would imagine her being petite et fragile, with very long black hair, and very long eyelashes. That's how I imagined her then. Today I would imagine her much better if I could listen to her sing Ramona again. But how can I get le disque where she sings Ramona? I don't even know her name.

When Papa listened to Ramona there were dreams in his eyes, I could see that, and I knew he was dreaming about his failed vocation.

He was dreaming, there in our drab and somber one-room apartment, ce misérable petit taudis of ours, where Papa and Maman and my two sisters, and me of course, lived, if one can call the sordid kind of existence we had living.

When Papa listened to Ramona, sitting in his old fauteuil à moitié défoncé, facing the phonograph, I could tell he was dreaming, I could tell he was making up stories about how he could have become un grand artiste if only...

Ah yes, if only...

I could see it in his eyes, but I could also feel it in the tips of his fingers, in his fingernails that traveled on my back, gently scratching my back when I said to him, Papa, *Tate* gratte-moi le dos, s'il-te-plaît, ça me gratte là, a little to the left where it itches.

Anyway, as I sat on the floor at Papa's feet, next to his old beat-up fauteuil vert, I listened to the phonograph play Ramona, while Papa's fingers scratched my back dreamily, and that's why I can say now that I knew he was dreaming, dreaming the great works of art he wanted to create and yet knew he would never have time to create.

Oh he had painted a few things that may even have had artistic value. Who knows. His friends, all of them struggling artists, said good things about his works of art, but he knew he had failed, failed to achieve the vocation inscribed in him, by his father, or some remote ancestor.

I think my father was the first ever to become an artist in our family. Yes, he was the first one to fail as an artist. All the others before him, his father, his grandfather and great-grandfather, all those who went before them, all of them losers. I once wrote a poem about the nothing, le rien-du-tout my father was. Here, let me give it to you, for whatever it's worth. It's called...

Before That

Some say, can say: my father was a farmer,
and his father before him, and his father
before that. We are of the earth.

Others say, can say: my father was a builder,
and his father before him, and his father
before that. We are of the stone.

And others can say: my father was a sailor,
and his father before him, and his father
before that. We are of the water.

They have been farmers, builders, sailors,
no doubt, since the time earth, stone, water
entered into the lives of men, and still are.

I am a writer, but I cannot say: my father
was a writer, nor his father before him,
nor his father before that. I have no antecedent.

My father, and his father before him, and his father
before that were neither of the earth, nor of the stone,
nor of the water. The world was indifferent to them.

I write, perhaps, so that one day my children can say:
my father was a writer, the first in our family.
We are now of the word. We are inscribed in the
world.

I feel I could write on the earth, on the stone.
It seems to me that I could even write on water.
I write to establish an antecedent for my children.

Five thousand years without writing in my family,
what can I do against this force which presses
me on? Say that I write to fill this void?

Say, I suppose, that of my father I cannot say anything,
except what I have invented to fill the immense gap
of his absence, and of his erasure from history.

No, I am wrong, you see, because I can say:
my father was a wanderer,
he came from nowhere and went nowhere.
He came without earth, stone, water, and he went
wordless.

While contemplating his failures, and absentmind-edly scratching my back, my father was perhaps thinking that his son, I mean me, would someday achieve the vocation he had failed to achieve. And so, gently, with the tip of his fingers ... already aware that his tuberculosis would soon kill him, or that some unforgivable catastrophe would erase him from history ... as he listened to that dying woman sing *Ramona je t'aimerai toute la vie* my father knew that soon he would change tense or the tenses would be changed for him in spite of himself and he would never achieve his vocation ... and so while gently scratching my left omoplate he would try to make me feel this yearning for greatness, he would try to transmit with the tips of his fingers this vo-cation into my body, into my skin, my flesh, my bones, and up here into my head.

As my father and I sat together listening to Ramona, Papa lost in his dreams, me slowly dozing off un-der the gentle touch of Papa's hand, he would in-fuse in me, transfer to me ... how shall I say it? ... He would give me my inheritance. His vocation. That's all he gave me. There in my head, Papa put the dreams he was dreaming while listening to a sad deep voice sing *Ramona je t'aimerai toute la vie...*

Well, I doubt I'll ever finish this, it's too sentimental, it'll remain among my abandoned works...

Now, I can go back to my pail...

As I was saying, every morning I went down three flights of stairs with that stinking pail to empty it at the far end of the courtyard, it was heavy you know, because during the night everybody had pissed or crapped in it, and I had to be really careful not to splash myself when I emptied it in the toilet hole in the ground, the shit house in the courtyard didn't have a seat like normal toilets, it was just a hole with a place marked for your feet, I think they call that un cabinet d'aisance Turc, there are still cafés in Paris with toilets like this where you have to crouch to do your thing, it's disgusting, you splash all over your legs when you take a leak, so you see why I had to be careful when I emptied my pail, otherwise I ended up with shit all over my shoes and legs, after that I had to rinse the pail under a small brass faucet near the water closet, in the winter the water was cold like hell and my hands were all red and frozen when I went back upstairs, you have no idea how much I hated that disgusting pail, but we had to make use of it, there was no way we were going to go down three stories to the W.C. in the middle of the night, when it was dark, of course it was easier for me and my father than for my mother and my sisters, because at least we could pee in the sink standing up, my mother complained all the time about that, saying that it's not hygienic to urinate in the same place where she prepares the food, and besides, it sets a bad example for the girls, and my sisters would really scream when we stepped on their bed, they would say, hiding their faces under the covers or covering their eyes with their hands, we're not looking, our eyes are closed, but me I think that Sarah, and even my little sister Jacqueline, they were cheating, I'm sure they were peeking through their fingers to look at our willies even though we were careful to hide it with one hand, of course we couldn't do le grand besoin in the sink therefore you understand the necessity of the chamber pot and the slop pail...

I hope I'm not boring you too much with what I'm telling you, but you have to know what kind of life we had before the war so you can understand why I became who I am today...

It's Jean-Paul Sartre who said, a life is a childhood mise à toutes les sauces, and according to him, we're all influenced by the lousy living conditions of our childhood, rich or poor doesn't matter, or to put it another way, we are impregnated by the fiddling about we were subjected to as kids...

Oh you're shrugging your shoulders and making a face, okay maybe it's not very profound nor very original but it's true nevertheless, and besides it's not me who said that, it's Sartre, so don't make a face at me, go tell Sartre he's full of shit, and let me go on with the story of our chamber pot and shit pail...

When you wanted to use the pail or the chamber pot you had to hide in the kitchen, or else go behind the curtain when the others were in the dining room, at night of course we didn't have to hide since it was dark, the best spot to use the pail was behind the heavy curtain of the bedroom, I told you, it was my mother who had that idea of dividing the room in two with that curtain, I think she thought of that when my sisters and I became old enough to understand what parents do sometimes in bed when they breathe heavily...

Have you ever caught your folks going at it, me I saw them a couple of times...

Anyway, if one of my sisters or me needed the pail during the night, we had to get it behind the curtain near my father's side of the bed because my father used it all the time, especially to spit in, my father didn't piss very often, he had trouble pissing because he had kidney stones, like Montaigne, did you know that Montaigne suffered from kidney stones, it's true, he talks about it in his essays, my father made a terrible fuss when he had to take a leak in the middle of the night, you could hear him moaning with pain behind the curtain, and on top of that he spat blood all the time because of his tuberculosis, and that's why when I was in school the other boys always called me fils-de-tubard, and nobody ever wanted to sit next to me because they were afraid of being infected, they said I had some kind of bug that was contagious, they called it the F virus, don't ask me why F virus...

Not because of my name, Namredef begins with an N not an F, maybe the F stood for foutu, you know fucked, or something like that, because I was really fucked up when I was a kid, but fuck is not French, maybe the F was for fainéant, yes, maybe that's what the F was for, because you know, I was really lazy as a kid, I never wanted to do anything, in school I was always the last one, and even now I'm lazy, I like doing nothing, just look at the sky and wonder how far it is, I suffer of Oblomovism, but that's normal because all great writers are lazy, no I'm serious, that's what I heard, and who knows, maybe some day I'll be a great writer...

Fils-de-tubard they called me...

You see, my father had one of his lungs removed, and in its place the doctors put a thing in his chest, it was like a little balloon called a pneumothorax, and once a week he had to go to the Montrouge Free Clinic to have oxygen pumped inside that thing, they used a syringe with a long needle and shoved it in his chest, I saw how they did it because I often went with my father to the dispensaire, at the end of the week, when the oxygen in his pneumothorax was running out, my father had trouble breathing, and at night when he was asleep he would make little whistling sounds that prevented the rest of us from sleeping, and then he would wake up to spit blood into the pail...

He had a rough life my father, he spent a large part of his life in hospitals before he was erased from history at the age of thirty-seven, he was an artist, I told you, a surrealist painter, but his paintings didn't sell, that's why my mother had to work as a cleaning woman to feed us, all that is so sad, my father was a loser, un artiste tubard, but you know what, in spite of his tuberculosis, he was quite a womanizer, I don't know for sure but my aunts and uncles used to say that he was unfaithful to my mother, it might be true because he was very handsome, tall, good-looking, with grey eyes, and always dressed sharp even though he never had any money, my aunts and uncles also said that my father was a gambler, that instead of working he wasted his time and money at the horse races or playing cards in the cafés, that's what they said all the time, I didn't know my father very well, he wasn't home much, and when he came home he always ended up having a fight with my mother or the rest of the family, because on top of everything else my old man he was a fanatic of politics, he argued with everybody about politics, but most of all with Léon, my father was a Communist, a Trotskyist, at least that's what they said, and Léon was more like a Fascist, but that's normal since Léon was rich and my father was always broke, that's why we kids were hungry all the time, and that explains why my mother had to clean other people's houses to feed us, and I even remember that during the great economic crisis in France, just before the war, I was seven or eight then, my mother took us to la soupe populaire, she was so ashamed my poor mother, but us kids we thought it was fun to wait in line with the other empty stomachs of the neighborhood...

I hope you're not too disturbed by the stuff I'm telling you, not that I'm preoccupied by the sordid aspects of life, like Zola, but I'm trying to create something moving, something touching, without tumbling into cheap misérabilisme, you know what I mean, so if I exaggerate a bit, if I spread the shit a bit thick, it's to better arouse my potential readers' compassion, of course I make it appear sadder and filthier than it really was, but in general I follow the main lines of my life, my real life or fictitious life, same thing, I make no distinction between the two...

But see, I just got lost again, I wanted to tell you about my visit to Aunt Marie and instead I literally fell into shit while talking about that damn pail, it's amazing how a little sentence, a word, a pail can lead you in the wrong direction just like that, but that's what free improvisation is, and I'm an improvisor, I suppose it's because I played jazz in America, did you know that, yes for a number of years I was a jazz musician, I played the tenor sax, when I was living in Detroit, maybe that's the reason why the stuff I'm telling you now is like a Bebop solo...

Oh I forgot to tell you that I played jazz, you want to hear more about that, it's a great story, ah jazz, that's what saved my life when I lived in Detroit, without jazz to comfort me I would probably have committed suicide I was so depressed, so lonely all the time, in the novel I'm writing now, you know the noodle story, there are many passages about my life as a jazzman in the ghettos of Detroit, want me to tell you, you'll see it's very American...

Not right now, you prefer to hear about my visit chez Tante Marie, alright I'll tell you about my life as a jazzman another day...

Hey listen, why don't we get out of here, let's go for a walk, I need to stretch my legs, and besides I tell my stories better when I walk than when I'm sitting on my ass, I told you the other day, I'm a pedestrian of literature...

Say, I hope you didn't forget to leave a tip, the guy was a good waiter, did you notice how he kept giving us extra bread...

Great weather today, look at that blue sky, it's good to be alive, and here I am telling you all these sordid stories, okay I'm going to be more cheerful, what do you say we go to Parc Montsouris, it's not far from here, that's where my mother used to take my sisters and I to play when we were kids, it's real nice, there's even a little zoo, it'll put me in a good mood to see that place again, one of the few happy places of my childhood, we used to ride the merry-go-round there...

Here, let's sit on this bench, look at those trees, I think they're marronniers, I love crème de marrons...

Ok, I continue, I arrived chez Marie's just before noon, everybody was there already, you should have seen their faces when they saw me enter the courtyard, what a sight, Aunt Rachel and Marco were at the second floor window when I came into the courtyard, it was a nice sunny morning, remember, last Sunday, and Marco when he recognized me started shouting like the big asshole that he is, mais c'est Rémond, it's him, Schimele-Bubke-Zinn, c'est pas possible, look at him, what is he doing here, it's Rééémond, he came back from America my little twerp of a cousin, and of course as soon as the rest of the family heard all that racket they rushed to the other windows, there were five windows in Marie's apartment, five big windows, what a sight, you should have seen that, a real bunch of dummies, like puppets framed in the windows, and me, well, I just stood there in the courtyard, like a schmuck, yeah like a jerk, a nitwit, un cornichon...

Yeah a cornichon, a pickle, that's what Léon also called me when I was a kid, cornichon, shows what he thought of me, so I just stood there with a big dumb smile on my face, waving at them, asking myself what the fuck I was doing there, and if I shouldn't just turn around and get the hell out of there and forget about them once and for all, but then they all started screaming in unison, it's true, it's Rémond, it's him, where does he come from, he's supposed to be in America, as if I were a ghost or something, what a joke, I even heard my Aunt Sarah say, oh look how he's grown, he's so much taller than when he left...

Can you believe the crap a guy has to hear, I was eighteen when I left for America, I had already reached my adult size, five feet nine, but they still saw me as a little kid, it's unbelievable, me the great explorer who crossed the Atlantic Ocean to discover the New World, me the adventurer who suffered in every corner of America, me the paratrooper who jumped out of airplanes, me the G.I. who crossed the Pacific to go fight the war in the Far East against the Chinetoques...

Yes, I was a paratrooper, with the 82nd Airborne Division in North Carolina, if you read **Take It or Leave It**, you'll see, it's another one of my stories about my life as a soldier, then one day they sent me overseas to fight the Korean War...

And look how the family treats me...

Me who worked like a slave in the factories of Detroit, on the line at Chrysler, me who played tenor sax with guys like Tommy Flanagan, Kenny Burrell, Frank Foster, the giants of jazz, and once Charlie Parker himself played my saxophone, unbelievable but true, I'm not kidding, it was at the Blue Bird in Detroit, I describe that historic moment in the noodle novel, what a scene, what an unforgettable event, you have to read that, *remembering Charlie Parker or how to get it out of your system*, that's what I call that chapter, yeah me who played poker and black jack and shot craps in Las Vegas, me who even tried to be a movie star in Hollywood, no I'm not kidding, okay it didn't work out but still I tried, I auditioned for a big part in a war movie, me who fucked dozens of little bow-legged Japanese girls with slanted eyes in Shimbashi, me who had done all this, and the fucking family still treats me like a dumb kid, it's unbelievable...

So here they are, all of them screaming at the same time, hurry up, come upstairs, hurry mon grand so we can see how you look and give you a kiss, as if they were happy to see me, yeah right, sure they were happy, they were probably wondering if I wasn't here to remind them of all the crap they put me through, they were probably wondering if I wasn't here to settle the score, if I wasn't here to dot their i's and cross their t's, or better yet to punch them in the face or kick them in the ass like they deserved because of all the dirty tricks they played on me, but me instead of going upstairs right away, I stood there in the courtyard for them to take a good look at me, I was wearing my best jacket, a navy blue blazer, and my grey flannel pants, I even put on a tie that day to impress them, a silk tie I stole in a department store in New York, yes I stole it, so what, I couldn't afford such an expensive silk tie, and I had polished my shoes to make them look good as new, even though I was broke I could still present well, I wanted to show them that I hadn't done too badly in America, sure, I know, they say you cannot judge a man by his clothes, but I looked damn good in my American clothes even though the pants and blazer were a bit worn, and there were holes in my socks...

Oh, you don't think I need to specify what I was wearing that day, you want me to skip the sartorial stuff and go faster, you're a pain in the ass you know, you're in a hurry, you have a date with your girlfriend, I think these details are extremely important because that day I wanted to make a good impression, anyway we can always erase these details later, before publication, if the editors insist on it, but there's no way I'm going to undress the guy I was the day I went to visit the family just because Monsieur thinks I'm wasting time, I think it's essential that I explain the way I looked, the guy they saw, that's why it's necessary that I describe the outfit, oh and I forgot to mention the white handkerchief I put in the breast pocket of my jacket to look more stylish...

Speaking of details, I'd like to add something, a little extra narrative detour, if you don't mind, I forgot to tell you that the only lovely thing in our crummy apartment on the third floor was the salamander-stove, the green salamander-stove with its tiny mica windows, it looked like a big puffed up toad sitting in a corner of the apartment, a nice friendly toad always staring at us with its big mica eyes, one of the little mica windows had a hole in it, so when the coal was burning inside the stove, that hole was all red like an eye, I would spend hours just staring at that red eye, I really don't know why that stove suddenly came back to my mind like that in the middle of what I was telling you, but since it came back I have to mention it, who knows, it might play an important part in this story, very often there are objects from our past that just stay hidden in the recesses of our mind until one day they suddenly reappear and take on a symbolic meaning that explains all the stuff about life, and these forgotten objects are important and useful especially if you're a poet because you can write poems with these objects hidden in you, you take these objects and you play with them, you transform them into what Francis Ponge calls *des objeux*, so that's why I mention our salamander-stove, maybe one of these days, when I am inspired, I'll make an *objeu* with it...

Hey talking about furniture, after the war, when I came back to Montrouge from the farm in the South where I was hiding for three years, I often wondered what had happened to the stuff in our apartment, everything was gone, the place had been totally stripped, everything inside had been removed, stolen, plundered, taken over, *by the neighbors,* that's what Léon told me, my eye, who was he kidding, I know it's them, les tontons et les tatas, who swiped all our belongings, everything, even though it was crummy stuff, it didn't take long for them to realize that my parents weren't coming back, and since they had no idea where I was, or if I was even alive, they helped themselves to our stuff like a bunch of crooks, they grabbed the furniture and all the rest in our pitiful hole, the curtains, the rug, so maybe it was not in good condition, but still it was our rug, our chairs, even if they were kind of wobbly, our table, my sisters' folding bed, my cot, and all the pots and pans, the forks, the knifes, every fucking thing, and even ... you won't believe this ... the chamber pot and my pail were gone, and the cute salamander-stove gone too, everything had been cleaned out, they must have sold it all at the flea market, my dear aunts and uncles must have told themselves, since they're not coming back, it would a shame to waste all this, so they grabbed everything, yes I'm sure it was them, and of course when I showed up after the war, still alive, they were ashamed to admit it...

You know, I often wondered how come everything chez Marie and Léon was still there, intact, untouched, just like before the war, nothing had changed, nothing had moved, every piece of furniture was in place, as if there had been no war, no defeat, no occupation, no deportation, no extermination, of course those bastards had the money to pay somebody to watch over their shit while they were hiding in some village in the free zone, while my parents and sisters were being remade into lampshades, but still that doesn't explain why their apartment remained intact while ours was completely ransacked, it's not fair, don't you agree it's unfair...

Dammit five o'clock already, shit I've got to go...

I have to meet my British girl at Place d'Italie, that's where she works, in a travel agency, I forgot to tell you, she wants to talk to me, I have no idea what it's all about, but must be serious because she sounded so nervous on the phone, I suppose it's about the thing, how to get rid of it...

Tomorrow ... oh no I can't, it's not possible, we can't meet, I'm having lunch chez Monsieur Laplume, dans le 16ème arrondissement...

That's right, the writer, Jean-Louis Laplume, you know him...

What ... I didn't know the guy was famous, you met him...

Oh, you just heard about him, but you never read his books...

You're surprised that I know him, we met on the plane coming over, he was in America for the publication of his new book, we were sitting next to each other and talked, he's very nice, and when he told me he was a writer, I told him I was writing a novel myself, he seemed inter-ested and asked what it's about, so I told him about the noodles, and he thought it was a fantastic idea, when we parted at the airport he said he would invite me for lunch one of these days, and now he did, I was so surprised when he got in touch with me, so tomorrow I'm going to lunch chez Monsieur Laplume, he said there would be all kinds of literary people I might be interested to meet, can you imagine that, me, I'm going to eat with Jean-Louis Laplume and a whole bunch of literary people, how about that, you bet I'm going to take advantage of the situation, I can already picture myself surrounded by all these famous writers, telling them my stories, telling them about America, I know they'll be impressed...

So we can't meet tomorrow, but the day after, okay, same place, same time, and I'll tell you what happened chez Laplume, and also I'll go on with my stories, don't be late...

Alright, I leave you here, and I leave myself here too, I mean in the courtyard of my old building looking up at that bunch of assholes up there in the windows, next time I'll tell you what happened when I went upstairs for lunch, what a scene...

Hey, it'll be kind of funny because next time I'll have two lunches to tell you, lunch number one with the family, and lunch number two with Laplume and his buddies, and who knows, maybe I'll be able to make a symbolic connection between these two lunches...

We'll see, sorry to leave you in suspense like that...

so long...

WHILE THE STORYTELLER IS HAVING
LUNCH CHEZ LAPLUME
THE LISTENER HAS A FREE DAY...

OH YOU ARE SURPRISED
CHÈRE MADAME...

You find it surprising, Madame, that an American like me speaks French so well, and without a trace of an accent. Let 's say that I have a gift for languages, and when I was younger I was awarded a special fellowship to study French literature à la Sorbonne.

I am teasing you, chère Madame. I was born in France, right here in Paris. I am French, but I've been living in the United States for the past ten years. I left France when I was eighteen to finish my studies in literature and philosophy at Columbia University in New York City.

Oh you understand English, well maybe we'll have the opportunity one day to share an intimate conversation in the eloquent language of Shakespeare.

I went abroad to study, and I became so enchanted with America, I decided to stay. It's a wonderful country you know. Have you ever been there?

Not yet, but you are planning a trip to New York next year ... Ah, with your husband. You are married then. I thought perhaps you were ... Well you'll see what an amazing city New York is. I must give you my telephone number, and when you come I'll take you on a grand tour of my adopted city. I'll show you Manhattan, and you'll see those magnificent buildings that reach up into the sky.

No, that's not so, people have a tendency to exaggerate the violence in the streets of New York. It's like any other major city, like any other place where there is a dense population, and where different ethnic groups are cramped together. It's bound to happen. But I can assure you that you won't have any problems in New York, except of course in certain neighborhoods, at night, but one doesn't wander alone in those dangerous places.

Me, I live on Riverside Drive. In a beautiful neighborhood. My apartment overlooks the Hudson River. It's very close to Columbia University where I got my doctorate, and where I taught for a while, in the Faculty of Comparative Literature.

That's right, I am, or rather I should say, I was a comparatist, because of my gift for languages. You're smiling. See what a teaser I am.

No, I don't teach anymore. I gave up the academic world. I now devote all my time to writing. I am a novelist.

Oh my friend Jean-Louis Laplume told you I was a writer, an American writer. Yes, that's right. I write mostly in English, but sometimes also in French when I get the urge. All the same, I must admit, it isn't easy to write in a language other than your own, not easy at all to adopt words that aren't your own, words that resist you because they are strangers to you. But you learn to love them anyway, these foreign words, you manage to make them your own, and they become part of you. Somewhat like a hen who has lost her chicks and adopts a duckling. Ignoring its yellow down and its flat bill, she teaches him to sift through the sand and to peck at earthworms. Well, I too learned to peck at the English words in what I write, but of course without ever forgetting my mother tongue.

True, sometimes I mix these two tongues rattling in my mouth, these two tongues that keep playing hide and seek and often play tricks on me.

As Gilles Deleuze put it so well, I am sure you know the work of this fine philosopher, the creation of a style in a foreign language, he said, passes through different stages, the first is a decomposition of the mother tongue, which soon becomes convulsive and starts stammering, stuttering, subsequently transforming and metamorphosing itself, to reemerge as a new tongue, a new syntax. Well that's what is happening in the novel I am now in the process of writing. It is written in this new tongue which I am sure my French compatriots would consider a linguistic defection.

Oh Jean-Louis mentioned the novel I am working on. The noodle novel. That's right. **A Time of Noodles!** That's the working title. It's an odd funny story, at once serious and profound, precisely because of the new syntax I invented. I call it paginal syntax rather than grammatical syntax.

No, it's not really a novel about noodles, it's just that the person who's writing the book survives on noodles for an entire year locked in a room where, as he says himself about his situation, he stands siege.

No, I'm not the one who eats noodles, it's the protagonist of the novel who is himself a novelist. He is the one who survives on noodles. If it seems confusing it's because what I'm writing is un roman en abîme.

Exactly, like Les Faux-Monnayeurs of André Gide. I see that you know your literature. Are you a writer too?

Oh you work for a publishing house!...

You are ... really ... what a marvelous coincidence, you are the literary director of a publishing house! Well, I am delighted to meet you, Madame. A writer is always thrilled to meet someone, especially a lady as charming as yourself, who publishes books. Now I understand why Jean-Louis had me sit next to you at this delightful lunch. How thoughtful of him. He knows that I don't know too many people in Paris, I mean people in our profession, and he probably wanted me to tell you about my novel. But perhaps I shouldn't bother you with this during lunch. We are here to enjoy this sumptuous food, and not to discuss business. Don't you find the wine exquisite? It's a Saint-Emilion you know, a very good year too. Allow me to drink to your health, and to your beauty if I may. Who knows, maybe we'll have the opportunity of discussing my novel professionally some other time.

In your office! Next week, Wednesday! Aux Éditions de l'Amour Fou. Really, Madame you are too kind, you fill me with joy. It'll be my pleasure. It's so good of you. I'm so grateful. You see how your kindness touches me. Look at me, I'm all flushed I'm so excited. I will be there, and we'll be able to discuss my work in private. And who knows, maybe by then you'll find yourself in my novel. I do that all the time, put people I like, interesting people I mean, in my stories.

All right then, you are too kind. In your office next Wednesday at ten. I make a note right here dans mon carnet de rendez-vous ... But tell me, all these people here today, are they all...

Really! All of them are renowned writers and publishers, and the gentleman sitting next to Madame Laplume is the chief editor of ... I can't believe it! Monsieur Bouquin lui-même. And across from him Monsieur Gallimard. Gaston Gallimard! Wow! Am I impressed. Well, I'd better watch my language.

Excuse me, Chère Madame, could you please pass the salt. This roast is simply delicious, but it needs a pinch of salt. Don't you think?

You understand, in Paris I know few people in the literary world. After all it is in America that I am recognized as a writer.

Do I have family in Paris? Oh certainly. Aunts, uncles, cousins. As a matter of fact, it's in order to see them that I come back to France every year. I am so fond of my family, especially on my mother's side. They all were so kind to me after the war ... when ... when I was left on my own at the age of thirteen. Especially my Aunt Rachel. Ah, my Aunt Rachel. I'll have to tell you about her one of these days. Her life was like a novel. I mean when she was younger. She was a dancer. Classical ballet. She traveled all over the world. What a fascinating woman. Someday I shall write the story of her life.

My parents? No ... you see, I lost my parents when I was very young. Both my father and mother, and also my two sisters. They disappeared during the war. An accident.

No, not a car accident. An unfortunate accident of war.

I know, it's sad, but one gets used to being alone. One gets used to absence. Gradually, one tries to forget those who loved you. You see, the greatest lessening of the self, the most humiliating form of suffering is when one no longer suffers from that absence anymore.

One always manages to survive when one has to. Life is a little like a boxing match. It's a matter of being able to keep going, to remain standing despite all the blows. I think it was Marcus Aurelius, that stoic emperor-philosopher, who said, living requires the art of the boxer and not that of the dancer. Holding your ground, staying up, that's what matters, no need to take pretty steps. Well, Madame, in my life, after the disappearance of my parents, I lived a bit like a boxer who, in the ring of life, refuses to be defeated, refuses to fall, especially in America where life is not always easy, particularly for a writer who refuses to compromise his work, a writer who seeks posterity rather than prosperity. Finally, I am sure you know this, but America is a very anti-intellectual country, and writers are not as respected as they should be. Writing is mostly considered a hobby, a recreational activity. It's not unusual for someone to ask what else you do if you say you are a writer. What else do you do, what kind of job do you have, as if spending time locked in a room writing isn't enough to justify your existence.

Well, writing for me is a deep and essential necessity. You see, there are in life insurmountable cataclysms from which one never recovers. And no matter what, you are unable to get out of this horror nor talk about anything else, that constitutes a regrettable constraint for a novelist. Yet, that's what informs my writing. What I call the Unforgivable Enormity that occurred during the war and caused a chasm in me by the erasure of those I loved and who loved me. It is that absence, that emptiness, that gap in me that controls my work and gives it its

urgency. That's what the Americans don't always understand. Especially those who are obsessed with the idea of success, financial success, I mean. They don't understand that one writes because one has to. Mind you, I don't want to give you the impression that I spend my life in despair. Far from it. No one knows better than I how to walk the tightrope between excessive despair and the mad passion for life.

In fact, what I write situates itself between this despair and this lust for life. Between the black fire and the white fire. Between sadness and laughter. And sometimes I wonder if one day I'll be able to free myself from those sad stories, if telling them will help me get rid of them for good, or if on the contrary, it will be disgust and lassitude that will free me.

You're smiling. But you must know yourself, since you are a literary person, that the work of fiction is always a form of recovery of the past, even if that past has to be falsified to seem real. The act of recalling the past in what we write doesn't mean knowing the way it really was, but rather becoming the master of memories as they burn in the perilous instant of creation.

You see, what I write is simply a mixture of memories and lies, well, if not lies, distortions, but of course every lie has a little part of truth, one has to learn to listen. Life, like an old worn-out coat, always has a lining of fiction that is a little ripped.

Of course, for a story to be convincing it has to be credible. Realistic to some degree. Well, if not realistic, at least believable. But verisimilitude isn't always the truth, and the truth isn't always convincing.

But you see how I've let myself go on and on. Please, forgive me. I don't want to sadden you with my personal history, and bore you with my crooked ideas about writing. Besides, I don't want you to think that I am not happy in America. On the contrary. Anyway I didn't mean to talk about my work today, we'll do that next Wednesday. In your office. Let's talk about you instead.

Tell me Chère Madame, where do you live in Paris?

Oh in the Seizième! Rue des Belles-Feuilles.

Yes, of course, I know where that is. Very elegant neighborhood. And what a pretty name for a street. Most appropriate for a literary person to live on a street called Beautiful Leaves.

Oh you don't like to talk about yourself, it makes you uncomfortable. Don't tell me you're shy.

That's not it. You're more intimidated than shy. You think your life isn't as interesting as mine. But of course it is, every existence is interesting and has its own mystery. I'm sure yours too has its little mystery, you just have to learn to explore it. That's what writers do, they explore, or better yet, they exploit mysteries. But you know all this better than I since you are one of those who decide about literature.

All right, I won't insist, I see you are a woman of great sensitivity. You prefer that I tell you more about America. Let's talk about America, then.

America, well, I know that country in depth because for the past ten years I've lived not only in New York, but also in Chicago, San Francisco, Los Angeles, and even Detroit. Oh do I know Detroit well. It's a fascinating city, very pleasant in a way, and at the same time quite depressing. It's the city where cars are made. A city where the entire population devotes its existence to the manufacturing of those elegant and comfortable American cars. Ah, the pleasures of an American car!

Oh, you don't like big American cars, you find them cumbersome. I understand, but in America, because of the space and the long distances between cities, we need these big comfortable cars. That's probably the most striking aspect of America, its space. Everything is spacious there, the streets, the highways, the cities, the forests, the deserts. And even the houses often have ten or twelve rooms. As a matter of fact, my own apartment in New York has four rooms, and the bathroom is almost as large as this dining room. And I live alone in that flat.

No, I'm not married, not yet. I haven't found the ideal mate, the woman who will be able to live with my whims and put up with my idiosyncrasies. And I have many, you know, crazes and idiosyncrasies, as most writers do, that species of beings who create what we call literature. Ah literature, what suffering it causes to those who devote themselves to it. But see how I get carried away again.

You're too nice. You say that I am full of verve and witty eloquence. You find me amusing and profound at the same time. Madame, I am flattered. One should never take oneself too seriously. What I reproach to intellectuals, especially French intellectuals, is that they are interested only in human miseries, all they do is explain to us the suffering of humanity. But why not care also about the little goldfish, for instance, they too are part of creation, and probably suffer as much as we do.

I made you laugh. Good. Your eyes sparkle when you laugh. And now I made you blush. Ok, let's be serious and let me go on a moment with what I was saying about space in America...

May I pour you another glass of wine?

All right. It's probably because we Americans are so used to spaciousness that when we come to Europe, here in France too, and enter an apartment, we immediately feel somewhat cramped. You see, even in this beautiful apartment of Monsieur Laplume, I have to admit that I feel ... how shall I say ... a little tight, squeezed ... un peu ... compressé. Can one say that, **con-pressé?** You understand what I mean, don't you?

Oh, the word *compressé* cannot be used this way in French, or at least not in that sense. You see how these two languages I have in me play tricks on me. In any case, I don't want you to imagine, that I'm not feeling at ease right now, especially in your charming company, talking with you so pleasantly. On the contrary, I do feel good, but still, a short while ago when I had to go to the ... Oh forgive me, one is not supposed to mention such places at the table.

It's awful how that relaxed side of America at times makes you lose your sense of decorum, *le sens de la bienséance*, as they used to say in the seventeenth century. Ten years of exile in that country, still wild, still somewhat uncivilized, and here I am, almost forgetting my good manners. I hope you'll forgive me.

Anyway, as I was saying, the most fascinating aspect of America is space. Especially when you travel West, toward the great skies of the Far West. The big sky, as it is called out there in the Far West.

If I were asked to find the one word that best expresses what America is all about, I would not choose the word *liberty*, as most people would, no it is not that word-cliché that defines that country best, although it is true that liberty, freedom prevails in America. But it is not, at least for me, what characterizes America. What characterizes that country is space. Yes vast unending space, and...

Oh excuse me! I didn't see you Jean-Louis. No thank you, I already ate too much of that delicious roast. My compliments to your wife. Oh, certainly, I'll have another glass of this superb wine. Thank you, thank you, that's plenty ... Everything is going superbly. I cannot tell you how delighted I am to be sitting next to this charming lovely lady who has made me feel as loquacious as **Le Bavard** de Louis-René des Forêts. We're having an exquisite conversation. And do you know what, Jean-Louis, we have already arranged a rendez-vous for next Wednesday to discuss my novel. Next Wednesday, aux Éditions de l'Amour Fou. The novel about the ... Yes of course, I'll come and chat with you and your wife in a moment. I want to thank you both for giving me the opportunity to meet such fine people.

What a delightful man!

Ah he publishes with you! Aux Éditions de l'Amour Fou. What! His last novel won Le Prix Goncourt. Really! How wonderful. I didn't know. And I haven't read it yet. I must get a copy immediately.

Oh, you are too kind. Really, you'll give me a copy next week in your office. Fantastic. I am sure Jean-Louis will be happy to sign it for me next time I see him. What a splendid day I'm having.

Shall we go on with our conversation? I am not boring you, am I?

No. Good. We were talking about space in America, and when talking about space one must also consider mobility. Yes mobility. What I'm telling you now is based on my own personal experience because you see I traveled a great deal in America from the East Coast to the West Coast. Go West Young Man, that's what they always tell you in America, because it's in the West that all the great adventures take place, in the West that supposedly you become rich and famous. At least that's what the Hollywood movies tell you.

Mobility, that's the most interesting aspect of America, and by mobility, I not only mean physical or geographical mobility but also social and economic mobility.

Social and economic mobility. Let me explain. In America, if one has the courage, the ambition, and the ability, one can move horizontally as well as vertically, that is to say, from one corner of the country to the other, from one state to another, therefore horizontally, and from one social or economic level to another, hence vertically.

Certainly, it's possible also in France, but not for everyone, not to the same extent, because in France most people are often stuck in their social milieu, in their family, in their neighborhood even, in their profession, in their education or lack of education, in their fortune or lack of it, in their heritage in other words, whereas in America since we are all, more or less, transplanted people, we are free to move wherever we want, and therefore we are able to take advantage of all the social and economic opportunities that present themselves. That is why America is called The Land of Opportunity.

You don't seem to agree. You think that I am generalizing too much. Well, speaking from my own experience, I am convinced that had I stayed in France after the war I would not have gone very far in life. I don't think I could have managed to escape the great tragedy that fell upon me. After the war, I found myself with nothing, no family, no education, no money. Nothing. It's

America that helped me become what I am today, that gave me the opportunity to become somebody, and do what I really wanted to do. What could I have done here without a family, with no education, no means, jostled out of my social environment by the tumultuous events of World War II, alone on the edge of the great precipice of the future?

Of course, Chère Madame, it's impossible to predict the future or to contemplate it retrospectively, but we still have to admit that it always comes disguised. Falsified. If the future came naked, we would be terrified by what we would see. And that's the reason why I often wonder what my future would have been had I stayed in France. Probably a tragicomedy.

Here, let me give you an example that will illustrate what I mean. It's about a friend of mine, a French friend who like me decided to emigrate to America after the war. He too lost his entire family during the Occupation. A great and painful tragedy for him.

No, not in a bombardment, in a concentration camp. He is ... Jewish, you understand. Well this young man arrived in America with absolutely nothing. No money, no family, no friends, no education. Before the war, his parents were very poor. I think his father was a tailor, and his mother worked as a cleaning woman in order to feed her children. So as soon as he arrived in America he was forced to work for several years in a factory in Detroit. In fact, that's where I met him, in Detroit. In those days, I was playing jazz, and I traveled a great deal from one city to another with my sextet.

Yes, I was a jazz musician for a while before becoming a professor, and then a writer. I played the saxophone. Tenor and Alto. I still play from time to time with friends, but not professionally, just for my own pleasure.

So you see, in America you can do anything you want, as long as you have some talent and ambition.

Do you like jazz?

In the novel I will bring you Wednesday, the noodle novel, there are several passages describing the life of jazz musicians in the black ghettos of Detroit and New York. There is even a scene that recounts how, one evening, as I was playing in a jazz club in Detroit with my combo, Charlie Parker himself came and joined us. He borrowed my tenor saxophone because, as you probably know, normally he played the alto, but that evening he didn't have his instrument with him. But Yardbird, as he was known, was as brilliant and innovative on the tenor as he was on the alto. He played it with the same audacity and dexterity. It was an unforgettable evening which I immortalized in my novel.

But see how I get all excited when I talk about jazz, so much so that I just can't stop. I am incorrigible. Always digressing. Allow me to finish the story of my friend, who like me, went to America after the war. He is about my age.

As I was saying, soon after he arrived he found himself working on the assembly line in an automobile factory. I believe it was a Chrysler factory.

Do you know what assembly line means? It's when you do the same work, the same exact gestures for eight hours in a row, screwing on a nut or making a hole in a piece of sheet metal. I believe we call these factory workers des travailleurs à la chaine in French. Isn't that right?

By the way do you know the Charlie Chaplin movie called **Modern Times**? Well, that's exactly what it is.

You saw it several times. It's a great movie. The novel, **A Time For Noodles**, the one I'll bring you Wednesday, does in a sense play somewhat on this Chaplinesque side of the absurdity of certain human activities. But in this case, it is the act of writing itself that is questioned and even ridiculed, because to write, to a certain extent, is to do the same thing, the same gestures every day, day after day in front of the typewriter, or bent over a sheet of paper, contemplating what Mallarmé called the white agony.

I'm sure you know that wonderful sonnet of Mallarmé that begins: *Le vierge, le vivace et le bel aujourd'hui va-t-il* ... and later asks if *ce cygne d'autrefois*, that swan of yesteryears will succeed in freeing itself from this *blanche agonie* ... Ah, the white agony of the sheet of paper ... But I'm wandering again.

I was telling you about my friend who worked in a factory in Detroit. Well, do you know what he is today? A professor. A distinguished professor in one of the Ivy League Universities. Professor of Comparative Literature. He knows French and American literature in depth. He was a voracious reader. He couldn't stop reading. Even when he worked in the factory, whenever he had a chance he would read, at night instead of sleeping, on the bus taking him to work, even while eating. He read all the time. And in less than ten years, he went from the bottom to the top. From the factory to the ivory tower. During these difficult years, not only did he obtain his doctorate, but he also wrote an important and original study of the fiction of Samuel Beckett. I had the pleasure of reading the manuscript even before the book was published. I myself am a fervent reader of Mister Beckett's fiction which has greatly influenced my own work. He's an outstanding writer. In my opinion, the most important writer of our time.

Yes, you found the perfect expression. A sublime writer.

Mister Beckett read my friend's study and wrote him a warm letter thanking him for having taken the time to write about his work. My friend showed me that letter. I remember exactly what Mister Beckett said: *I thank you, Sir, for having paid attention to the shape of my sentences rather than their meaning.*

Isn't it beautiful?

In the last few years my friend, whose name, by the way, is Ramon Hombre de la Pluma, he comes from Spanish Sephardic origin, has since published several books of criticism much appreciated in literary circles. You see America made it possible for him to escape his situation as a worker and to reveal his ability as a scholar.

I doubt, Madame, that if he had remained in France he could have succeeded in such a way. Do you really think that he could have risen so easily and so rapidly from the lower depth of society to the top of academia? Certainly not. And that's what I mean by mobility in America. It's what allows you to have access to what is only a vain chimera here.

You say this is an isolated case. You believe that the same opportunities exist in France. Well I cannot agree, because you see, in America, it is possible to erase the distance between people, between social environments, between ethnic groups. I don't think that it is as easily accomplished in France. Here, it seems to me these distances are always prescribed and usually inviolable. It is somewhat like the distance between the *tu* and the *vous* in French, the *vous* that can only become *tu* when...

What do I mean? Well, for instance, right now you and I are using the formal *vous* to address each other. Therefore, there is between us a certain distance dictated by our present social situation.

You are smiling. Yes, I do remember what André Gide said on that subject, that one can address one's partner with the *tu* — for Gide it probably didn't matter if it was a man or a woman — only after having slept with that person. Forgive me for being so direct.

Yet this distance between the *tu* and the *vous* defines human relations, here in France.

True, in English there is the archaic *thou*, but the *thou* is as formal as the *you*. It does not express the intimacy of the French *tu*.

Here, let me relate an incident that happened to me right here in Paris a few days ago. I think it will clearly illustrate what I mean.

Last Friday, I hailed a taxi to go to the airport to pick up a friend who was arriving from the States. A charming beautiful young lady, but very American. You know. Blonde, blue-grey eyes, rather tall, elegant, stylish. Her first trip to Europe.

She's from Boston. Good old family of Irish origin. We met at Columbia University where she studied Anglo-Saxon literature. Anyway, I hailed this taxi at Place Denfert Rochereau. I was in a good mood that morning since I was going to see Susan again. That's her name, Susan. Except that suddenly it starts raining, and I don't have my umbrella. That was last Friday. You probably remember that downpour.

Yes, it rained all day.

In any case, after several minutes of waiting, and watching busy taxis speed past me, a taxi stops abruptly in front of me, splashing the bottom of my pants. It bothered me a lot because I wanted to look my best to greet my friend. So I get into the taxi mumbling to myself when the driver exclaims — even before I had time to settle into the seat — 4 *Rue Louis Rolland, that's where you're going, buddy, right!* I'm dumbfounded.

Why? You see, 4 Rue Louis Rolland is the address where I lived before the war. In Montrouge. That's where I spent my youth. Can you imagine how surprised I was when this taxi driver that I didn't even know tells me, more than ten years after I left for America, the address where I lived during my childhood.

This young man, who is wearing a worker's cap, notices my hesitation and says to me, using the *tu* form, can you believe that, en me tutoyant ... *hey machin, don't you remember me and you we lived on the same street, you lived at number 4, the house with the big courtyard in front, & me I lived at number 42, next to the tannery where my old man slaved before the factory burned down, don't you remember that fire ... you, your father, I think he was an artist, a painter, yeah, I can still remember, he was a strange man, un étranger...*

You understand, Madame, I'm trying to imitate as best I can this taxi driver's common way of speaking to give you a better idea of the kind of person he was. And he goes on ... *we went to school together, shit don't you remember, the boys' school Rue d'Bagneux, we were in the same class, yeah Madame Lalouche's class, man was she mean and ugly that old cow, she wore glasses La Mère Lalouche, her clothes were always wrinkled, & her stockings were forever falling down, she taught arithmetic, remember ... merde, it's so funny that you and me we meet again like this in my taxi ... must be a coincidence, don't you think...*

All of a sudden, as the taxi starts moving and the driver keeps talking on and on about the school, I see in my mind the ugly face of this mean old teacher who used to hit us on the fingers with a wooden ruler when we didn't behave, and who forced us to stand in a corner of the classroom, facing the wall with our hands crossed on top of our head, but I still do not recognize this taxi driver who keeps on reminding me of things and people I have forgotten. Intentionally I must say.

Absolutely, you said it for me. The situation was disturbing. But allow me to continue. Or rather let *him* continue.

... you had two sisters, & also a cousin ... oh what was his name ... who lived in the same building with you, I remember, we used to play football together in the street with your cousin & you & the other copains from the neighborhood, there was Gugusse, Marius' son, remember Marius, the owner of the café Avenue d'Orléans, Chez Marius it was called, & also there was Mimile who played with us, remember, Mimile, he had a sister who was a knockout, we all had eyes for her, yeah, did we have fun when we played in the street, after school...

I cannot believe he remembers all this. For him, it is probably those childhood games that count the most in his life. So I let him go on, but he notices in his rear-view mirror that I look puzzled and do not seem to recognize him, so he says ... *mais si, I'm Robert, Robert Laurent, but everybody always calls me Robbie, & you, your name is ... it's ... ah damn ... wait ... wait don't say it, it's gonna come back, it starts with an R, yeah with an R, like my name ... no it's not Roger it's ... oh I have it on the tip of my tongue...*

Rémond, I say, to get him out of his awkward situation.

yeah ... that's it, Rémond, but I forgot your last name, what's your last name...

I tell him my last name.

...yes yes, now I remember it was a foreign name, I know it didn't sound French, your father was a foreigner, un étranger, right...

I have to tell you, Madame, my paternal grandfather was Russian. A white Russian aristocrat. He came to France during the Bolshevik revolution. In fact, he fought the First World War as an officer in the French army, and was even decorated. Unfortunately, I never knew him, he died before I was born, but I was told he was a remarkable man.

Anyway, I interrupt this taxi driver who claims to be an old classmate to tell him that I am in a hurry and that I am not going to Montrouge but to Orly Airport to pick up someone.

...ah you're in a rush, okay okay, I'll step on it, je fonce, full speed direction Orly, but you know when it rains cat and dogs like this there are traffic jams on the autoroute sometimes, and you know what Rémond it's not fun to drive in this rotten city ... I dunno but that filthy weather we've been having for months now must have something to do with the atomic bomb, what do you think, they say it's the atomic bomb that fucked up the atmosphere, yeah, you know, since they have the atomic bomb the Amerloques & the Russkoffs, we live with death above our heads all the time, & you know it can drop on us any time, what a bunch of jerks these ... these politicians...

What an awful language. I apologize for having to repeat his words, but I want to give you a good idea of the situation. So I let him go on while gesturing with my hand that I want him to get going a bit faster. And now we are racing full speed on the autoroute du Sud toward Orly, in the midst of an incredible downpour.

I am afraid we are going to have an accident, especially since my driver keeps turning his head toward me sitting in the back seat as he continues to tell me all about his life, full speed as well. First, he tells me about his parents who are still alive but retired, and asks if I remember them.

He notices in his rear-view mirror that I vaguely shake my head, and he interprets this as an invitation to go on.

yeah, you understand mon pote ... he explains while glancing at me over his shoulder ... *we often wondered after the war why your parents had moved away 'cause we didn't see you anymore in the neighborhood, everybody wanted to know where you and your family had gone, but us we stayed in the same building, my parents & my sisters, remember I had four sisters, but now they're all gone, they live in the province, but me I stayed in the neighborhood, in the same house, but not with my folks, no 'cause you see me I'm married now & I even have a kid, he's eight years old, and you know what, life's not easy when you've got a kid & a wife to feed ... after the war I worked in a factory, a factory where they make tubes, you know tubes for toothpaste, it was in Vanves, but lemme tell you, what a crummy lousy job, I had to slog away ten fucking hours a day...*

I apologize again for using such language, but that's exactly how that taxi driver spoke. I assure you that even if we were effectively in the same class in grammar school, this is not the kind of person I associate with nowadays.

finally ... he continues ... *I got fed up with the damn factory, I tell you man, I had it up to here with the tubes, couldn't stand it no more, so I borrowed some dough from my old man to buy this taxi & now I'm free & I make a pretty good living driving around Paris, not a bad job, you know, you see I gotta save money 'cause my wife is gonna have another kid, yeah I knocked her up again ... hey, you must remember Josette, she's the girl who lived in the building across the street from yours, don't you remember, Josette, she was gorgeous, cute as a bug with her curly black hair, but lemme tell me you what a hot dish she was, everybody was saying that at least half the guys in the neighborhood lost it with her, but it's not true you know, they exaggerated ... hey say, how about you, Josette ... you didn't ... did you ... anyway after the war we got married me & her, we had to do it fast on top of that 'cause ... well, you know what I mean ... she was enceinte ... Josette she works in a shoe store, she sells shoes...*

He goes on telling me all about his life, his mediocre uninteresting life, while driving like a maniac in the torrential rain. Then he looks at me in his mirror and asks *... & you, what kind of job you do ... I mean, what do you do for a living...*

These are his exact words.

Yeah, what do you do for a living...

I hesitate to tell him who I am, where I come from, and what I do, especially now that we are in the middle of a traffic jam and my taxi driver, the old classmate, encountered by chance but whom I do not seem to know, focuses on the road as he overtakes a truck hurling insults at the driver, then turning to me without even looking at the road, he shouts ... *did ya see that ... what a fucking cretin, quel enfoiré, did ya see how the jerk drives, he almost crashed into me, no wonder there are so many accidents on the highways with these damned truck drivers, these guys always think they own the road, what a bunch of morons ... I tell you it's not easy to live in this stinking world...*

After this detour into vulgarity because of the truck, my driver returns to the attack ... *yeah, so what do you do in life...*

Alright, since he insists I quickly explain that I've been living in the United States for the past ten years, that I went there to study literature, and that now I am a writer, and also an American citizen.

... what, you're kidding, you're pulling my leg mon coco, you, living in America ... you, you're a Yankee, un Amerloque ... he breaks out into a sneer as he says that, obviously thinking that I am making this up, because for him America is probably only a fiction. The America he has seen in Hollywood movies. I don't insist, but it is obvious from the way he shakes his head and shrugs his shoulders as he accelerates to pass another truck that he does not believe what I told him.

... you, you write books, you're jerking me off...

I can see what he is thinking, for it's true that when I was a schoolboy the teachers always asked me if I was dreaming. I was quite a daydreamer as a child. That's probably why he thinks I am lying. You see, when I was young, before I found my vocation, I was always lost in dreams, and, I have to admit it, I was lazy. But then, isn't it true that all artists are somewhat lazy? It is said that artistic creation is often preceded by a long period of idleness and reverie. Well, I went through such a period before becoming a novelist and a poet. Yes, I also write poetry. Perhaps one of these days I'll have a chance to read you some of my poems. This way you'll have a better idea of who I am. But for the time being, let me tell you the rest of this strange encounter, and what my taxi driver said after I told him who I was and what I did.

... don't tell me you yap anglishe, ça alors that really floors me, it's a damn hard language l'anglishe, how do you manage with all these foreign words...

And he sniggers again. I have the impression that he still doesn't believe me. But then after a moment of silence, he asks.

... hey tell me, if you live in America you do like the Americans, I mean you only eat canned food ... that's what I heard ... that les Amerloques they only eat canned stuff & that's why they all look so ... so anaemic, see what I mean, a little weakly, & that's because they don't eat enough fresh food ... I'm not saying that you don't look well, no on the contrary you seem to be in good shape, but still the canned food, it lacks vitamins...

That's what my taxi driver tries to explain to me. Well, there is no need to make him understand that his vision of America is rather naive. So I say nothing. We are almost at Orly.

... say, which airline he arrives your buddy...

Pardon me?

... your friend, he arrives with which airline...

Oh! TWA. It's not a ... it's a young lady.

... Oh, it's a chick ... the one you're fucking...

I do not respond. Another moment of silence. My so-called old schoolmate must be trying to digest what I told him about myself, and all of a sudden he mumbles, as if talking to himself ... *ah it's your gonzesse who arrives from somewhere, where does she come from...*

I decide not to pursue this conversation any further. I take Susan's telegram out of my pocket and pretend to be reading it.

We finally arrive at Orly. I would have loved to get rid of this embarrassing taxi driver, but I feel somewhat compromised, so I tell him to wait for me, and once I find my friend he can take us back to town.

Because of the rain and the trouble I had finding a taxi, we arrived at Orly just when Susan's plane landed. So a few minutes later, after going through customs, Susan and I arrive at the taxi. When he sees us, the driver gets out of his seat to help with the luggage which he puts in the trunk, and that's when he notices that Susan and I are speaking English. All of a sudden he realizes that I may have told him the truth. He stares at us with a dumbfounded look.

Well, let me tell you quickly the end of this irritating encounter. We settle in the taxi, and I give the driver the address of where we are going, avoiding to say *tu* to him as it is possible to do in French when you don't know if you're supposed to use the familiar *tu* instead of the *vous*. As you know, there's always a way to construct a sentence without ever having to use the pronouns *tu* or *vous*.

Quite right. A way to bypass the person you're addressing in order to remain impersonal.

So, after having told him where we were going, I turn to Susan and we go on chatting in English. By the way, I should have mentioned that Susan doesn't know a word of French. She speaks very good Spanish, and even a bit of German, but has no French at all. The taxi starts and the driver asks me ... *Monsieur, huh ... excusez-moi ... but ... est-ce-que vous préférez ... do you want me to take the outer boulevards or l'Avenue du Général Leclerc?*

We were going to Montparnasse. That's where I live, right now, in Montparnasse, in a small but comfortable apartment.

So you see what happened. As soon as he heard me speak English this poor fellow suddenly couldn't address me with the *tu* anymore. He felt the distance between us, geographical and linguistic distance of course, but above all the social distance. We suddenly didn't live in the same world, and so it became impossible for him to say *tu* to me. That's what I meant by the distance which divides people in France. But that's not all.

We arrive at the address I indicated. He quickly gets out of his taxi to help with Susan's suitcases. I pay him, giving him a generous tip. Probably because I feel embarrassed by his confusion. And I see him hesitate. He stands there, on the sidewalk, his mouth half open, as if trying to find the right way of saying what he wants to say.

... but ... but, vi ... ve ve ... vien ... ve-nez quand même dîner un soir chez nous, toi & ..., enfin vous & votre amie ... but but you you ... sir you can still come to dinner one of these days, you ... I mean you sir & your friend...

I didn't reply. I simply nodded vaguely, the kind of gesture one makes when one doesn't mean either yes or no. I had no intention of going for dinner at his home. What would we have to say to each other? Finally he jumps in his taxi, slamming the door, and making the tires screech as he shoots off.

You see, what struck me, and still does today, is not as much the clumsy, tactless switch from the *tu* to the *vous* as his *quand même*, meaning I suppose, *in spite of all*. Yes, of course, what he meant is that despite the distance that now exists between us, despite all that happened since our childhood, and everything else, is it still possible to...?

Well. No need to continue. I am sure you understand what I'm trying to say. For me this incident was very revealing.

Oh, but I see that everyone is getting up from the table and moving to the salon. Chère Madame, it was a great pleasure talking with you, and now I look forward to seeing you again in a few days.

You too. Well I am very happy to hear that. I hope I didn't bore you too much with all my stories. It's the incurable storyteller in me.

Not at all! You're so kind.

Of course not, I won't forget. Next Wednesday in your office. Ten thirty, that's right. I'll be on time. I can't wait. Till Wednesday then. I'd better go now, I have to talk to Jean-Louis and his wife before leaving. I must thank them for inviting me today and above all for giving me the opportunity to meet such a charming lady. Au revoir. Goodbye. See you next week.

AH MY LUNCH CHEZ LAPLUME...

Want me to tell you about the lunch chez Laplume, okay, but I warn you, it wasn't funny at all, you can't imagine how boring it was, what a bunch of snobs those literary people, and all of them third-rate writers, you can see that at first glance, just a pack of pathetic writers who talk as if they have mashed potatoes in their mouths and a feather up their asses, you should have heard them...

So you see my deaar ... it bothers me so terribly chère Madame that a friend of mine should be treated that way ... that boy has such talent but it is wasted in self-indulgence ... oh yes he has all my admiration ... what a superb book it is but ... ah deaaar deaaarJean-Louis if only you knew ... mon cherrr machinchouette ... daarling ... oh Madame Trucmuche how I adored your last book...

That's the way those assholes talk, it's always Cher Monsieur here and Chère Madame there, and lick-my-boots here and kiss-my-ass there, and how excited they get when talking about their own books, with heavy sighs they say, *in my last book there's a love scene of breathtaking eroticism ... in the novel I am currently writing I devote more than twenty pages to the description of two lovers making mad mad...*

Mad bullshit, masturbating I'm sure, let me tell you, when those petty third-rate writers start to drivel on and on it's really chochotte machin, or as Flaubert said, that kind of ecstatic exaltation might look good in books, but one can doubt it is beneficial to literature, and you should have seen them, they all have cute effeminate hair cuts, some even with a pony tail, and little goatees too, you know the musketeer goatee, and of course they all wear the obligatory turtleneck sweater, as if long hair, a beard, and a turtleneck sweater make you a better writer, ah what a bunch of cretins, they put on airs just to impress one another, you should see how they eat, with their forks and knives daintily held between two fingers, unbelievable...

But to tell you the truth I had a good time finally, I wasn't bored because I spent most of the afternoon talking to a woman, quite an attractive gonzesse, sort of sexy, in her middle thirties, well put together, maybe a bit over-perfumed, and not too bright, but man she sure had a friendly ass...

No, I behaved, I didn't make a pass at her, I just let her know, in a rather subtle manner, that if...

I'm seeing her again next Wednesday in her office, because, you won't believe this, she's the literary director of a publishing house, and you know what, she wants me to bring her my novel, you know the one about the noodles...

It's true, really, I'm not kidding, I described the book to her, told her what it's about, and she got all excited, especially when I told her the story takes place in New York and it's about jazz, she loves jazz she said, so, imagine, it's possible that my Noodles will get published, and who knows maybe I'll have my name in all the newspapers of Paris, Le Monde, Le Figaro, La Quinzaine Littéraire, Les Lettres Françaises, and who knows where else, because I believe I'm writing a chef-d'oeuvre, well a little chef-d'oeuvre, nobody to my knowledge ever wrote a novel entirely based on boxes of noodles, don't you think it's a brilliant idea, and maybe I'll win a literary prize, doesn't matter which one, I don't care, even if it's only The Pasta Prize awarded by some international macaroni company...

Go ahead laugh, but he who laughs last laughs best as the saying goes, we'll see who laughs best when I'll be interviewed on television on Apostrophe, talking with Monsieur ... what's-his-name, that jackass ... Privat, Privot, Pridevot, Pinot, Pinard, damn I forgot his name, you know who I mean, the guy who wears his spectacles on the tip of his nose and thinks he knows everything about literature, another asshole...

I'm not exaggerating my friend, my noodle story will dazzle that sexy literary director, hey maybe she loves noodles, like me, anyway I'll bet you anything that if she'd had a contract in her purse we'd have signed it right there on the spot, that's how much she was excited by what I told her, I even recited one of my poems to her...

You should have seen how I impressed that charming lady with my knowledge and my lyricism, because me I remember everything I read, therefore it's all here in my head and I can make anything resurface anytime anywhere, the classics as well as the moderns, I can quote Boileau as well as René Char in the same sentence, for instance do you know that little classical saying, *La racine boit l'eau de la fontaine molière*, well there you have it, in one short sentence a complete seminar on the French literature of the Seventeenth Century...

You don't know that thing, I'll be darned, all the Parisian lycéens know that, you mean you never learned by heart the great lines of Corneille and Racine, wow you're not very cultivated, you never recited, *Rodrigue as-tu du coeur, non Papa j'ai du foie,* or better yet, *oh rage oh désespoir de se voir tout nu le soir dans le noir...*

You seem surprised, I know loads of stuff like that, the problem is that the more I remember the more it gets all mixed up in my head, and then it becomes scraps of memories...

Here, if you're interested I'll recite a passage from a prose poem I wrote the other day with the leftover crumbs of poetry that float in my head, you know all the poems they pounded into me in school, I put all these fragments together and made a poetic stew out of them, but with some subtle little changes here and there, it's called **Mémoires en Miettes**, you'll hear faraway echos of poetry that you too probably were forced to learn by heart, here listen...

———

**The Listener closes his eyes
and listens intently
to the poem**

Mémoires en Miettes

je trouve parmi les débris de ma vie déchirée par le temps un morceau de pensée qui pousse sur le crâne creux de ma géologie intime où ma végétation humide attend gentiment le vent de la vieillesse en se tordant les mains et tout à coup le rire se lève il faut tenter de respirer même s'il est impossible de voir l'insecte qui me gratte la fesse gauche tandis que sous ce toit tranquille où

cavalent des morpions mes souvenirs obscurs broutent
des fourmis rangées en spirales dirigeant leurs cercles
alchimiques vers des serpents tordus qui se dévorent eux-
même en se creusant la tête triangulaire ah la chair est
lasse hélas et j'ai lu tous les bouquins pornos mais je
m'en fous je partirai un doigt dans la bouche oh la la que
d'amours fous dans des nuits sans nuit je rêverai un
pied contre le coeur en écoutant celui qui pleure ici si
près de moi mais sois sage oh ma douleur et chatouille le
divin ennui de notre recueillement sans rage ni désespoir
de ne pouvoir savoir dans le noir revoir les bons soirs
remplis de nos noyés perdus dans les goémons verts et
pourtant je ne regrette pas les murs écroulés de mon passé
ah quelle boue gouffre de mon cou coupé dans la mémoire
d'outre-tombe où j'attends en vain de devenir un très
méchant fou suspendu à mon sperme tout seul me
regardant me voir dans les îles chaudes du coeur
croustillé d'or las de l'amer repos...

Okay that's enough, but you see how my stuff works, and it's only a short extract of a much longer poem, un morceau choisi, the kind of selected passage they fed us in school, what do you think, not bad...

What are you talking about, it's completely incoherent and disjointed, you're really something, sometimes I wonder why I go on telling you my stories, don't tell me you believe that poetry must have a meaning, a direction, be accessible, real poetry should never be rational and coherent, anyway I am not here to lecture you on poetry, I just wanted to give you an idea of the kind of stuff I write when I poetize, to show you how I impressed that sexy literary director, I recited that thing to her, and she loved it...

Believe me, she looked at me as if I were some kind of genius, she was fascinated by all the bullshit I threw at her, she must have taken me for a superbrain even though I was telling her a bunch of nonsense, especially when I recited that prose poem to her, just to amuse her...

You have to understand, when I tell my stories I don't have to respect the lies and truths I'm weaving together, I can modify, amplify, corrupt, alter, distort, falsify that canvas as much as I want, and of course digress and even regress when I feel like it, in other words I am free, yes free, even if sometimes it makes me come within an inch of catastrophe, but what do you think literary creation is, it's always a catastrophe, a happy catastrophe in fact, according to Monsieur Didier Anzieu...

Oh you don't know Didier Anzieu, nice name Anzieu, makes you think of the sky, les cieux, Anzieu is a guy who delves into people's skulls, even into dead people's skulls, he's a psychiatrist who writes literary criticism, he psychoanalyzes dead writers with Freudian crap, he was there at Laplume's lunch and we exchanged a few words, he wrote a book about Samuel Beckett, a stupid book, I read it, it's pulled out of a hat, psychiatrists scare the hell out of me, they invent things just to make you feel guilty, anyway I talked to him because his name intrigued me...

I don't know why I'm suddenly mentioning him, what is he doing here Anzieu in the middle of what I was telling you, so I met him and we talked about literary creation, but that's not a good enough reason to give him a place here, in this story, why on earth did I fall into that psychogazouillis, probably because I always come within a hair's breath of happy catastrophe when I tell my stories, after all we know for a fact that artistic creation can only be done in a state of excitement, you have to have an erection to be able to screw, you have to be excited about what you're doing otherwise it's like a premature ejaculation, but never mind that's not what I wanted to talk about, what I was trying to suggest before drifting into

126

the psychopathetic is that me, as a writer, I suffer from a surplus of pulsations, or if you prefer, I have a floating aggressive libido, and that's probably why I talk about sex all the time, and this brings me back to the subject of that charming literary director of Les Éditions de l'Amour Fou, to tell you the truth, I'd love to fuck her in the ass with my noodles, that's what I wanted to tell you before I got lost in that psychoshitstuff...

Oh, monsieur thinks I'm getting too vulgar, okay, you're right, but understand, that lunch yesterday really bugged the hell out of me, what a pain in the ass, and on top of that, the food was awful, that Madame Laplume she sure can't cook for shit, her roast beef was too well done and smelled burnt, the potatoes weren't cooked enough, and her crème caramel was dripping all over, only the wine wasn't too bad, Laplume served a decent St. Émilion, so in spite of all the assholes I had a good time telling my stories to that charming lady...

What did I tell her...

The story of my life of course, but I also invented stuff that never happened, or didn't happen yet, but will happen eventually, or stuff that happens in the noodle novel, because me I make no distinction between reality and fiction...

Some of my stories are based on my own experiences, and others come from my novel, that's the way I function, on one side I'm writing a novel in which my protagonist experiences my life, somewhat transformed and sublimated by imagination, and on the other, when I recount my life experiences, I mix in all kinds of fictitious elements, experiences that belong to the protagonist of my novel, the noodler, who's not me since he doesn't really exist, or rather exists only in words, whereas me I'm real since I'm sitting here in front of you, in flesh and blood, do you follow my reasoning, you look confused...

You say it's not clear, how can I project myself into something that didn't happen yet, wow I didn't think you were that dumb, that's why I have to stop all the time to explain what is self-evident...

Look, let me give you an example, I told that lady a crazy story about a taxi driver who just like that, out of the blue as they say in America, claimed that he knew me as a kid, that we went to school together, of course none of that is true, me I didn't know that guy, I invented him, I even told her that it was the taxi driver who took me to the airport to pick up Susan, but Susan, as you know, she hasn't arrived yet, she's arriving in two or three days, or is it four days, I forget what I told you before...

Oh I said five days, you sure have a good memory, that's great, because this way you can correct my mistakes, especially my chronological errors, when it comes to keeping track of time, I always get lost...

In any case, I told her the story of the taxi driver and of Susan's arrival even though it's not true, or it hasn't happened yet, but since I'm certain that something like that is going to happen soon, I mean the fortuitous encounter with the guy who will claim to be my childhood friend, well I just jumped a bit ahead into what I will probably tell you later, I simply leap-frogged into the future of my story, dans **Le Livre à Venir** as Maurice Blanchot calls it, all novelists do that, announce in advance what is going to happen later in the life of their characters, Stendhal did that all the time, just reread **Le Rouge et Le Noir** or **La Chartreuse de Parme**, and you'll see how the story leaps forward into the future of Julien Sorel and Fabrice del Dongo, so if sometimes I project myself into my own future, it's because I'm like a character in my own novel as well as the guy who invents the stuff, I talk about myself as if I were someone else, as if I were fictitious, so you see, I'm somewhat of a literary invention, I invent myself and the story of my life as I go along, and that's probably why that sexy lady was interested in me and in my noodles...

But enough of that, I'd better stop jumping around all over the place, otherwise we're going to waste another day of great storytelling, and we won't progress, today we must go forward because so far we've been stagnating too much, I have to get to the core of the story of my Aunt Rachel...

But before I go on, tell me, what did you do yesterday when we didn't see each other...

You went to the movies, what did you see...

A Sergio Leone film, which one, I love his movies, I love those Spaghetti Westerns...

Duck You Sucker, that's a good one, I must have seen it at least four times, in fact I saw all of Sergio Leone's movies, that guy is a genius, and you know what, he never set foot in America, everything he knows about Westerns he learned watching cowboy movies or reading books about the Far West, so he invents most of the stuff in his movies, shows you to what extent America is fictitious, in a way America doesn't really exist, I know, I live there, it was invented by Hollywood, America is all make-believe...

So you're a movie freak too, but you don't work, you don't do anything that you can afford to go to the movies during the week, how do you earn a living, you've got means...

You know what, I don't know anything about you, we met like that the other day in a café, became buddies right away, probably because you have a cheerful friendly face, and I suppose you must have found mine intriguing...

I see from your smile that you agree, it's your friendly pimp face that attracted me, but tell me what do you do in life...

You've got a girl who takes care of you, you're a gigolo, you're being kept, that's why you can spend your time listening to my stories...

No, that's not it...

What ... you're kidding, you're a professional listener of stories, that's what you do for a living, you go from one story to another and you listen, hey that's fantastic...

So perhaps our encounter was not accidental, were you looking for me, you know the expression, you wouldn't have found me if you hadn't been looking for me, well something like that, or maybe it's the reverse, doesn't matter, what really matters is that you're here and that you are listening to my stories, gives me a purpose, a reason to go on, even if I don't know where I'm going...

And since you're here to listen, I should tell you something nice today, something profound, exhilarating, what would you like to hear, do you want me to tell you about my British girl or do you want to know more about Susan...

Oh you want me to continue with the lunch chez Tante Marie, you're right, I almost forgot that I left you in the middle of that story, and myself standing like a jerk in the courtyard with a stupid grin on my face, all right then, back to Montrouge...

So, knowing that the whole family always got together on Sundays chez Marie, and having reached the point of no return, I decided to go see them, but let me tell you, I wasn't in a very good mood that day, that's for damn sure...

I know you've heard that part of the story, but I've got to step back a bit to be able to leap forward, otherwise the story won't take off in the right direction, so bear with me my dear listener, and we'll get back to 4 Rue Louis Rolland in a moment...

The other day I was telling you that to go to Montrouge, you have to take the métro to Porte d'Orléans, and then to get to Rue Louis Rolland it's a ten minute walk, you can either take l'Avenue d'Orléans or la Rue de Bagneux, one or the other, in the old days, when I was a kid, between the métro Porte d'Orléans and Montrouge there was La Zone, the slum belt, it was like that around the entire city of Paris, a wide stretch of wasteland where bums and thieves used to live, you know, the rabble, the canaille, the homeless, the jobless, they cooked their grub on campfires and slept on the ground wrapped in newspapers or in cardboard boxes, in the winter it was tough for them...

You bet it was a dangerous place, especially at night when you came home after an evening in Montparnasse or on the Champs Elysées, to see a movie or go to the resto, or even after a quickie in one of the bordels on Rue St. Denis, damn right it was dangerous to cross The Zone alone on foot, people used to walk together in groups from the métro, in groups of five or six, to protect themselves because they were scared to get mugged by the Sidis, that's what we called those bums who lived in La Zone, les Sidis, because you see most of them came from North Africa, they were Arabs from the colonies, and believe me Coco these guys were tough, you had to cool it with them otherwise psitt you were done for, your head lopped off or a blade between your shoulders...

I'm not exaggerating, you should have seen their faces, they all looked so mean and tough, they never washed, they all had thick mustaches, Arabs always have mustaches like that, thick and full of lice, but you know in the end these guys were nothing but poor slobs, poor bastards who came to La Belle France to get a job, their heads full of the beautiful images they had seen in glossy magazines about life in the Mother Country, except that nobody wanted to give them a job, so no wonder they had to sleep in La Zone, to be safe when you walked past them you always had to have some change in your pocket, this way if you gave them a little something, two, three sous, they smiled at you with rotten yellow teeth and thanked you like you were a millionaire...

No, these slums don't exist anymore, they were cleared out after the war, on that land they built huge modern buildings, blocks and blocks of luxury apartments for the bourgeois, all around the périphérique, but still I remember the way it was, and let me tell you, it wasn't pleasant, that's for sure, scary like hell, especially at night, but look, I'm not here to talk about geography or urban anthropology, that's not why I told you about La Zone, I just wanted to situate Montrouge for you...

I was telling you about my visit chez Tante Marie, so here we go, I enter the courtyard and there I see my cousin Marco doing some gardening...

Last time I said he was at the second floor window with my Aunt Rachel, then I was mistaken because I'm certain he was gardening in the courtyard when I arrived,

but it doesn't matter, who cares if he was in the courtyard or at the window, I was there and that's what really matters, right...

By the way I've got to clarify something, the courtyard in
front of the house, it wasn't really a courtyard, it was more
like a little garden, because once Uncle Léon planted a
tree in the middle of the courtyard, with a flower bed
around it, it was quite an event the day Léon planted his
tree, I was still a kid but I remember that day so clearly,
everybody in the building was watching from the windows and shouting encouragements, he had taken off his
veston, Uncle Léon always wore a jacket, even at the table
while eating, it made him feel like a big shot, but in reality he was only a mediocre tailor in the suburbs, in any
case, that day he took off his jacket, rolled up his shirt
sleeves, and he started digging like a lunatic, sweating
all over, I remember his purple suspenders, I don't know
why I remember those purple suspenders, the same as
Adolphe's, you know, Adolphe in **La Nausée**, the bar-
man au Rendez-vous des Cheminots who made
Roquentin feel sick to his stomach with his purple suspenders, and man did Léon sweat that day, he looked
like he was going to pass out any moment, but when he
finished planting his tree and the flowers, he leaned on
his shovel with a proud look on his red face and stood
there admiring the fruits of his labor, and it was hard work
for him, don't forget Léon was only a tailor, so he wasn't
that strong, he wasn't built for that kind of manual labor, so all of us at the windows we applauded him, but
to tell you the truth, that tree never grew, it always looked
like it was dying, it looked like the tree in Godot, yes
Léon's tree didn't look too healthy, rather piss poor, like
Léon himself, moche and chétif, I mean not very good-
looking, in fact Léon looked just like Fernandel...

Fernandel, the famous actor, you don't remember him,
he was a damned good actor, and very funny, tall and

gangling, just like my Uncle Léon, everybody in our neighborhood used to say that Léon had Fernandel's mug, and they knew what they were talking about because every Thursday Fernandel came to pay a visit to a rich lady who lived in a beautiful house surrounded by a tall green fence, number 19 Rue Louis Rolland, very close to where I lived, we called her la Comtesse de Montrouge, she looked rich, she wore chic clothes, in the winter she would go out wearing a huge expensive-looking fur coat, on Thursdays when we played in the street, in those days there was no school on Thursdays, so we could play in the street, we would see Fernandel's big black Citroën traction avant arrive with the chauffeur behind the wheel, and we could look at him, but not too close because we didn't want to bother him, movie stars don't like to be stared at from too close, but every Thursday without exception, at one o'clock sharp he arrived with his traction avant and his chauffeur, and he quickly went inside the beautiful house, his hat pulled down over his eyes and the collar of his coat turned up to his ears, he looked like a spy, and he stayed there chez la Comtesse until his chauffeur came back to get him at five o'clock sharp, I swear it's true, everybody in Montrouge knew that Fernandel frequented our neighborhood...

What was Fernandel doing there, how naive can you be, what do you think he was doing, obviously he didn't come to play dominos with Madame la Comtesse, or to tell her the story of his life, use your brains, everybody in the neighborhood knew what he was doing there, and that's why we were able to notice the resemblance between my Uncle Léon and Fernandel...

You're right, we could have seen the resemblance by going to the movies, but this way it was more real seeing Fernandel in person...

You want me to tell you something, Fernandel in person, without his make-up and all the shit movie stars put on their faces to look better, he was sort of ugly, and Léon he was even more ugly with his big glassy eyes, his thick lips, his hooked nose with hair coming out of it, and on top of that he was always yelling, always arguing with everybody, especially with my father, Léon used to say that my father was a nobody, a lazy bum, a good-for-nothing, artists are useless to society, he would say...

I told you, didn't I, that my father was an artist, and that he had tuberculosis...

But to come back to Léon's tree, it was rather scraggly, it never grew more than three meters tall, every Spring people in the building wondered if it was going to come back to life, but that little tree was stubborn, and each Spring, it sprouted its four puny little leaves, I loved that tree, I think that tree was suffering like the rest of humanity...

What are you mumbling about, oh I see, Monsieur says that he didn't come here to listen to me talk about nature, okay no need to jump on your high horse just because I embarked on a tree story and digressed into Fernandel and his mistress, if my detours bug you so much that means you don't understand my aesthetic system, you don't see that my recitation is more like dancing than walking...

Listen carefully because what I'm going to tell you now is very important, so pay attention, you see, one always walks for a reason, when you walk it's because you're going somewhere, to work, to the grocery store to do your shopping, to your girlfriend's house for a quickie, to walk your dog, and even if you're going nowhere, if you don't have a real destination, there's always a reason for walking, to stretch your legs, to exercise, to ponder your future, whereas one dances for nothing, only for the beauty of dancing, for the form, because one can never tell the dancer from the dance, as Yeats put it so well, the walker always walks for a reason, it's the reason that makes him walk, good or bad, useful or useless, doesn't matter, ah but one dances for no reason, that's what you have to understand if you're going to stay and listen to me, I'm not walking here, I'm dancing, get it, I'm doing acrobatics, I don't tell my stories in order to get somewhere, I tell them for the simple pleasure of telling, no more no less, and if you're listening in order to find out what's going to happen at the end, you're wasting your time, you have to listen just for the pleasure of listening to my voice, to the dancing of my voice if you prefer...

So now, let me make a nice entre-chat in the staircase of 4 Rue Louis Rolland and hop here we are in Tante Marie's apartment...

No, wait a minute, let's go back downstairs in the courtyard to better place the whole family at the windows, and my cousin Marco in the garden planting his radishes, they always grew radishes in their courtyard...

So there they are leaning out of the windows, my Aunt Marie, Aunt Fanny, Aunt Rachel, Aunt Sarah, and Uncle Léon trying to squeeze his ugly head between the other heads, what a puppet gallery, amazing how even after ten years of absence I still recognize them all, even though they all look older, their hair greyer, their faces more wrinkled...

Tante Rachel who was so beautiful ten years ago now looks like an old lady, but Marco hasn't changed a bit, same handsome face, same black curly hair slicked with brilliantine and plastered down on the sides, Marco's friends always called him Casanova, I saw him in action before I left for America, when from time to time I tagged along when he went to Montparnasse or on the Champs-Elysées to pick up a piece of ass, Marco always managed to get laid, but not me because, as I told you, I was terribly shy when I was younger, shy and naive...

Don't get nervous, I'm getting back to the story, so here I'm in the garden, Marco stares at me stupefied, as if I was a ghost or something, and then he shouts, I'll be damned, c'est pas croyable, c'est l'Amerloque, that little jerk of a cousin, it's Réémond, he came back my blockhead of a cousin, hey did you find gold over there in the streets of America, are you a millionaire, do you drive a Cadillac...

I almost ran out of there, but I couldn't move, I was frozen in place, I felt just like Léon's miserable tree...

Look at that, Marco is now next to me feeling the quality of the cloth of my jacket, nice schmates, he sneers, doesn't he look chic my little cousin with his American ready-to-wear navy blue blazer and his baggy American trousers, who is your tailor over there, Rockefeller...

You see, that's how he treated me all the time, always got a kick out of treating me like a piece of shit, as if I was inferior, destined to be a failure, ah did he make me suffer Marco before the war, when we lived in the same house...

I should have told him, go fuck yourself you second-rate tailor, go to hell, I should have turned around and left for good...

Meanwhile Aunt Marie shouts from the second floor window, hurry, hurry, come on up my boy, as if she's happy to see me...

I must admit that Tante Marie, before the war, sometimes took care of me and my sisters when my mother went to clean other people's houses and we didn't have enough to eat, Marie would give us a little bit of food, on the sly, nothing much, un morceau de pain avec un tout petit bout de fromage, you know, a piece of bread with a slice of cheese, she would slip it into our hands in the staircase when we came home from school, whispering in a hushed voice, shh hurry take this upstairs before Tonton Léon sees you...

Yes, she looks happy to see me Tante Marie, and the other Aunts too, Tante Rachel especially, because they all scream together, it's Rémond, Margot's son, look how well dressed he is, so elegant, he looks like a real American, hurry up, come upstairs so we can take a good look at you and give you a kiss...

I think that even Marco is happy to see me again, even though I'm sure he knows how much I hated his guts and how jealous I was of him when we were kids, so after having made fun of my clothes he gives me a big slap on the back, puts his arms around my shoulders to hug me, and tells me, come on upstairs Schimele-Bubke-Zinn, let's have some lunch and you can tell us everything you did over there in America...

So together, my cousin and I, we go up the stairs to the second floor...

I should mention that after I left for America, I never wrote to any of them, not even to my Aunt Rachel who had been so kind to me, so generous, as you will hear when I get to that part of the story, so they had no idea what I had become, what I was doing, and I'm sure they didn't give a damn...

In any case, here I am going up the stairs, the same old stairs I climbed so many times when I was a boy, the same old stairs that smelled of overcooked cabbage and rancid piss...

Of course not, there is no elevator in that house, what do you think, it's an old building, must have been built in the nineteenth century, probably even before that, so the staircase is really dark and narrow, and always that awful smell of rancid piss and overcooked cauliflower, that's the first thing I notice as I enter the corridor, the smell, but you know, that smell gave me a shock, right here, a little flicker in the heart, as if climbing up these stairs was like going down into my childhood, do you know what I mean, a kind of reverse ascension, in depth, except that the stink was a lot worse now than back then, and as I enter Aunt Marie's apartment, I notice how the parquet isn't as shiny as it used to be before the war, but still my first reflex is to put my feet on the cloth pads near the door in the entry, amazing the old habits one has in one's blood, how conditioned we are to repeat the same old gestures even though meaningless and irrelevant now, and so here I am sliding on the floor from one Aunt to the next kissing them and letting them kiss me...

What strikes me right away is how this apartment which seemed so spacious, so luxurious and sumptuous before I left for America, now looks small, confined, dusty and seedy, although I can tell that Léon and Marie are still plenty rich, the silver on the table, the oriental carpets, all this smells of money, I notice this while everybody embraces me, and my Aunts nod to one another approvingly, look how handsome, how healthy he looks, he must have a good life in America, he looks so well-fed, and take a look at his clothes, he's really become an American...

Aunt Rachel squeezes me real tight in her arms, she has tears in her eyes, he looks so much like his poor mother, she says tilting her head back to better look at me, then she hugs me again and kisses me hard, wetting my cheeks with her tears, ah if only you knew what a saint your mother was, she squeezes me harder against her as she says that, and all of sudden, even though I'm trying to restrain myself, I feel moved...

No, I didn't cry...

I know I told you that I hate the whole damned family, but with Tante Rachel it's different, she's an exception, let me tell you why...

I'm going to skip all the details of the hugging and kissing and all the emotional stuff, the banalities one says to a nephew who's been away for ten years, and before we all sit down to eat Tante Marie's lunch, I'm going to tell you the story of Tante Rachel, and you'll understand why she's so special to me...

It's a great story, I hope you're not in a hurry, because it's going to be a long detour, but essential, wait till you hear...

Okay, sit back and listen while I plunge into the history of my family...

In 1910, I think it was 1910, you may want to verify that in a history book, or in the city archives, there was a great flood in Paris, the Seine overflowed, so for weeks it became difficult to move about in the city since there was water all over, my grandfather, on my mother's side, was a shoemaker, and in spite of the inundation he had to go to work because of the children, the eight children he and my grandmother had brought into this world, they had to feed these kids, that's what happens when you screw too much, you have to suffer the consequences, so one cold rainy morning my grandfather left home to go to work, with water up to his knees, and he never came back, nobody ever knew what became of him...

He just disappeared, and when us kids asked where our grandfather was, we were always told that he perished in the flood, that he probably fell into a big hole full of water and was never found, you can believe that story if you want to, personally I think my grandfather took off, he was fed up with the wife and the kids and the misery, he couldn't take it any more, so he abandoned them all, just like that...

That's what I think he did, he took off, maybe with some young woman, I understand he was quite a womanizer, like my father, but whatever the case, my grandfather disappeared in 1910, so now my grandmother suddenly finds herself without a husband, and eight kids to raise, the youngest, Sarah, only six months old at the time, and the oldest, Aunt Marie, fourteen, my mother was seven then, that's the family situation in 1910...

Of course, it's my mother who told us all that, so what I'm telling you now comes from her, or else from my grandmother and the rest of the family when they reminisced about what happened before I was born, so none of it is really verifiable...

In any case, suddenly finding herself alone with eight children to feed and no money, my grandmother is forced to put three of the children in an orphanage, Aunt Rachel, four years old, Uncle Maurice, six, and my mother, seven...

I know, it's sad that my mother was raised in an orphanage, maybe that's why I was destined to be orphaned too...

Okay, three kids in the orphanage, Rachel, Maurice, and my mother Marguerite, four, six, and seven, I think I got the ages more or less right, I'm forced to approximate because I'm not sure any more when all these children were born, but the orphanage that's the truth, it's real, and according to what my mother told us, it was like a prison...

Oh you want to know about the other children, well, the two youngest, the six months old Sarah, and Lea who was two, of course my grandmother keeps them with her since they're still babies, but the three oldest, Marie, Fanny, and Jean, fourteen, thirteen, and eleven, they are forced to go to work in a factory, a factory where they made toothpaste tubes, I think that's what it was, but I may be confusing it with some other factory...

Damn right it wasn't fun for them, but somehow they all had to survive, and in those days children were sent to work when there was no other way to put food on the table...

It's sad, yes it's sad, but stop interrupting me when I'm launched like this, I'm trying to tell this in one breath in order to create more tension and emotion...

Ok, let's forget the two babies who stayed with the grandmother, those two don't count, and also the three oldest who went to work in a factory, even though it was hell for them, and let's concentrate on the three kids who were dumped in the orphanage...

My mother and Maurice stayed in that place until the age of eighteen, and they suffered plenty in that prison, you should have heard the stories my mother told us about the eleven years she spent there, how hard she had to work scrubbing floors on her knees, doing laundry, washing pots and pans in the kitchen, and how the women who took care of the kids used to beat them for no reason, just to teach them how to behave, but mostly because these women who run orphanages hate children, it's well-known, these women are all failed mothers, but look, I won't go on about the miseries my mother endured in that orphanage or I'll make you weep, I don't want to redo Les Misérables of Victor Hugo, it's already been overdone, and besides it's not about my mother I want to tell you, it's about my Aunt Rachel...

But perhaps a few more words about my mother, just to set the scene in the orphanage...

Being the oldest of the three kids, she was the one who took care of the other two, as best she could for a little seven year old girl, she mended their clothes when they were ripped, she darned their socks when there were holes in them, because you know the kids didn't get a lot of clothes in that orphanage, she gave up her own portion to put a little more food on Rachel and Maurice's plates, she combed their hair, wiped their tears when they were crying at night before falling asleep, she was like a mother to them, and that's why Uncle Maurice and Aunt Rachel always said that my mother was a saint, that does her a lot of good now...

It must have been hell in that sordid orphanage, instead of taking care of the kids, instead of preparing them for the world, those harpies beat the shit out of them, they didn't miss an occasion to hit them, it was like they were always mad at the kids, so my mother suffered for eleven years in that horrible place, eleven years of martyrdom...

No it was not a catholic joint with nuns, it's not because I say martyrdom that immediately you have to make a connection with the Christian martyrs of ancient Rome who were fed to the lions, it was a Jewish orphanage, there are Jewish orphanages too you know, this one was called La Maison Rothschild...

I don't think it still exists, the Germans and the fucking Pétainistes got rid of it during the Occupation, they probably made a regular prison out of it for political undesirables, you know, foreigners, les étrangers, les Maquisards, Les Communistes, after having dispatched all the kids to you know where, I never saw that place, my mother never took us there, she didn't want us to see it, but she talked about it all the time, and always with tears in her eyes...

My poor mother, she cried all the time, her big black eyes were always full of tears, that's all I remember about her, how she cried all the time, quietly...

My soft-voiced mother wept for everyone, but not for long, her beautiful black hair never turned white, her big black eyes became stone...

You see how incorrigible I am, wandering again, this time with Paul Célan, I just can't get to what I want to tell you, the story of my Aunt Rachel...

No more wandering, let's forget my mother with her eyes full of tears, maybe later I'll tell you more about her...

At the age of thirteen Rachel sneaks out of the orphanage and takes off, just like that, one night when everyone is asleep...

It happened all the time that kids ran away from that horrible place in the middle of the night...

The only one little Rachel, shivering with fear, says goodbye to before leaving is my mother...

144

My mother is in bed, it's the middle of the night, Rachel comes and kneels next to her bed to kiss her, she has put her few miserable rags in a paper bag, and she's carrying her big ugly black orphan boots in her hand, and while kissing her sister she begs her to come with her...

Come Margot, come hurry get dressed, let's run away together, she says, you'll see we'll manage, together we'll make it, let's leave this terrible place...

But my mother who was shy, and not very daring, not as resourceful as Rachel who was, from what I've heard, quite adventurous, tells her little sister that she can't, that she's too scared, and besides she must stay to take care of Maurice who was a sickly little boy, but while they're embracing each other, with tears running down their cheeks, my mother murmurs to Rachel in a hushed voice, go, go my little Rachel, go my little sister, hurry run away, and make a good life for yourself dans la liberté...

Well, I don't know if it's exactly what my mother said to her sister, but probably something like that, and that's how Rachel took off, one night, with my mother's words to drive her on towards freedom...

From what my mother told us, it wasn't easy to escape from that orphanage, there was a tall wall surrounding the yard, I told you it was like a prison, but Rachel did it, she jumped that wall, she was thirteen then, this was in 1919...

Remember, everything I'm telling you about the orphanage happened before I was born, all of it was told to me, so I'm merely repeating what I heard when I was a child, and it's quite possible that what I was told had already been distorted, altered by bad memory, because you

145

know the stories your parents tell you about their life, I mean what happened to them before you were born, are often half forgotten stories, or else they have been improved, transformed, beautified, uglified even to make them sound sadder than they were, that's why one can only imagine what really happened, the past is always made of distorted recollections that can never be trusted...

Anyway, that night, after having cried with my mother, and after having kissed her for the last time ever, Rachel escapes from the orphanage, it was during the winter of 1919...

How do I know it was winter, I just know, it had to be winter, it makes the story more dramatic if it's winter...

The winter of 1919, pay attention, are you asleep, I told you my grandfather disappeared in 1910 during the great flood, and that my mother was seven at the time, Uncle Maurice six, and Aunt Rachel four when they were dumped in the orphanage, so if Rachel escapes at the age of thirteen, nine years later, it brings us to 1919, you see how easy it is to do that kind of calculation, but don't start imagining that because I'm giving such precise dates my story is going to organize itself chronologically, no way, I don't give a damn about chronology, I can stroll with my words in the past, the present, as well as in the future, the immediate future, the future perfect, the future anterior, doesn't matter to me, but to make it easier for you to follow me, and those who eventually may want to listen to this story, I have to give some exact points of reference in time, otherwise the critics are going to attack me like wild animals, you probably don't know this, but for the critics the notion of time is sacred, ah time, that two-headed monster...

You want me to tell you something, I think that the guy who invented time really goofed, he got us stuck with the worst load of shit ever, and on top of that, that idiot could only conceive of time moving in one direction, from left to right, from past to future, just imagine, imagine for a moment how life would be far more exciting if time could go in any direction, up and down, sideways, even backwards, and things and events could undo themselves instead of always shaping miserably in the same direction...

Hey, what a fantastic idea, don't you think so, we could call it **the reverse of timeness**, just as old Sam invented **the reverse of farness**, I now invent **the reverse of timeness,** maybe that'll make me famous after I've changed tense, that's all it takes sometimes, a wild idea...

In the reverse of timeness, instead of flaunting its ugly face at us, time would show us its lovely ass, wouldn't that be great...

Okay, forget this inadvertent digression, and let's get back to Tante Rachel...

In 1919, she vanishes, and for more than fifteen years, no news from Rachel, nothing, nobody knows where she is and what's she doing...

Often, when I was a little boy, and the aunts and uncles got together, they would talk about their missing sister, and even wonder if she was still alive, after all a little thirteen year old girl, all alone in the world, with no money, little education, no experience of life since she had spent almost ten years behind the walls of that orphanage, they wondered how she could have survived, maybe she was sold as a slave in Africa, a little sex toy, because you know in those days there were children-kidnappers, des malabars, des pimps, des gangsters, especially in Marseille, who stole little girls to sell them to the rich Arabs, or to put them in the colonies' bordellos for the colonialists to enjoy, they called that la traîte des petites blanches, these Pashas in the colonies loved to deflower little white virgins...

Well, that's what my aunts and uncles were whispering when they got together on Sundays in Bubbe's tiny apartment Rue Vercingétorix dans le Quatorzième Arrondissement...

Bubbe, hey I just remembered that's what we used to call my grandmother, it came back to me all of a sudden, out of nowhere, isn't that funny...

That's where the whole family used to meet, chez Bubbe, before she died in her own bed at the age of sixty-six, then the reunions moved chez Marie, and that's when she took over and became the matriarch of the family...

As I was saying, when we went chez Bubbe, on Sundays, me, my sisters and my dumb cousins, even though we didn't know this missing Aunt Rachel, and had never seen her, we wanted to know where she was and what she was doing, because when all the aunts and uncles were gossiping while drinking hot tea in glasses with slices of lemon floating in it, and crunching on sugar cubes they dipped into the tea, us little children we listened to the conversation while playing on the floor with the toys Tonton Maurice brought us every Sunday, and we would ask, qui c'est Tante Rachel, qu'est-ce qu'elle fait, we wanted to know where she was this Aunt Rachel they talked about all the time, and what she was doing...

We were curious, but all we got was, oh Tante Rachel, she travels a lot in far away places, that's why you never see her, now go play and stop bothering us with your questions...

So we went on playing with the toys Uncle Maurice gave us on Sundays and we never got to know more about that mysterious Tante Rachel...

Maybe I should make a little narrative detour to tell you about Uncle Maurice, our favorite Uncle because of the toys, he also plays a part in this story, and after all, since he also suffered in the orphanage, he deserves a little place here...

Maurice, after he left the orphanage at the age of eighteen, he became a pushcart merchant, you know guys who go on Sundays with their buggies from one open market to another to sell their stuff, well Uncle Maurice sold dishes, kitchen utensils, pots and pans of all sorts, but also toys, dolls, little wooden cars, trains, tin soldiers, all kinds of junk like that, and every Sunday when he was finished selling his camelote, as he called it, he would join the rest of the clique, and he always brought a toy for the children, he never forgot, he was nice to us kids, especially to me and my sisters, I suppose because he remembered how my mother took care of him in the orphanage, so every Sunday he gave each of us a toy, not a big expensive toy, a little one, but he never forgot, I was fond of my Uncle Maurice, even though later, like the others, he screwed me too...

I know I keep repeating that this damned family played all these dirty tricks on me after the war and that's why I left for America, and I know you would like me to tell you what kind of dirty tricks, but first I've got to give you the background of the family, make you see what they were, before I can tell you how they ripped me off, so if you don't mind I'd like to finish with Maurice and get back to Rachel's story...

The amazing thing about Maurice, who was, as I told you, a shy and sickly little boy at the orphanage, is that

149

when he came out he became quite smart, débrouillard, and with Aunt Marie he was the richest of the family, finally I think the orphanage did him good, it taught him how to make it in life...

He had a small truck and he went from one marché to the other in the suburbs to sell his junk, the problem is that on Sundays, we always had to wait for him and Nénette to come back from the market before we could eat lunch, and us children, even though we knew Maurice and Nénette were going to bring us toys, we moaned and groaned the whole time because we were starving, and so...

Nénette ... beautiful Tante Nénette, I have to tell you about her too, since it's the first time I mention her...

Nénette was Maurice's wife, well, not officially his wife because they weren't really married, that's because Nénette wasn't Jewish, and even though Maurice wasn't a believer, simply out of respect for his mother while she was still alive, he couldn't marry Nénette, and even after Bubbe died, they never got married, out of respect for her memory, isn't it unbelievable how religion makes you do stupid things, how religion prevents you from doing what you would like to do, what you should do, ah religion, talk to me about it, the great calamity, the great affliction of society, I know what I'm talking about, it's because of their religion, which they never practiced, that my parents were erased from history, as a Communist my father was a fervent atheist, so my sisters and I we were brought up without any religion, even though my mother, who had been conditioned to believe in that religious rigmarole in her Jewish orphanage, tried, from time to time, when my father was not around, to make us believe in le Bon Dieu...

In any case, Jewish or not, everybody in the family adored Tata Nénette, even my grandmother, she was wonderful Nénette, so kind, so gentle, and beautiful too, well, when she was younger, a dazzling blonde with big blue eyes, very slender and elegant, Maurice was crazy about her, but they never got married, what a pity to believe in such bullshit...

Wow, do I have stuff to tell you, I hope you're not too tired, or too lost in all that, anyway, enough about Maurice and Nénette, let's get back to Aunt Rachel...

While the children were playing on the floor with the toys, the Aunts and Uncles were discussing family affairs, and of course they were always wondering where their sister could be, or if she was still alive...

But not a word from Rachel for more than fifteen years, nothing at all, nobody had any idea where she was, then one day, it was a Sunday, I remember that very well, I was six or seven years old at the time, everybody was there, and suddenly Bubbe announces...

Wait, I should have told you that when the family got together, everybody, my mother too since she was out of the orphanage, what I'm telling you now happened after the orphanage, since I was already born and my sisters too, so we're in the thirties now, I should have told you that when the aunts and uncles met for the Sunday lunch, they didn't speak French, because my grandmother who had come from Poland never really learned French, just a few words which nobody could understand anyway because of the way she pronounced these words, she spoke mostly Yiddish, which I could understand a little at the time, but not anymore, I've forgotten everything except for a few swear words my father used when he argued with Léon, so they all spoke Yiddish together, and that day, that Sunday, my grandmother said, in Yiddish then, I'm translating for you, she said, with a sob in her voice and a few tears in her eyes, yesterday I got a letter from Rachel, a letter from India, from Calcutta...

From Calcutta, everybody shouted in chorus, even us grandchildren, from Calcutta, and immediately everybody wanted to see the letter, so my grandmother took it out of the drawer where she kept the money Maurice and Marie gave her on Sunday to pay the rent and buy food, all the aunts and uncles tried to grab the letter, except my mother who just sat there at the table with tears welling up in her eyes...

You see, my mother was like that, instead of being happy to learn that her little sister was still alive and well, it made her sad, and she started crying, so my sisters and I went to console her, and she held us tight against her...

No, my father wasn't there, he never came with us to these Sunday lunches, everybody on my mother's side hated him, and it was reciprocal, my old man hated their guts as much as they hated his, he fought with them all the time, and if he happened to pass Uncle Léon in the staircase of the house where we all lived, Rue Louis Rolland, you could be sure there was going to be an argument, and man were they both foul-mouthed, when Léon and Papa argued we kids didn't stick around, because let me tell you all hell broke loose, that's how I learned those Yiddish swear words...

But back to Rachel's letter which was circulating from hand to hand...

While reading the letter they were all making ahs and ohs and oys of joy and surprise, they all seemed happy to learn that their sister was still alive...

What was she doing in Quel-cul-ta, that's how we pronounced the name of that place, even us kids said it that way ... patience, I'm coming to that, we're now getting to the heart of this story, just listen, it's going to get better and better...

After that first sign of life from India, the letters kept coming regularly, and almost every Sunday Bubbe would announce, I got another letter from Rachel, but this time from Singapore...

Singapore, all the children repeated while playing on the floor with our toys, where is Singapore, and the answer was, Singapore, it's very far, very far from here, but it wasn't a good enough answer, we wanted to know more, what is she doing over there so far in Singapore Tante Rachel...

Tante Rachel, we were told, is a dancer, a famous international ballet dancer, and that's why she has to travel all over the world...

Yeah right, sure, a dancer, a belly dancer maybe, you can imagine what they all thought, the comments the aunts and uncles whispered to each other about their sister Rachel, but the best was the day Bubbe announced she received a big money order from Rachel, of course immediately everybody wanted to know how much, how much did she send...

I don't remember how much grandmother said, but I can tell you it must have been a large sum of money, because you should have seen the reaction around the dining room table...

I even remember what Léon whispered in Nathan's ear, Nathan was my Aunt Fanny's husband, we called him the family idiot, not because he was stupid, but because he was crazy, seriously, he had a loose screw up there in his head, and in fact, after the war he ended up in an insane asylum, anyway I clearly heard what Léon said, I was under the table playing with my tin soldiers, that's why I could hear him, he said, it's easy to accumulate a fortune in the colonies when you have a nice ass...

I don't know how he knew that my Aunt Rachel had a nice ass since he'd never seen it, but that shows the way Léon was, always mean and ugly, always criticizing, knocking everybody, I hated him, not because he was a sonofabitch, but because only money was important to him, he didn't give a damn about people, not even his own family...

In any event, during my entire childhood, I'm talking before the war now, everybody in the family wondered how Rachel had become so rich in those far-away places, and everybody wanted to know when she would come back to France, since she always said in her letters that she was planning on coming to live in Paris soon...

But then the war started, and the letters stopped, once again no more news from Rachel, that's because during the German occupation Jews were not allowed to receive mail from foreign countries...

Oh you didn't know that, it's true, us Jews, before we were exported to the death camps to be exterminated, we lost all our rights, there were many things we couldn't do, for example we were not allowed to go to libraries, we couldn't go swimming in the municipal pool, for me it was terrible because I used to love to swim, we couldn't go to the post office, the movies, the theaters, all public places were forbidden to us, it wasn't funny you know, and on top of that, all the Jews had to wear a yellow star on all their clothes, I was so ashamed of that yellow humiliation, but as you can see I survived, I'm still alive...

You don't mind do you when I talk about the Jews, you're not an anti-Semite, I hope...

Good, I got scared for a moment, one never knows...

On the contrary, you understand, you sympathize, some of your best friends are Jewish, that's good, you have compassion for us, well I'm glad to hear that, so I can talk about the Jews without any fear...

Okay, the war started, and no more news from Tante Rachel...

The saddest is that my mother died without ever seeing her little sister again, the last time she saw her, you remember, was when Rachel said goodbye to her, the night she ran away from the orphanage...

But before the war, after that first letter from Calcutta, historical letter, postcards, letters, money orders arrived regularly in the mail from every corner of the world, one week from Bangkok, the next from Manilla, then from Tokyo, Hong Kong, even Timbuktu, and us grandchildren we kept dreaming about this famous and wealthy Aunt Rachel who traveled like a great adventuress all over the world...

Especially me, since I was more of a dreamer than the others, I imagined myself sailing on one of those huge liners, standing on the deck next to my Aunt, my hair blowing in the wind, a cigarette dangling from my lips, my arms around my Aunt's shoulders because she was shivering in the sea breeze, I held her tight against me to warm her, she was beautiful my Aunt Rachel in my imaginings with her big black eyes and her long dark curly hair, I pictured her like one of those voluptuous Jewesses described in the Bible, ah did I love those exotic Jewish beauties from the Old Testament...

My mother made us read that book sometimes when Papa was not home, for our education, she would tell us...

That's how I visualized my Aunt Rachel, voluptuous, exotic, and capable of great passion, but at the same time experienced enough, for having traveled so much in the world, to be able to hide her natural inclination toward sensual pleasures, I think secretly I was in love with her...

How do I know Rachel was beautiful, because my mother had a picture of her, it was the only picture of Rachel she had, it dated back to the time when they were in the orphanage, it was an old faded picture, with one of the corners torn, but still we could see how beautiful she was even though she was wearing her sad orphan clothes, a black apron and ugly boots with laces that came up above her ankles, she must have been nine or ten in that picture, but in my imagination I had transformed that little girl into a sophisticated, elegant woman, I kept seeing her, in my dreams especially, at night, wearing colorful exotic dresses, big hats and splendid jewelry glittering on her soft tanned skin, she was so gorgeous...

Rachel never sent pictures of herself while she was traveling, I have no idea why, maybe she didn't want the family to see what she looked like, you know, very often your face reveals what you do in life...

No, it's true, for instance you, the first time I saw you, I understood right away that you were some kind of sponger, don't be insulted, I don't say that in a bad way, but your face shows that you feed on others, I'm not talking about food here, in your case I'm talking about intellectual nourishment, since you live on other people's stories you are the curious type, your profession is curiosity, and your face reveals it...

You're probably not going to believe this, but once some-body told me that I must be a writer or an artist because of the way I combed my hair, and also because of the beard I was sporting at the time, the guy who told me that didn't know a thing about me, we had never met before, I was sitting next to him on a bus on my way to Chicago, we started talking, and right away he said to me, you must be a writer or somebody like that, just by looking at my face, so maybe that's the reason why my Aunt Rachel didn't want to show her face on photo-graphs...

So I never saw pictures of Rachel as a woman, it's when she arrived in Paris after the war that I saw her for the first time, before that I only knew her from that torn faded photo of the little orphan girl, but deep inside I knew she had become a beautiful woman, like a movie star, I was convinced of that...

Tata Rachel, ah TaTaa Raa-Chel, I would whisper in my dreams, sucking in my mouth each of the sweet syllables of her name as if they were pieces of candy, and in my dreams I could see her, touch her, I could guess under her tunic with the plunging neckline, the delicate con-tours of her heavy rounded dark breasts, I saw her in my nocturnal dreams like a plant, a tree, a young fig tree with its supple branches and its delicious plump juicy fruits, wow was I dumb and romantic when I be-came old enough to dream of all the treasures hidden under a woman's dress...

I know it's not right, it's not normal to think of your Aunt in such a way, but that's the way I was as a kid, I was hot in the pants, and still am, I make no secret of it, but it's not a crime, it's even normal to get aroused at the sight of a beautiful woman, even if she exists only in your dreams, I think that the guys who don't react when

157

they see a good-looking woman are half-dead sexless zombies, I always get a hard-on whenever I see a nice ass, and Aunt Rachel's ass, well, the one I contemplated in my dreams, it was divine, round and firm...

When I reached puberty, you know, when I started to have erections at night in my bed under the blankets, I sometimes imagined Rachel dancing, she was wearing a very short skirt, black stockings, red silk panties, and golden shoes, I always saw her in my dreams dressed as a night-club dancer, probably because I had seen pictures of dancers dressed like this in magazines, and one night I even dreamt that I was dancing with her, and at the end of the dance, I think it was a tango, she kissed me, but not on the cheek like my other Aunts always did, no, right smack on the lips, and I even felt the tip of her tongue entering my mouth and rubbing against mine, and suddenly we were in bed together on top of each other, both naked in a big bed floating like a boat on a river, well, what I'm telling you now was just a dream of course, she was dark-skinned my Aunt Rachel, with lots of black hair under her armpits and between her legs, and me I was trying my best to put my willy inside her black triangle, but it wasn't working at all, my little red penis couldn't find the way, suddenly I felt Aunt Rachel's two fingers gently grab my wandering prick and guide it into the right place, but just when the feverish tip was about to penetrate her dark and mysterious cave, I ejaculated and I awoke, my thighs all wet and my sheets soiled, I tried to wipe the stain, because I didn't want my mother to see the cochonneries I did at night, but she probably knew anyway because my sheets were always covered with yellow spots when I was a boy...

I see you make a face, don't tell me you never beat your meat when you got old enough to feel your cock stand at attention as soon as you saw a woman's ass, what do you take me for, and don't tell me either that you don't do it anymore, that you stopped jerking off, it would be like giving up on life, like the end...

Anyway, you see how Aunt Rachel excited me even before I saw her in real life, and I'll even tell you that during the war when I was alone on the farm, in the South, and I felt sad and homesick, I often dreamt about her at night in my bed of loneliness, dreamt of my Aunt Rachel instead of dreaming about my mother or my father, as I should have, since they were no longer here, and probably suffering a great deal where they had been taken, instead, I was dreaming of Aunt Rachel's ass and her black fur, what a filthy little jerk I was, I should be ashamed to tell you all this, but don't forget that the stories I'm telling you aren't all true, and even if they are, I embellish them, I make them more fictitious, I sublimate, I glorify, I exaggerate, but these stories still excite me, that's because, as I explained before, literary creation always happens in the fervor of excitement...

Shit, I've to stop for a moment, I feel dizzy, see what I mean, what I just told you got me so worked-up I feel kind of funny, too much emotion ... all ... how shall I put it ... exhilarated ... see how excited I am, look I'm trembling ... literary creation is really exhausting you know...

Listen, I'm going to go to the toilet to re-compose myself, I have to relieve the tension, you stay here and wait for me, give me five minutes and I'll be right back to tell you the rest of the story, okay, don't go away...

———

OKAY ... SO LET'S GO ON...

I feel better now, wow I thought I was going to pass out I was so worked up, okay let's go on with the story...

At the end of the war, when I returned to Paris, everybody on my mother's side was surprised to see that I was still alive, they thought I had been deported with my parents and sisters, they didn't know I escaped and ended up in La Zone Libre in the South where I worked on a farm until the Americans liberated France, nobody knew I was alive, they all thought I had been exterminated, but I wasn't, as you can see, so when I showed up in Paris after La Libération, they were shocked, they must have thought I was a ghost or something...

How did I escape, oh that's another story I've told many times, too bad you weren't around then, I'm not going to repeat it just for you, it's not my fault that you arrived too late in my stories, besides I'm tired of telling the same old thing over and over again, what I'm telling you now is new stuff, stuff I've never told before...

So after escaping from the great round-up of July '42, La Grande Rafle, I find myself working on a farm in the Lot-et-Garonne, not far from Villeneuve-sur-Lot, in a little hicktown, in the middle of nowhere, called Monflanquin...

No don't insist, I am not going to tell you what happened before I landed on that farm after I jumped off a freight train which was probably taking me to my final solution, no I'm not going to go into that again...

Let's forget that story, instead I'm going to tell you about the farm...

Did I suffer on that farm for more than three years, remember I was only twelve years old when my parents were taken away, and a shy little city boy who had never seen a cow or a pig up close, who didn't know anything about plucking a dead chicken's feathers, or how animals climb on top of each other to fornicate, here I was on that farm with manure up to my knees, milking the cows, cultivating the land with a pair of oxen hitched to a plow, feeding the pigs, the chickens, the rabbits, the geese, the goats, I sure saw them close the cows and the pigs and the rest of the farm menagerie, I won't go into too many details about the fucking animals, I already told parts of the farm story in the noodle novel when I was doing some flashback, all you have to do is visit the noodle novel when we're finished here, and you'll see for yourself how I suffered in my youth, in that novel I tell everything, the war, the occupation, the yellow star, La Grande Rafle, the collaboration, the deportation, the trains, the camps, the extermination, La Libération, and finally, finally America and jazz, and all the loneliness...

America, I almost forgot it, it's been a while since I mentioned America, did you notice, the deeper I go into the stories of my childhood, the more I lose sight of America, it's been at least three days since I talked about that place, same thing for Susan, I haven't mentioned her since I told you about her telegram, doesn't matter, we'll get back to America soon enough...

In any case, the noodle novel deals more or less with my life-story, my noodle life, so to speak, because you understand that even though the noodles in that novel are fictitiously real, since the guy who's writing the novel within the novel survives only on noodles for a whole year, they are also symbolic, and from the symbolic point of view they represent the improvised aspect of the novel, the noodling element...

Let me explain...

When a jazz musician improvises a solo, and don't forget that I played jazz, the tenor sax, so I know what I'm talking about, we say that he's noodling, to noodle in the language of jazz means to improvise, and that's exactly what I'm doing in my novel, I noodle along on the basis of my own life, just like I'm doing for you, now if symbolically you transpose jazz improvisations to writing, I mean the kind of writing that ignores the rules and regulations of grammar and syntax, then you can say that I noodle when I write, or if you prefer, I doodle, you know, noodling doodling, same thing...

What, you don't know what doodling means, boy you're really dumb, you don't know much about anything, sometimes I wonder if I shouldn't find myself another listener, a smarter guy who could follow all my detours, I know it takes a strong temperament to keep up with my rambling, but probably less than one would need for *the soliloquy battle* as the great Sam used to say, and so for your patience and determination I salute you, you are a tenacious listener...

But enough of that, let's get back to the farm, revenons à nos moutons, as the judge kept saying to Maître Pathelin in the farce by that name, though in this case, he would have to say, revenons à nos vaches et nos cochons...

I was telling you about the farm, but in fact I was telling you that I was not going to talk any more about that farm, I simply wanted to tell you that after I left there I went back to Paris, and all the aunts and uncles, on my mother's side, because on my father's side there was nobody left, they were stupefied to see that I was still alive, they didn't know that I jumped off a train, and that's how I landed on that farm where I worked like a slave, from five in the morning till late into the night when I would collapse into my cauchemars, yes every night I had nightmares, and did I work hard, like a beast of burden for more than three years, my hands and feet aching, bleeding all the time...

You say why don't I tell all that right now because you think that the story of the train and the farm would interest the public, you must be kidding, the public doesn't give a shit about my little story of survival, what the public wants is ass stories, and that's why I'd better get back to Aunt Rachel's story...

So quiet and listen, I'll tell you about that other stuff maybe next week, there's no hurry...

Wait, all things considered maybe I should tell you a bit about the farmer's wife, because you see, when I arrived on that farm, in the middle of the war, there was only the farmer's wife and her old father-in-law to do all the work, so they were glad to have another pair of hands, so to speak, to help in the fields and with the chores, but that bastard of a father-in-law did he make me suffer, that old geezer was so mean, even with the wife's four year old kid, a little redheaded snotty-nosed brat who whined all the time, he used to beat the shit out of him...

You have to understand, during the Occupation, there were only women and old people left to do the work on the farms, or else displaced children like me lost in the great tumult of the war, so the women, the old folks, the children, the crippled, the disabled, the lame did the farming, that's because the stupid Germans had sent all the strong and able men to *Deutschland Über Alles* to make cannons, rifles, machine guns, tanks, bombs, bayonets in their factories, and that's where the husband was, in Germany, and that's why the wife and the old fart did all the work, so when I showed up in Monflanquin, nobody asked where I came from and why I was alone, instead they hired me on the spot, no money of course, just food and a bed full of bed bugs, there I was on that farm with the old man and the pretty farmer's wife...

Oh, was she pretty, and sexy too, plump, nicely rounded, big boobs, she must have been twenty-five or twenty-six at the time, and me, well me, I was only twelve and a half when I arrived there, but I was already starting to feel a little something inside my pants whenever I saw a beautiful woman, and the farmer's wife, even though she didn't wash every day, made me so horny, and the harder I worked the stronger and the harder I became, and don't forget, I stayed more than three years on that farm, by the time I left I was fifteen, all that hard work made me grow up fast in all directions...

What, here he goes again with his ass stories you say, but of course, what do you think, everything in life has to do with the ass, with sex, but if you really don't want to hear what happened with the farmer's wife, fine with me, I'll just skip the whole thing...

Oh, you changed your mind, you think it might be interesting and relevant...

You make me laugh you know, on the one hand you pretend to be disinterested, you make a fuss when I talk about sex, and on the other hand you get a big kick listening to my little cochonneries, all right then, the farmer's wife, but quickly, only the essential...

So here I am on this farm during the Occupation, can you picture me cultivating the land, I didn't know a damn thing about agriculture, and I didn't know much about le cul either, but let me tell you, you learn fast on a farm, up before the sun to milk the cows, shovel the manure out of the barn, feed the pigs, the cows, the chickens, the ducks, the rabbits, the whole damn zoo of those so-called domesticated animals who spend their lives doing nothing but eating and crapping all day and all night long, until we kill them to eat them and defecate them in turn, man is there ever a lot of shit on a farm, tons and tons of it, but you know it's a damn good system nature, it's amazing how it functions, how it keeps renewing itself with shit, yeah, with shit...

You see, first you cultivate the earth to make things grow, hay, wheat, vegetables, all the stuff you feed the animals to fatten them up so that afterwards you can slaughter them and stuff yourself with their meat, but before they die those animals, wow can they shit, and of course we shit too after we devour them, and eventually all that shit is returned to the soil to enrich it, to make the things that grow in the earth bigger, more nourishing, more fattening because of the manure, and so it goes until the end of time, or until we humans are destroyed by nature, or until we destroy ourselves, what a beautiful system nature is, don't you think, it keeps jump starting itself with shit, but on the farm nature needs our help to keep going, therefore every day, Sundays included, five o'clock in the morning, the old man came to get me out of the sack, and off I went still half asleep, with my nightly nightmares still whirling in my head, off I went to the barn to sink in the manure up to my knees, and then to the fields to cultivate the soil till nightfall, harvesting the wheat, cutting the hay, scything the grass, plowing the fields, digging holes, gathering the potatoes, the beets, the beans, the turnips, cutting trees down, well you know, everything there is to do on a farm in order to grow enough food to feed the fucking animals so they can shit, and then we kill them and eat their meat after having sprinkled the fields with manure, and it's like that every day, Sundays included, except that on Sunday morning, after taking care of the animals, the farmer's wife and the old guy had a quick wash, put on their fancy Sunday's best, and off they went to church...

And me too, yes me too I had to put on the clean pair of pants and the clean shirt the farmer's wife had washed, to go to church with them...

I'm not kidding, me the little Yid from Paris, le Youpin, I went to church with the farmers every Sunday morning, the three of us, or rather the four of us, I keep forgetting the little redheaded whiner, yes the four of us, with the kid in a big basket on the back of the old geezer's bike, we trudged twelve kilometers to go to mass in the Monflanquin church, every Sunday morning we prayed and listened to the priest's bullshit...

By the way, do you know that it's in the steeple of this church, during the Hundred Years War, that the British Black Prince was kept prisoner after he was defeated by the French in 1356, that's how old that church was...

How do I know, it's the curé of Montflanquin who told me, he took a liking to me, he told me all kinds of stuff like that...

Oh no, he didn't know I was Jewish, and neither did the hicks, they never asked me, and me I never told them, but I remember the first Sunday morning after I arrived on the farm, the old man told me I had to wash up and put on clean clothes for church, just like that, he didn't even bother asking if I was interested, but me I said with enthusiasm, *church, oh yes yes of course, I'm a good Catholic*, and after that, every Sunday I went to mass with them, you should have heard me recite the *dominus vobiscum tummtumm spirituuuum sanctus tammtamm deo gratias sanctus chewing gummm*, anything went since I hadn't the faintest idea what the fuck I was saying, I was just pretending, ah the crap you have to hear in church about THE SEVEN DEADLY SINS, THE GOOD LORD, THE DEVIL, PARADISE, HELL, PUNISHMENT, REDEMPTION, CONTRIBUTIONS, always in capital letters, I tell you, unbelievable how that priest brainwashed those dumb peasants, and on top of that, he was a filthy collaborator, in his sermons he kept repeating that we must behave with the Germans, obey them, respect them, admire them, and thank them even for protecting us from Communism, and above all, he insisted, never ever hide food from the Germans in the barn or in the loft, because they need all our food to win the war, and he went on and on repeating what Pierre Laval had said to the factory and farm workers who were shipped to Germany to slave in the factories, yeah, like a parrot he repeated what Laval said, *I wish victory for Germany, because tomorrow, without her, Bolshevism will spread everywhere like a plague...*

That's exactly what that fucking Fascist Laval said, and what that cul-terreux curate kept preaching to us, and man did the Krauts help themselves, they came with trucks to take the food away, les sales Boches, les Doryphores, as we called them, they weren't shy, but they always came accompanied by Pétain's Militia, yes it was Maréchal Fart-one's henchmen who collected the grub for the Germans, while the Mütter-Fuckers waited in their trucks smoking cigarettes, singing their Nazi songs, and laughing their heads off, but whenever those potato-bugs came, I always managed to be somewhere out in the fields or in the woods, away from the farm house, you understand why, I didn't want to show my historical hooked nose, it was easy to know when the Krauts were coming, because from the farm we could see their trucks come down the big dirt road...

In any event, on Sunday morning in the Monflanquin church, you wouldn't believe the kind of crap the priest spewed in his sermons, that Lavaliste traitor shouted at us all the time, he would tell us, well to the bumpkins rather, because me I wasn't really listening, I was daydreaming while he was bellowing his sermon, he would say, us French we are dying not only from the great military thrashing we just sustained, but also from inveterate alcoholism, chronic guzzling, from an excess of Youpinerie, and especially from a lack of belief in the great Aryan and Christian race, I tell you, he sounded just like Céline, I'm convinced that instead of studying his prayer book, that miserable traitor was spending all his time reading Céline's *Bagatelles* or some other filthy stuff like that, sometimes it was frightening to hear what he had to say, he kept saying that we had to rebuild France, restore the Catholic and Mystic Absolutes, whatever the fuck that meant, and stay true to our beautiful Gallic tradition, what a load of shit, no need to tell you that the country hicks had no idea what he was talking about, and he always ended his sermons-kick-in-the-ass shouting that thank goodness the Germans are going to put us back on the right path and lead us back to faith, and he would conclude, or rather expire, by spitting on us and ordering us to kneel before the cross and pray for the victory of France and Germany...

I'm sure the sonofabitch kept a picture of Hilter inside his prayer book...

That's what that priest said to us every Sunday, but me, as I told you, I wasn't really listening, instead I was day-dreaming about the future, since I had no more past, or else I was glancing sideways at the farmer's wife's knees who sat next to me, eyes half closed listening to the priest's sermon her hands clasped in front of her, I loved the porcelain of her knees sticking out from underneath the faded flower-patterned dress she always wore on Sundays to church, she was really beautiful for a coun-try girl, except that she smelled, she smelled like rancid cider...

Well, that's enough, I'm not going to tell you everything that happened on that farm during the Occupation, as for the Krauts, let's forget about them too, as you know, they eventually ended up going back to the *Vaterland* with their tails between their legs to rethink their sordid history, but I do want to tell you a bit more about what happened between the farmer's wife and me...

But first let me describe the farm to you...

It was a big farm, with a large herd of cows, and pigs, goats, sheep, four horses, chickens, rabbits, ducks, even geese and turkeys, and huge fields everywhere, it was a rich farm, with two barns, but the house itself wasn't very spacious, so they didn't have a room for me to sleep in, I slept in a corner of the kitchen under the staircase that went up to the loft where we kept the harvest of wheat and oats, I slept there on a folding cot, and in that loft there were rats, loads of big grey rats with long whiskers, during the night those ugly rats came down into the kitchen to look for food, as if all that grain up there in the loft wasn't enough for them, so me, all curled up in my narrow bed I could hear them slide down alongside the walls to come and creep in the kitchen, some of them even scampered about on my bed as if they wanted to nibble my ears or the tip of my nose, I was so scared, don't forget, I was just a shy fearful little Parisian boy with no experience whatsoever of country life, there were no rats in our apartment in Montrouge, only cute little mice, and lots of cockroaches, but rats that's another thing, they really scared me...

You too, that's not unusual, I know lots of people who are afraid of rats, even if it's only a picture of a rat in a book, it frightens them and they close their eyes not to see, these people suffer from ratophobia, and I too suffered from that same affliction on the farm...

But to go on with my folding cot, in the evening, when it was time to go to bed, the farmer's wife would go in the corner of the kitchen under the staircase to make my bed, and while she unfolded it and straightened the sheets, I stood behind her and watched her leaning over my bed to tuck in the blankets, and when she leaned over like that I could see part of her big thighs under her skirt, and it really excited me, here let's say for the sake of the story, even though I may be distorting the facts a bit, that she always wore very short skirts, therefore I could see most of her thighs, almost up to her buttocks, which were nicely rounded and firm, and man did I enjoy the sight, every night I got an eyeful, but I never touched her, I didn't dare, though I am sure she was aware that I...

Listen, I think I told you enough already about the farmer's wife, you can imagine by yourself what happened, or what could have happened, and so let's go directly to the end of the war when I went back to Paris...

Well, maybe I'd better tell you a bit more about that farm and the farmer's wife so you can get an idea of how much I suffered, physically, mentally, and sexually for more than three years, this way you'll understand how I was marked by the war when I was still young, naive, and virgin, how every day I was assailed by death and fornication...

Yes, death and fucking, that's what goes on all the time on a farm, I was only a boy then but I saw how easy it is to die, or to fuck, that's all the animals did, they kept mounting each other, in the courtyard, in the barns, in the fields, whenever they felt like it, and every day one of these creatures croaked, either from fatigue, old age, or because we had to kill it so we could eat its meat, death was always around us, ah, I tell you, the simplicity of death, but sometimes you know it's kind of funny too...

Here, let me describe what I once saw, the farmer's wife was going to kill a chicken to cook in her pot, she took a big kitchen knife in one hand, she wedged the chicken between her round knees and held its head with the other hand stretching its neck, I remember it was a huge colorful rooster with a lovely red crest, and when I saw how she stretched that poor cock's neck and swish-swash with the knife cut the head off I gagged and almost fainted...

Of course it bleeds, what do you think, that chickens don't have blood like us, but the funniest is that even beheaded the rooster was still struggling for a few moments before dying, and you won't believe this, but after she lobbed the rooster's head off, the poor thing fidgeted about so furiously it managed to slip free of her knees and it fell to the ground, and this chicken without a head hotfooted around the kitchen flapping its wings for a good two minutes before it collapsed and dropped dead in a corner, I was horrified when I saw that, but at the same time I burst into laughter, so you see how simple and downright funny death can be...

172

But most of the time I was sad and depressed on the farm, always alone, except for the animals who were my companions in misfortune, mostly I talked with the cows, the goats, the horses, but especially with the dog who followed me everywhere I went, an ugly mutt, half shepherd half terrier, I think he was lonely too, and he was scared of the old man who always kicked him just because he was half blind, that dog had only one good eye, the other eye was just white without an iris, but he was smart, gentle, obedient, I called him Bigleux, it wasn't his real name, but that's what I called him, and whenever I said come here Bigleux, he would rush immediately to lick my hands, and every time he saw the old bastard coming towards us he would hide behind me, you know what, I'm convinced that dog understood everything I was saying, it's with him I talked the most, because you know the farmer's wife and the father-in-law, they didn't speak much, and when they happened to say a few words it sounded more like grunts, ah was I sad, lonely, homesick, depressed, demoralized, exhausted all the time on that farm, and to make it worse, my hands were always hurting, and my feet too, because you see I wore clogs, yes for more than three years I wore wooden clogs like a farmer, well let me tell you, it takes time to get used to these sabots, in the winter we stuffed them with straw to keep our bare feet warm, you should have seen me trudging along with my clogs, I felt so klutzy, so rustic, it's not easy to walk with these damn things, after an entire day tramping through the cow dung in the barn or in the muddy fields my feet were so sore and bloody I couldn't sleep at night...

Speaking of those clogs, that reminds me how one morning I found a rat in one of them, no kidding, five o'clock, I hear the morning grunts of the old geezer, I wake up, I sit on the edge of my bed still half asleep trying to emerge out of my nightmare, I slip my feet into my clogs but I feel something warm moving inside, quickly I remove my foot and what do I see lurching out, an enormous grey rat who quickly disappears into the wall, wow did it scare the hell out of me, I screamed, I bet I scared the rat too...

Of course I screamed, and the old fart, who was still in the kitchen drinking his early morning glass of pinard rouge, came to see what the big fuss was about, and when I told him there was a rat in my clog, he laughed and called me a cretin, a jerk, a sissy, un trouillard, a little fag, and then he shouted, get your fucking feet inside those clogs and get your ass into the barn on the double before I kick your lazy ass, so I did what I was told, I put my feet in my clogs that smelled of rat, and off I went to the barn to milk the cows, with manure up to my knees, and the rest of that day I felt a strange painful tickling sensation in my clogs...

So you see how my feet suffered on that farm, and my hands even more, my poor hands, at the beginning when I was still learning how to use a pitchfork, a rake, or a spade, you know, the tools you need to cultivate the earth, clean the barn for the cows, pile up the manure in the dung-cart, my hands hurt all the time, they were always red and swollen, covered with cuts and scrapes and blisters, you wouldn't believe what a klutz I was when I was kid, and still am, I'm a person of the mind not of the hands, to give you an idea, if you ask me to hang a painting on the wall, not only am I going to demolish half the wall with the hammer trying to hit the fucking nail, but by the time I'm finished my fingernails have turned black from hitting them with the hammer, now you understand how little I knew about their earthly activities, I knew zilch about that farming stuff...

But by the end of the war I had become a good farmer, and when I told the old man that I was leaving, that I was going back to Paris, he said, it's too bad you've got to leave, you're a good farmer now, maybe one of these days you can marry the neighbor's daughter and settle down here, make children with her, she has a nice round ass, and then when her old man kicks the bucket the farm will be yours...

You know what, I hesitated for a moment, for a moment I contemplated my future as a farmer, can you believe that, but then I shook my head no, can you see me today, a farmer in the Lot-et-Garonne, with half a dozen little brats with a nose like mine running around like a bunch of chickens...

It was the first time the old motherfucker addressed me without yelling at me, first time he spoke more than two words, a whole sentence, probably the only real sentence I heard coming out of his mouth the whole time I was on that farm...

You can keep your fucking farm and the neighbor's ugly daughter who looks like a fat cow, I didn't say that, but I must have thought it, the next day I left...

You sure learn fast on a farm, you get old fast too, I mean your body becomes older than you really are, and even though my dick was always straight up in front of me, my intellect hadn't caught up with my body, it took a long time before the two coincided, and that's why I suppose after only a few weeks on the farm I started getting horny whenever I was alone with the farmer's wife, and so every night I stood behind her and watched her lean over my bed to tuck in the blankets, and I got an eyeful, but I never touched her, I was too shy, except once, here's how it happened, but first I have to flashback to something that I saw by accident a couple days before which finally gave me the courage to reach for her ass and ask her if maybe, maybe...

So this is how it happened, one afternoon, it was summertime, I remember because it was a real scorcher that day, I was working in the fields, cutting the hay or something like that, when the tool I was using broke, I don't remember what kind of a tool it was, a rake, a fork, a scythe, it's not important, so I had to go back to the farm to get another one...

Oh by the way, I should mention that when it was hot like that, the old sonofabitch always took a nap in the barn in the afternoon, so that day I was the only one working in the fields...

The farmer's wife had announced during lunch that in the afternoon she was going to do the laundry, so I arrive in the courtyard, and head for the toolshed to get another tool, but I notice a bike resting against the wall next to the kitchen door, I recognize it right away because I had seen it many times before, it was the postman's bike, it wasn't unusual for the farmers to give a drink to the postman whenever he brought the mail, and often the farmer's wife offered him a glass of wine or cider, I didn't think much of it since it was such a hot day, I figured she had probably invited him into the kitchen to cool off, I was ready to go back to work with the good tool when I told myself, hey maybe I should also get me a cold drink in the kitchen, so I head for the house, and as I get closer to the kitchen window what do I see, the postman with his pants down, his striped underwear around his feet and his white ass up in the air, going at it full blast with the farmer's wife, she was leaning forward on the edge of the table, her skirt hitched up all the way exposing her big round rump, the postman was screwing her from behind, en levrette, yes that's what I saw that day through the kitchen window, but they didn't see me, they were so involved in what they were doing...

Are you crazy, of course not, I didn't go in, I told you they hadn't seen me, I just took off in a hurry and went back to work in the field, but I felt strange, I don't know why but I felt sadness, you see it was the first time I saw humans fucking, animals, I saw them all the time, all the different species, but a man and a woman screwing, that was the first time, it gave me a funny feeling, I don't know how to say it, a kind of alien feeling, it didn't excite me at all, well, at least not right away, later of course when I got to think about it, but back in the fields, cutting the hay all alone, I was disturbed, confused, lost in incomprehension, I didn't know what to think...

Okay, so now we'll go back to the day I finally touched her ass and asked if maybe, well you know what I mean, it was two days after the scene with le facteur...

It's evening, the old geezer is snoring away in his bedroom, he always went to bed with the chickens, so as usual the farmer's wife goes under the staircase to unfold my cot, I follow her, and when she leans over I can't resist, I reach, slide my hand under her skirt from behind, and feel her ass, she starts and turns around, she's all flushed, at first I think she's going to slap me across the face, I step back, but she doesn't move, she stands there next to the bed staring at me, I don't know if it's a look of surprise, anger, stupefaction, amazement at my dexterity, or simply an inquiring look, I must have been fourteen by then, but I wasn't very good at deciphering the messages women send with their eyes, so me, dumb little puceau that I was, I say to her, without thinking, just like that, *if monsieur le facteur can do it why can't I do it too*...

I swear, that's exactly what I said to her, and this time she really turned red in the face, but she didn't say a word, she just put her index finger on her lips, and with the other hand pointed in the direction of the old man's room to make me understand that I'd better keep my mouth shut, and then she walked past me and went to the sink to do the dishes, she didn't even finish making my bed, I felt like an idiot, a jerk, so I got into the bed and tried to sleep, I could hear her moving about in the kitchen, she was finishing the dishes, then she turned off the light, I was drifting into sleep when suddenly I felt a hand slip under the covers and fondle my prick until it stiffened and...

Well no need to go into the details, but after that memorable evening, she came regularly to caress me under the blankets before I fell asleep, but she never got into my bed and I never dared ask her, almost every night she would make me feel good with her hand, a bit like a mother who consoles her sad child with caresses and kisses to put him to sleep, except that the farmer's wife and I never kissed, never, maybe it never occurred to us to try, but she did once suck my cock, just before I left the farm to go back to Paris, a kind of farewell present, I suppose...

I think she was my first love, or maybe I should say, my first sexual failure because with her I remained far from **The Origin of the World** so beautifully recreated by Courbet...

Have you ever seen that gorgeous cunt Courbet painted to remind us whence we come...

Yes a failure since with the farmer's wife there was no penetration, or if I may permit myself a little pun, as I look back to the little jerk that I was then, I missed my first penistration, it's later, when I was back in Paris that I explored **The Origin of the World**, that of a putain dans un bordel de la Rue Saint-Denis, with her I went all the way to the end of the world, and man was that a trip...

178

Many years later I wrote a little thing in remembrance of that memorable night when the farmer's wife sucked my cock, you want to hear it, I know it by heart, listen...

A Day of Rare Intensity

At dawn half-awake he sees himself as a young jerk knee deep in manure being undumbed for the first time by a pretty country lady...

she masturbates him and then she gathers in her lovely wide-open mouth his young virginal cock ... it is a grandiose moment of rare intensity ... and that exquisite image remains engraved in his memory forever...

You like it...

Maybe before we leave the farm, I should tell you about some other fantastic dreams I had each night after the farmer's wife's visitations to my private parts, they were amazing dreams, you see after she started giving me pleasure like this, my nightmares stopped, I had only lovely dreams...

Can I tell you one of them, there is a good one which I've never forgotten, it was so complicated and so beautiful, it was like a poem, and very patriotic, here listen...

In the dream I see myself dressed as a legionnaire wearing a navy blue uniform and a kepi with a square piece of white fabric covering the back of my neck, in my hand I'm holding a bayonet, in front of me there is a shape, I cannot tell if it's human, animal, or just a thing, it looks like a box, so daring legionnaire that I am, I stick my bayonet forward, you know, my dick-bayonet of course, this is a dream, and anything can happen in dreams,

179

and I plunge it into the shape before me, as I lunge forward to push deeper into the shape I feel as if I'm no longer held down on the earth by the force of gravity, it feels like I'm being elevated by some mysterious force, I am floating on air, I feel light, alive, like a bird flying, that's how I feel in the dream, but I don't know why, maybe because I feel so good, so flottant, I burst into mad laughter, or rather, j'éclate en fourire, since I am dreaming this in French, then a torrent of ecstasy rushes in me as my weapon, what else can I call it, emerges on the other side of the blurry ashy shape I'm bayoneting, suddenly the shape turns into a bouquet of flowers just as the moon emerges from behind a cloud above my head, I drop my bayonet and reach for the flowers with my hands, when I touch them they take the shape of a body, a feminine body, I think, but when I try to embrace this body, it changes form again and becomes a soft delicate pearly fur, like my Aunt Rachel's fur...

Holy shit, did you hear what I just said, I was in the middle of telling you that terrific dream I had when I was on the farm, and unconsciously I reeled into Aunt Rachel's mysterious fur, wow, can you imagine the psychological possibilities of such an inadvertent deviation, the complexity of this transfer into furry divergence, are you following me...

Of course at the time, on the farm, I didn't know how to dream as well as I do now, I mean I didn't know anything about all that Freudian stuff, my dreams didn't mean much then, except for the lovely sensations they gave me while dreaming, but to finish with that one dream, the cute little legionnaire suddenly vanished and his prick-bayonet with him, this is still the same dream, it was a dream in two chapters, and everything went black inside my head, like inside a dark tunnel, I didn't even have a chance to dream the end of my dream, but then something amazing happened, it was like an explosion, and everything became bright, I'm still talking about the same dream, in the brightness a huge American flag appeared, you know with stars and stripes, and now I was dressed like a paratrooper, I heard bombastic music, so I stood at attention and saluted the flag, I had tears in my eyes, all this in the dream of course...

Now try to explain all this, it shows how confused I was on the farm...

Well, to go on with the farmer's wife, even though she never came into my bed, and I never ejaculated inside of her, so to speak, her hand made my body and mind feel so good in those moments of loneliness...

You know, the guy who invented us, the creator, he understood that the genitals are supposed to be the center of pleasure, not the head, the head is the center of intelligence, reason, logic, and it never gives pleasure, on the contrary it makes you suffer, but when your cock or your cunt comes, your entire body feels and delights in this exquisite rush of orgasmic pleasure, in fact it's the only part of you that can give pleasure to the rest of your body...

What do you mean, it's not so, that there are other extremities capable of exciting the rest of our body when we touch them...

The top of the head and the bottom of the feet...

Really, you must be joking...

I'm serious, try, rub the top of your head with your hand in a circular motion, and you'll see, the rest of your body will feel it, or tickle the sole of your feet, and I assure you, your entire body will enjoy it and will even burst into laughter...

181

Still, I think it's mostly through the genitals that we get the most and best pleasure, I know that for a fact, because my farmer's wife's hand knew a lot about giving such pleasure, she was very talented in that region, and yet, despite her soothing hands, I was always sad, I had no sense of who I was or what I wanted to become, I was just a poor miserable farmer, not by choice of course, but a farmer still, always dirty and unhappy, the rough and ordinary ways of these people had become my life, it had invaded my frail Parisian body, I had no idea what I was doing there, I didn't understand the cold simplicity and constant violence of reproduction and death that I witnessed every day, I merely existed, like a dumb plant outside of human reality, on that farm, reality began where meaning stopped...

But worst of all was the filth, I felt dirty all the time, you cannot imagine how grimy you become when you work on a farm...

In the beginning during the first few weeks, I washed my face and brushed my teeth every morning, like I used to do at home, but the old man and the farmer's wife made so much fun of me that I soon stopped, I even threw my toothbrush in the hole in the ground in the little shack behind the barn, the shit house...

Where did that toothbrush come from, that's an interesting question, it's obvious that when I escaped the big round-up and reached the free zone hidden in a freight train, I didn't have a toothbrush, what can I say, I don't know how I got that toothbrush when I arrived on the farm, I forget, I guess I've got a mental block, it's normal you know, people often block out their miseries, I suppose that toothbrush will remain a mystery in my life, but I do remember throwing it inside the shit hole one morning, after the old bastard laughed while I was brushing my teeth in the kitchen sink...

Did I suffer on that farm, especially from all the filth around me, on me, in me, I'm not trying to sound like an Existentialist, but let me tell you, *mon surmoi et mon enmoi* didn't look and smell too good at the time, indifferent to myself and the sordid affairs of the world, I couldn't imagine anything about myself and my future, I was stuck in that filthy present, cut off from my short past that didn't even have a meaning yet, and unable to contemplate my future, prisoner as I was of my filth in the crude timelessness in which I was stranded, that's the way I was on that farm, my life nothing but a long confused emotion...

Excuse the pseudo-philo-linguistic acrobatics but I'm trying to get out of that farm, I'm tired of telling you these depressing stories, perhaps if I stop talking about it, that miserable farm will vanish from my mind...

Oh you like what I said about the farm, you found it fascinating, touching even, I'm delighted, makes me feel like I didn't waste my time, nor yours, you know there are so many things I could still tell you, especially about the old geezer who, you won't believe this, I swear it's true, fucked the cows...

I saw him myself once, in the barn, he was standing on a little stool behind a heifer, shoving his old shriveled dick in this cute little cow's crack, I saw that by accident, I was going into the barn to get something, I don't remember what, and there he was standing on a three legged stool doing it to the cow, it really blew my mind to see that old sonofabitch sodomizing a cow, even today I can't erase that image from my mind, I still see that old vicious bastard taking advantage of that poor animal's nudity...

See how I get all worked up when I talk about what happened on that farm, I think that's enough about this sad and pathetic period of my life, so let's drop it because I want to finish telling you the beautiful story of my Aunt Rachel, otherwise we're going to get lost again for sure, it's been at least two hours since I started talking about the farm, and I almost forgot where I was in Rachel's story, besides you must be exhausted, it's some job to listen to me, it requires a lot of concentration, doesn't it...

Hey why don't we go have a bite somewhere, it'll do us good, I know a nice little restaurant near La Bastille, Chez Jule et Juliette, the food is fantastic, and not expensive, they make the best crème caramel in the world, and the éclairs au chocolat are out of this world too, let's go, we'll order a bottle of Bandol...

No, you dimwit, it is not a wine qui te fait bander, Bandol it's the name of the château in Provence where they make that wine, you'll see it's a great wine, light but very dry, nicely rounded, my treat this time, how about that, doesn't matter if I'm broke, I'll get some dough from Susan when she arrives, come on don't worry, let's catch le métro, and La Bastille here we come, wait till you taste those éclairs...

———

IT WAS GOOD ... WASN'T IT...

How did you like it, wasn't it great, I told you the food is terrific here, you want some coffee, I'll go on with the story while we're having our coffee...

Garçon, deux cafés s'il-vous-plaît...

You want a Calva...

Monsieur, two Calvados with the coffees...

Okay, you ready...

Excuse me, what did you say, I didn't hear you, stop mumbling...

Oh, you noticed the different tone of voice when I was talking about the farm, you say I was speaking in a softer, quieter, gentler tone, but that's normal when you deal with a situation charged with emotion, I always feel a little sentimental when I tumble back into sad memories, besides you know as well as I do that your moods change according to the stories you tell, sometimes you get mellow, other times angry, all worked up, and other times you're in a joking mood, and there are moments when you feel sentimental and nostalgic, when that happens you become more reserved, you take refuge in tenderness, and occasionally you even retreat into silence, it's always like that when you tell stories, it's all part of the creative rambling, but that doesn't prevent you from saying anything you please in any old way, the reason I change tone in my stories is because I change moods like the weather, understand...

Okay enough of this self-reflexive sentimentality, let's go on with the story, I'll pick it up where I deviated, I mean before I backtracked to the farm...

The war is over, I'm back in Montrouge, hello, coucou, here I am, it's me, haha, still alive...

I enter the courtyard of the house, 4 Rue Louis Rolland, it's July, or maybe August, doesn't matter, it's a lovely sunny day with a great big blue sky, a day when it feels good to be alive, and by pure coincidence it happens to be a Sunday, so the whole family is there looking out of the windows of Tante Marie's apartment taking in the sun, except my parents and sisters of course, and when I come into the courtyard they recognize me and they all start shouting, it's Rémond, le petit Rémond, le fils de Margot, c'est pas possible, we thought he was ... where does he come from...

You should have seen their faces, they looked flabbergasted, as if they had just seen a ghost...

So, here I am in the courtyard in a pair of shorts, an old short-sleeve shirt too small for me, and torn espadrilles on my feet, my sole possessions, and of course not a centime in my pockets, that's how I appeared in front of them, I'm fifteen, but have I already seen a lot of shit in my short life...

After listening for a moment to all these puppets screaming upstairs at the windows, shouting their surprise to see me, I rush up the stairs three at a time to the second floor and enter Tante Marie's apartment, and they're all around me, staring at me, touching me to make sure they're not dreaming, and that it's really me, then one of the aunts says, the poor boy must be starved, look at him, and it's true that I probably looked like hell when I reappeared that day, like a starving survivor, so Tante Marie goes to the kitchen to get me a little something to eat, yes I probably looked like a living corpse, I was so skinny, you know, even on the farm we didn't have much to eat because the Collabos and the Krauts took all the food, they grabbed everything, and the dumb farmers were afraid to open their mouths, they didn't dare kick up a fuss, so that's why I looked like I'd been starving to death when I returned home after the war...

Anyway, after the hugging and the kissing, they shoved a slice of bread with a piece of cheese at me, and a glass of tap water, to show me I suppose that they still care for me, or maybe to ease their guilty conscience, but let me tell you, it wasn't much of a snack, one lousy slice of stale bread with a tiny piece of rotten cheese that stank like a dead rat...

Isn't it funny that I still remember that the bread and cheese they gave me weren't fresh, it may seem like an insignificant detail, but it has to be mentioned, that kind of detail reveals the mentality of these people...

Okay, you're right, they probably didn't have much to eat themselves since even after La Libération food was still rationed in France, the fucking Nazis didn't leave much behind, empty stores and ruined lives...

While chewing away on the bread and cheese, I start telling them how I managed to escape when the French police and the Gestapo came to arrest us, ah *la-j'ai-ta-peau*, as Max Jacob used to call Hitler's private hit men, yes they were there too, but instead of letting me talk, they interrupt to tell me the pathetic little story of their survival, they tell me how **THEY** escaped the great round-up and went to hide in the free zone where **THEY** suffered from hunger and how frightened **THEY** were to be arrested and deported like the other Jews, and they go on and on explaining how surprised **THEY** were when **THEY** returned at the end of the war to see that most of the things **THEY** had left behind were still here, and while they're telling me their bullshit miseries, I try to tell them how much I suffered, how I jumped off a train and almost killed myself and how I ended up on a farm in the South where I worked like a slave from five in the morning till ten at night, every fucking day, even on Sundays, but they don't care, they're not listening to what I have to say, they keep shoving their cowardly flight at me, they don't even let me finish my story, instead they tell me that children like me don't suffer as much as adults because kids don't really understand what's going on in a war, can you believe that, yes that's what they tell me those ... those bastards ... and they keep on moaning and whining about their little ordeal, and how they almost got arrested like my parents, ah poor Marguerite, but not a word of regret for my father or my sisters, that's how they are, ah my family, and they insist on the fact that it really was pure luck that they were able to escape, my eye, they didn't stick around too long after they heard there was going to be a round-up, they took off full speed, their suitcases full of dough and silver, and abandoned us because they didn't want to be burdened with five more mouths to feed, finally I got so disgusted with their pitiful story and their phoney suffering, I got up from the table and left slamming the door behind me, and I went up to **my** apartment on the third floor...

You know I think the Germans exterminated six millions Jews to make them suffer, but what those dumb Germans didn't realize is that the dead don't suffer, I mean they can't suffer anymore once they're dead, the dead don't feel anything, it's the people who are left behind who suffer from the death of their dead, or pretend to suffer, maybe that's what the Germans wanted, to make us survivors suffer even after their defeat, after their sordid history will be erased from memory...

So I went upstairs to our old apartment, it was totally empty, there was nothing left in it, nothing but dust that looked like ashes, everything had been plundered, ransacked, the door had been smashed in, there was no lock, when I saw that there wasn't anything left, not a piece of furniture, not even a chair, or a pot to piss in, I went back down to Marie's apartment to ask what had happened to my parents' stuff, and they all mumbled in chorus, uh, ugh, oh, you know, it's probably the Germans or the neighbors who took everything, we lost a lot too, you should see our place now...

Yeah right, and me I was so stupid I didn't say anything when they told me that, nothing, what a dumb ass I was, I could have asked why everything looked the same in Marie's apartment, why everything had been left untouched, but instead I didn't say a fucking thing, I just left and slammed the door again and went back upstairs, after all it was still my home, even though it was empty, and I lived there in that empty space, until I left for America two years later...

It bugged the hell out of them that I lived upstairs, above their heads, like their conscience, their guilty conscience, especially on Sundays when they all came for lunch chez Marie, I could hear them whisper their wailing, I would lie flat on the floor and press my ear against the parquet to better hear them whine their lamentations, ah did it bother them to have a survivor upstairs, a kid who should have been dead, an overgrown boy who had confronted his own death, and decided he was not ready for it, and who came back like a revenant to tell about it...

There I was, above them, like a judge reminding them day after day of their guilt, their fear, their cowardice, their sin, I was there as a reminder of the final sentence that awaited them, and did I enjoy being up there, sometimes I would burst into mad laughter, just like that, so they could hear and not forget how they had ditched us, how they all took off to save their miserable asses and left us behind penniless, and so for the next two years I kept on laughing, just to torment them...

No, I didn't work, I didn't have a job, I did nothing, I just roamed the streets, at night mostly, I searched in trash cans for something to eat, I even begged in the streets so I could buy a piece of bread, I stole food from markets...

Of course I could have asked them to help me, but I didn't want anything from them, nothing, eventually I started to sell things on the black market with some guys I met in a Montparnasse café, the black market was still going strong after the war, and that's how I kept alive...

Are you crazy, pay rent to live upstairs, no way I was going to give them money to live in my home, even if the house belonged to Léon and Marie, besides, as I told you, there was absolutely nothing left in that crummy pad, except cockroaches, it was like a huge empty hole, but there in that hole at night, lying on a rotten mattress I had gotten at the flea-market, I thought of my parents and sisters, and in my skull, when everything went dark, une étincelle y pensait à mes absents, or to put it another way, a yellow feather in my head kept scribbling the names of my lost ones...

Une étincelle y pense à mes absents, isn't it beautiful, I wish I had invented that line, but it belongs to Valéry, damn how the hell did he think of that...

You don't know Valéry, you mean you never read Le Cimetière Marin, that great sad poem about death, I'll be darned, the guy never heard of Paul Valéry, unbelievable, everybody knows who he is, what kind of professional listener are you, what sort of stuff do you listen to, the writers whose stories you visited before must not have been very cultivated if they didn't quote the great classics from time to time, all writers borrow from each other, I've already explained that, all writers are word-thieves, and you don't have to reveal what you steal, that's part of the game, *a text is only a text when it hides at first glance the principle of its composition and the rules of its game*, that's the way my landsman Derrida explains it...

Well, I don't totally agree with Derrida, I think that a text, like a beautiful woman, should always show its ass, otherwise it's a frigid text, and as for the rules of my game, it consists of flagrant playgiarism, le plajeu en pleine vue if you prefer, in everything I say there's borrowed stuff, and maybe even more stolen stuff than borrowed, because, as Lautréamont once put it, and I wouldn't be surprised if he too stole that from somebody else, *in the process of literary creation plagiarism is not only advisable but recommended*, and he added, *minor writers borrow, great writers steal...*

Well, who knows maybe someday I'll become a great word-thief too...

But to get back to my empty hole on the third floor, I had a lot of time there to contemplate my misfortunes, the void is the perfect place to meditate on one's misery...

What bugged me is that in Léon and Marie's apartment everything was still there, intact, and there was even more stuff than before, things they had taken out of our apartment, even my shit pail had moved to their place, and I'm pretty sure the other aunts took their share of my inheritance, ah mes tontons et mes tatas, they sure helped themselves, and on top of that I learned later that right after the war ended they also pocketed the reparation money given by the Germans for the members of the family who had perished in the camps, I mean my mother father and sisters, and I wouldn't be surprised if they also collected money for my own death since they thought for sure I had been reduced to ashes, that's what they believed, until I showed up, still alive, they sure didn't waste a minute to help themselves to our stuff those money-grubbing salauds...

How do I know they were the ones who collected the reparation money, I did some investigating, I went the National Federation of Prisoners of War and Deportees, and also to the Ministry responsible for the Victims of the War, I got all kinds of documents, and I spent hours arguing with the fonctionnaires in charge of paying the compensation to the survivors, since I was the sole survivor of my family I was entitled to that money, but I was told that someone had already applied for the payment, and the money had been paid, of course I asked who got the dough I was entitled to, but the people at the Federation and the Ministry refused to answer under the pretext that these matters were confidential...

Confidential, my ass, can you believe this...

I'm convinced that it was my darling aunts and uncles who grabbed the money that was mine by right, and once again, the shy little twerp that I was never dared ask about it, and when I showed up they were ashamed to tell me they had pocketed my money...

My reparation money was probably hidden under their mattresses, reparation, what a joke, money in exchange for ashes...

My aunts and uncles got even richer on our tragedy even though they were crapping in their pants when they took off just before the round-up...

They probably paid someone, a neighbor, not Jewish, to keep an eye on their furniture and the rest of their possessions, that's why everything was still there in their apartment, but in my place, nothing, absolutely nothing, so I slept on the floor, on that old mattress, with no sheets and no pillow, only an old tattered army blanket that smelled like shit, and was it cold in the winter, there was no heat of course since our cute salamander-stove had also vanished with the rest of our furniture...

Tante Marie wanted to give me some old useless broken stuff they kept in the basement, she even tried to shove some sheets and a clean blanket in my arms as I was going up the stairs one day, but I refused, I threw the stuff down the stairs, I didn't want anything from them, I just wanted to be left alone in my hole, because you see, in my empty miserable room on the third floor above their heads I was there to remind them how they had abandoned us, how two days before the great round-up, they had cleared out during the night, Léon Marie Marco and all the others, without even warning my parents of what was about to happen, and that's why they felt guilty, guilty to be alive, because they knew they could have helped us escape, but they didn't, that's because they hated my father, and knew that if they had asked my mother to take the kids and come with them without him, she would have spat in their faces...

Sure they could have helped us, even if they hated my father's guts because he was a lazy good-for-nothing-womanizing-gambler, after all he was part of the family...

Wait, I'm going to tell you something so despicable that just the thought of it makes me sick to my stomach...

They told me that they had the names of my mother and sisters inscribed on the family tombstone au Cimetière de Bagneux, but not my father's, they told me that last Sunday when I went for lunch chez Marie, remember, when I couldn't take it anymore because I hadn't had anything to eat for days...

I hope you're not lost, I know it's difficult sometimes to follow me when I wander all over the place in time and space, it's easy to get confused...

You see, I learned about the family tombstone not when I came back from the farm, but when I returned from America...

So last Sunday, just like that, proudly, they announced that they had my mother's and sisters' names inscribed on the family tombstone, and they pleaded with me to go and see how beautiful it looked, you can imagine my reaction, wow did I get pissed when I heard that, and I told them how I felt about it, what the hell do you take me for, I shouted, I don't give a damn about your fucking tombstone, do you really expect me to go and cry on an empty hole, the hole where you buried your guilt, fuck you all, how dare you ask me to go and cleanse your filthy conscience with my tears, I know why you left us behind, you were ashamed of us, of our poverty, you wanted us to be erased from the family, you didn't expect me to come back, did you, it bugs the hell out of you that I'm still here to tell you the truth, that's what I told them, and then I left, that was last Sunday...

You have to understand that most of the Jews in Paris knew that something bad was going to happen, everybody knew that Pétain and his clique were planning with the Germans to get rid of the Jews, so those who had the money, like my aunts and uncles on my mother's side, they packed their things and took off for the free zone two days before La Grande Rafle du Vel d'Hiv, but those who didn't have money, the schleps, they stayed and waited, and eventually off they went by freight train to exchange their rags for striped pyjamas...

And us, you know, with my tubercular father who could barely work on his paintings he was so weak, and my poor mother who slaved as a cleaning woman to feed the kids, what could we do, we couldn't even afford regular train tickets to get away, let me tell you we didn't get to go on vacation very often when I was a kid...

For the rich Jews who took off for the free zone it was as though they were going on vacation with their suitcases full of jewelry and silverware, and what a coincidence that the round-up should take place in July, the perfect time for them to go to the beach or the mountain, pour se bronzer les fesses, just as they always did before the war...

How did we know about the round-up, there were guys who worked for the Germans, it doesn't mean they were collaborators, no, for them it was just a way like any other to make a living, and that's why they knew in advance what was going to happen, in fact I learned later that it was Marius, the owner of the café at the corner of Rue Louis Rolland and Avenue d'Orléans, who warned

Uncle Léon, because you see Marius had a brother-in-law who was a policeman, and that's who told Marius that all the Jews in the neighborhood were going to be arrested, and since Léon the tailor from time to time made a pair of pants for Marius in exchange for black-market food, Marius was known in the neighborhood as le roi du marché noir, this guy could get you anything you wanted, eggs, meat, soap, sugar, silk stockings, chocolate, cigarettes, capotes Anglaises even, you know all the things you couldn't get in the stores anymore, so because of the pants Marius and Léon were buddies in a way, and when his brother-in-law told him about the round-up he came right away to warn Léon and Marie, but they didn't tell us, because they couldn't stand my old man, and also because it would have cost them to take the five of us with them, it would have meant five more mouths to feed...

What has not been told enough about the Unforgivable Enormity is that those who were sent to their death in the camps were the poor Jews, like my parents, those who couldn't afford to buy train tickets to get away, those who didn't have anything to sell or pawn, no jewelry, no silverware, no cash hidden under the mattress, because you know if you didn't have money to pay the smugglers who led you across the demarcation line to the free zone, often with the help of the Krauts who pocketed half of the money, well you ended up taking the free train you know where...

The rich fat Jews on the other hand, they all took off for the free zone to enjoy their vacation, but only until the Yankees landed in North Africa, I think it was in November of '42, I don't remember the exact day, then the Germans immediately invaded the rest of France, and no more free zone, after that a lot of those hiding in the South of France were caught and exterminated together with the poor, the gas chambers didn't make a distinction between rich and poor, still many, like my aunts and uncles on my mother's side, managed to stay hidden, and that's how they survived, but on my father's side they all got wiped out...

Ah my father, the starving artist, he didn't last long, and he sure didn't leave me much of an inheritance...

Well, he did leave me something, his artistic temperament, and his sentimentality too, it's because of my father that I know something about the plastic arts, I have an eye for painting, if I hadn't become a writer I probably would have been a painter, or maybe a sculptor, yes a sculptor because sculptors have to be violent, they have to fight with their material, I would have done dirty erotic art, I would have created obscene scatological objects to symbolize the great crime of our century...

I love to look at paintings, ancient, modern, concrete, abstract, it's all the same to me, I can spend hours admiring a painting, I always try to figure out how the painter managed to fool us just with lines and colors, how he managed to make us believe that these illusions are real...

I once wrote a poem about painting, it was published in a magazine called **TXT**, just like that **TXT**, a great name for a magazine, do you know it ... You want to see the poem, it shows how much I know about *les bozards*...

But first let me explain that what inspired me to write that poem is the obsession artists have with the ass, the human ass...

Wait, let me finish, I know I was talking about my family's dirty tricks and that suddenly here I am again digressing into asses, but these are precisely the central themes of my story, the family and the ass, the ass and the family...

Ah the ass, **le cul**, so many great words to name it, to describe that splendid and welcoming part of our body, here is a nice little list for you...

Ass
Posterior
fanny
tush
rear
butt
buns
behind
bottom
buttocks
poop chute
waste basket
fart factory
asshole
butt hole
butt crack
bunghole
rear end
derriere
rump
pot
tail
seat
barrel
backside
fundament

You look puzzled, you don't get all that, you don't know American slang, how about if I translate all these English asses into French culs, maybe you'd understand better, okay here we go again...

le cul
le tonneau
le croupion
le fouettard
le gros ballon
les fesses
le fendu
le popotin
le fessier
le fondement
le panier à crotte
l'envers du devant
la voie anale
les doudounes
le saint~séant
l'arrière-train
le derrière
la praline
la croupe
le train
le pétard
le troufignon
l'usine à gaz
le foirard
le derche
le fût
le Q

ah le **Q**, the 17th letter of the alphabet, what a wonderful subject for art, as you'll see in my poem, without the ass the story I'm telling you would have no center, my story is above all an ass-story, it's like literary ass-fucking...

Okay, here's the poem...

[please turn the page]

The Museum of Imaginary Asses

When one thinks of the millions and millions of people who have dreamed before Leonardo's MONA LISA, one can imagine their sweet smiles had he painted her ASS instead of her face. The ASS has captivated artists throughout the ages, and in their attempts to capture the delights of this ever-changing shape they have given us an amazing collection of ASSES, for instance:

the obscure asses of Rembrandt
the celluloid asses of Rubens
the pyriform and whiny asses of Cranach
the geometrical asses of Picasso's Cubist period
the long and supple asses of Modigliani
the exotic well-rounded asses of Gauguin
the mischievous asses of Fragonard
the morbid asses of Signorelli's Resurrection
the rustic but vicious asses of Ingres
the sumptuous asses of Tintoretto
the suggestive asses of Poussin
the gracefully balanced asses of Maillol
the asses-within-asses of Moore
the blossomy asses of Renoir
the skimpy asses of Dubuffet
the nervous asses of Goya
the angular asses of Holbein
the shriveled asses of Brueghel
the lyrical asses of Chassériau
the gushy asses of Bellmer
the shy asses of Matisse
the vulgar asses of Toulouse-Lautrec
the hollow asses of Giacometti
the intrepid asses of Schiele
the disfigured asses of Magritte
the insolent asses of Salvador Dali
the immense asses of Lipchitz
the shapely asses of Courbet

the slick asses of Arp
the elongated asses of El Greco
the non-existent asses of Motherwell
the nondescript asses of Pissaro
the invisible asses of De Kooning
the minuscule asses of the miniaturists
the complicated asses of the Baroque painters
the puritanical posteriors of Copley
the elegant derrières of Tissot
and all the glorious and anonymous buttocks of the
Apocrypha.

What do you think, have you ever seen a list of asses like that, you know it wasn't an easy thing to write, I did all kinds of research, I spent hours and hours in museums and libraries looking at original paintings and reproductions, I took notes, it's a serious educational exercise...

You make a face, don't you like it...

Oh you do, for once you make me happy, I'll make a copy of it for you and I'll sign it...

Okay, let's forget poetry, I'd better stop all that ass-wandering and go on with Tante Rachel's arrival in Paris, all that stuff I've been telling you so far was simply to give you a better idea of the family situation, and mine too, before the return of the world-famous dancer, Rachel...

But before I describe Rachel's triumphant arrival, there is something else I have to tell you about Marius, so just one more detour, it's really funny, it's about something that happened in his café, in fact that's what I was about to tell you before I got distracted with asses, but maybe there is a connection...

Quickly then...

One day, or rather one night, some thieves burglarized
Marius' bistro, it was a neat place you know, un bureau
de tabac also, with an old zinc counter, and a pool table
in the back, of course us kids were not allowed to go
into that café, only the adults could go in to drink and
get drunk, but me I got to go inside whenever my father
needed cigarettes, he smoked a lot, des Gitanes, isn't it
amazing that I still remember the brand he smoked,
Gitanes, without filter-tips of course since filters hadn't
been invented, anyway that's what my father smoked
even though it made him cough like mad at night because of his tuberculosis, my mother used to tell him,
those damned cigarettes will kill you, well finally it
wasn't cigarette smoke that killed him, but some other
kind of smoke, so one Sunday...

How do I know it was Sunday, because there was no
school that day, what I'm telling you now happened
before the war, I was seven or eight years old, and that
Sunday morning three police cars stopped in front of
Marius' café, when the people in the neighborhood heard
the pin pon of the police sirens they rushed to see what
the racket was all about, and the cops explained that
there was a burglary during the night, some thieves
broke a window, went inside and stole bottles of wine,
cognac, beer, you know, all the booze one normally finds
in a bistro, but not only that, they also stole all the money
in Marius' safe...

Wait, I'm coming to the good part...

During the robbery, one of the thieves took a shit on top
of the billiard table, and that's the first thing Marius
noticed when he opened the bistro early that morning,
that big turd right there in the middle of his pool table,
he almost passed out, and when the cops saw that lovely

pile of shit they just laughed, of course it didn't take long before the entire neighborhood heard about it, and everybody wanted to have a look at the big dump on Marius' billiard table, well let me tell you, it was quite a show, a lot more entertaining than the lousy movies they showed at the Montrouge cinéma, Place de la République, pretty soon there was a long line of people in the street waiting to go into the café, the street became so crowded the cops had to direct traffic, letting only a few people go in at a time, you should have seen how the people shoved and pushed, without the cops it would have turned into a riot, this way this way the cops kept saying, pointing at the pool table in the back of the café, come on move it, go around the table, a little faster over there, don't be selfish, let the others see too, and that day even the children were allowed to go in...

I tell you, this was the happiest day of my childhood...

Poor Marius, you should have seen his face, he was so embarrassed, so ashamed, he was sitting at a table, his head between his hands, I think he was crying, he was so ugly Marius, he had a monkey's face, he looked like a hairy ape, you know a marmoset with tufts of hair on his ears...

That pile of shit haunted him for the rest of his life, everybody kept reminding him of it, when people came into his café they always asked, hey Marius how is your big piece of shit, what did you do with it, did you put it in the fridge, did you cook it, did you give it to the museum...

You don't think it's a funny story, you find it too scatological, oh, the man knows his science of shit, I'm impressed, okay forget it, but me I have never forgotten that great big lump of merde in the middle of Marius' pool table, it's one of my fondest childhood memories...

Alright, enough, no more digressions...

As I was saying, every Sunday, the entire family got together chez Marie instead of my grandmother's since she died...

How did she die, didn't I tell you, she died of natural causes somewhere in the free zone during the war, I don't know exactly where, wherever my aunts and uncles had taken her...

Anyway whether she died a natural death or artificial death doesn't matter, because to tell you the truth, I didn't like her very much, and she didn't like us either, I mean my sisters and I, you see, Marco was her favorite, he was Bubbe's Kleine Chouchou because not only was he the oldest of the grandchildren but also the richest, I mean his parents were the richest in the family, and Marie kept giving Bubbe money on the sly, without Léon knowing of course, but now that she was dead the family met on Sundays chez Marie, and since I was there, upstairs in my hole, sometimes Marie would come up and beg me to come down and eat with them, she would plead, come, come and have lunch with us, it's no use sulking like that all alone, it doesn't help, it just makes things worse, I know it's sad that your mother and your sisters didn't come back, but what can we do, it's life, don't be stubborn...

Too late, I would tell her, and I always refused to go eat with them because I didn't want to hear once again how they had suffered during the war, that's all they talked about, their suffering, or else they complained that they had lost so much, they were so poor now they had to work like slaves, night and day just to be able to buy a little food, what bullshit, that's what they told each other on Sunday...

I couldn't stand their sniveling, it made me sick to my stomach, although one Sunday, I did come down, I was flat broke and I hadn't eaten anything for three days, I couldn't take it anymore, the smell of cooking coming up through the floor drove me crazy, I was hallucinating, so I went down to eat with them, and during the meal Tante Marie announced that she had just received a letter from Tante Rachel, who was now living in Senegal, saying that she was coming to Paris in a week to see and embrace the brothers and sisters she hadn't seen in so many years...

You should have seen how they all went berserk when they heard that Rachel was coming...

But instead of being happy about seeing a sister they hadn't seen in more than twenty-five years, right away they all started speculating about how rich Rachel must be to travel like that all over the world...

It had been twenty-five years since Rachel escaped from the orphanage, remember, in 1919, at the age of fourteen, and what I'm telling you now happened during the winter of 1945, after La Libération, I think it was January when the letter from Rachel arrived announcing that she was coming, that means that she was now thirty-nine years old...

I don't suppose you were born yet when Paris was liberated, no you're too young to have witnessed that glorious day of August 23rd, 1944, when General de Gaulle walked up the Champs-Elysées in front of his army, ah what a day, thousands and thousands of people on the sidewalks crying and cheering, and singing la Marseillaise, too bad you didn't get to see that...

I was still on the farm when de Gaulle paraded triumphantly up the Champs-Elysées with all his medals pinned on his chest, but I heard about it, everybody heard about it, all the farmers were listening on the radio, and that's why I can tell you about that historic day...

Anyway, immediately after Paris was liberated, Tante Rachel wrote from Dakar, where she was now the owner of two hotels, that's what she said in her letter, yes two hotels in Dakar, don't ask me what kind of hotels, she wrote to find out what had happened to the family, if all her brothers and sisters whom she hadn't seen since she ran away from the orphanage were still alive, she was worried and concerned...

She sent that letter to my grandmother, because she didn't know she was dead, but it's Marie who got it and who answered, explaining that everybody was fine, except for Marguerite and her children...

You see, I found out later that Marie had answered Rachel's letter before I showed up in Paris, explaining that everybody was fine, except for poor Margot and her children who disappeared, I suppose they thought I was dead too...

Well, I don't know how Marie put it, something like that, it's Tante Rachel who told me what Marie wrote, and that's why she was surprised to see me when she arrived, but I'm anticipating here, let's go back to the day Marie announced that Rachel was coming to Paris...

Immediately the whole conversation turned to the question of how that little sister who ran away from the orphanage at the age of fourteen with her miserable bundle of clothes under her arm made her fortune in Senegal, and how much money she had, and what kind of hotels she owned...

One thing for sure, I didn't believe anymore about Rachel being a dancer, neither did the rest of the family, in fact during the conversation Léon sneered, in front of the kids, I mean in front of all my dumb little cousins, it's easy to get rich when you prostitute yourself all over the world, especially in those far away countries where people screw like animals, if you've got a nice ass you can become a millionaire in the colonies...

Personally I didn't give a damn if Léon thought that my Aunt Rachel was a prostitute, and besides how did he know she had a nice ass, me I just wanted to meet that great adventuress, she intrigued me, and even if she had fucked for money in the colonies, it made no difference to me, if she hadn't been dumped in the orphanage at the age of four maybe she would have become a good bourgeoise like her sisters...

So the day of her arrival, I decided that I would get out of my hole and join the rest of the tribe to meet la putain du Sénégal, as Léon called her...

Oh you want to know if I also thought that Aunt Rachel was a prostitute, une fille de joie, rather than a dancer, to be frank I didn't think anything, you must understand my dear professional listener that to think is to ask oneself if, and if always implies doubt, or if you prefer, as Herder put it, to think always expresses incertitude...

Herder who...

Johann Gottfried Herder, you've never heard of that eighteenth-century German nihilist, one of the first pseudo-prophets of Nazism, well according to him, to think is to be perplexed, so to answer your question, my Aunt Rachel left me perplexed, that's why I wanted so much to get to know her...

Okay it's now one week later, the day of Tante Rachel's arrival...

She called from her hotel to say that she would arrive chez Marie by taxi around two o'clock in the afternoon, on a Sunday...

It seems that all the important events in my life happen on a Sunday, curious coincidence, in fact you may not know this but I was born on a Sunday, May 15, at 3:00 o'clock in the afternoon, this may not mean much to you, but it does to me, I was born to be lazy, Sundays are made for laziness...

But it's true that there are a lot of Sundays in my story, that's because Sunday is not just another day, something always happens to me on Sunday, Sundays are like a hiatus, a discontinuity in the web of my existence, in the drama of my living days...

Okay I don't want to be carried away with this little Sunday digression, but once again it was a Sunday, and they were all there lined up on the sidewalk in front of the building waiting for the taxi to arrive, they were all there, the uncles, the aunts, the cousins, all dressed to kill, with overcoats and hats, because that day it was cold as hell, wow was it cold the day Tante Rachel arrived, but me, since I had nothing to wear, I came down from my third-floor hole with my torn military blanket wrapped around my shoulders, you cannot imagine how cold it was that day...

When Tante Marie saw me with that khaki blanket on my shoulders she said, listen I'll go get one of Marco's overcoats, you can't possibly...

I can't possibly what, look like a bum, like a starving filthy disgusting bum to meet my aunt from Africa, I shouted to Marie, leave me alone, I'm not ashamed of my poverty, and I stood there on the sidewalk with the rest of them waiting for the arrival of my mother's little sister...

She had said two o'clock, but it was past four when a taxi finally stopped in front of the house, we were all frozen from having waited in the cold for more than two hours, stomping our feet, rubbing our hands and ears...

On va attraper la crève, Léon kept saying...

So let him catch his death, I mumbled to myself...

Meanwhile all the little cousins kept whining, why can't we wait inside...

The taxi stops, they all rush towards the curb, but I stay in the back, against the wall of the building...

The children had been told to behave and to give Tante Rachel a big kiss when she arrives, and if she hands out presents not to forget to thank her, and if she gives nothing, since she doesn't really know how many nieces and nephews she has, because she left so long ago, then the children should not say anything...

Except for Marco who was older, all my other cousins were younger than me, and they always acted like a bunch of spoiled brats, I couldn't stand them, especially Giselle, Aunt Léa and Uncle Nathan's daughter, she was only twelve but she put on airs because her parents owned a fancy shoe store in Clichy, she always wore a stupid pink bow in her hair, and lace panties she kept flaunting in everybody's face, the little bitch, she got on my nerves with her stuck-up manners...

Well, I'm not going to describe all those little brats, only four of them all told, a rather sterile family on that side, except for my mother who had given birth to three children, but they were all there the cousins the day our aunt from Senegal finally arrived...

Ah, Tante Rachel, I'll have to describe her, but not right now, I want to keep you in suspense for a while...

So, a little after four, a taxi turns into our street from Avenue d'Orléans and comes towards us, they all push and shove to be the first to kiss la putain du Sénégal, bunch of hypocrites, but Marie gets mad, back off, back off, she yells, don't you have any manners, I'm the oldest and this is my house, I'll be the first to kiss our sister, so everybody moves back because when Marie speaks nobody dares argue, she was tough, and you didn't mess with her...

The whole scene is happening on the sidewalk in front of the house, what a pathetic reception committee, you would have laughed had you seen us, but me I don't care if I am the first or the last to embrace my Aunt Rachel, I am here because I want to see how she looks, if she resembles the beautiful exotic dancer of my dreams...

Well let me tell you, Tante Rachel was stunning, incredibly beautiful, resplendent like a movie star, I'm not exaggerating, and so chic...

She gets out of the cab wrapped in an extraordinary fur coat, I mean a fur coat so elegant, of such thickness and richness it was a marvel, let me put it this way, that coat was not only beautiful it was sexy, I don't know if it was mink or bear or beaver or rabbit, but that coat was impressive, a luxuriant deep grey, superbeau et superchaud, of course it's understandable since Rachel lived in Africa that she had gotten the warmest coat to come to Paris in the middle of winter, you should have seen the dumbfounded expression on everybody's face when she came out of the taxi, they stood there open-mouthed, gaping in admiration, staring at Rachel with big round eyes, as if they had just seen a fairy queen, I tell you it was just like a movie...

Here, let me go back a few frames and describe how Tante Rachel first emerged from the taxi, I'm going to zoom in and replay the whole scene in slow motion, like a Cecil B. De Mille movie, or better yet, à la Fellini, it's more modern...

The taxi stops, the back door opens slowly, first we see a golden shoe with stiletto heels slip out of the car, and then a long slender leg in black nylons settles on the sidewalk and hesitates for an instant, the toe pointing, a gorgeous slim shapely leg, with a leg like that, I marvel, it's possible that Tante Rachel was a dancer, the second leg comes out and then the fur coat, I cannot begin to tell you how magnificent it was, how sumptuous, sen-suous it was, she is holding the coat tight around her with both arms as if embracing herself, and she's wear-ing a jaunty little black hat with a veil that covers half her face, so at first I cannot really see how beautiful she is, it's only when she lifts the veil to kiss her sisters, broth-ers, sisters-in-law, brothers-in-law, nieces and nephews, that I get to see her exquisite face, I'll describe it in a moment, but first I want to finish the scene on the side-walk, I re-zoom...

Since I'm standing against the wall of the building, away from the curb, I can see everything that's happening in front of me, that's why I'm able to replay the entire scene for you, in a way I'm like a movie director, and at that moment I realized that perhaps someday I might make a movie of all that, or else write a novel...

So to continue, while Rachel goes from one person to the next to be embraced hugged and kissed, her sisters and sisters-in-law are surrounding her, fondling her coat, oohing and aahing in admiration and stupefaction, whispering to each other, look at that coat, here touch it, it feels like it's still alive, it must have cost her a fortune, our little sister knows how to spend money, looks like she only gets the best...

Meanwhile Léon and the other uncles stay out of the way, waiting for their turn to be kissed, that's normal, women first...

Me, I smile and shake my head watching the whole scene, especially when I hear Léon whispering in Marco's ear, let me tell you that coat is no fake, must be worth ten or fifteen grand...

After the hugging and kissing with her brothers and sisters, who all wipe a few crocodile tears, Rachel embraces the sisters-in-law and brothers-in-law she doesn't know since they all became part of the family after she ran away from the orphanage, and then it's the nieces and nephews' turn, all born during her absence, she asks each of them their name, she tells them how cute they are as she pinches each cheek gently, of course that little bitch Giselle takes advantage of the occasion to brag about her excellent work at school to show Aunt Rachel how smart and well behaved she is, I feel like kicking her in her lace panties...

Suddenly Tante Rachel notices me standing alone against the wall, she comes towards me and asks, what's wrong with this one, is he sick, why is he wearing a blanket, who is he, he's not part of the family, is he, a neighbor, a curious neighbor who wants to see the beautiful lady from Africa, who is he, but before anyone can answer, she exclaims, no it can't be, no ... it's not ... oh my god, it's Margot's son, I can't believe it, he looks exactly like her, same eyes, same mouth, he must be the same age she was the last time I saw her, ah poor Margot, and suddenly she covers her face with both hands and starts sobbing quietly, right there on the sidewalk, in front of me, I almost burst into tears myself, she's crying for my mother, I never saw my other aunts cry for my mother, and suddenly I feel like a fool because I don't know what to do, what to say, I just stand there like a dummy with my blanket around my shoulders, holding back the tears...

After a while she calms down, she slips a finger under her veil to wipe the tears from her face, yes it's Rémond, Margot's son, Marie says, he came back all alone, we had no idea where he was, the poor boy we thought he was dead too, somehow he managed to escape, but not Margot and the girls, it's so sad, we tried to save them too you know, but we couldn't, there was nothing we could do, it's pure chance he escaped, and now he lives upstairs, we take care of him...

Listen, I have to stop a moment to put myself back together, I'm so choked-up, I'm losing control, I feel all mushy remembering how my Aunt Rachel cried when she saw me with that beat-up blanket on my shoulders and said that I looked just like my mother, look how I'm shaking...

No stay, I'll be okay...

Yes thanks, get me a glass of water ... no, bring me a beer instead, but hurry because I want to tell you what happened next...

I get so emotionally worked-up when I talk about all that, I'm so hyper-sensitive, but I feel better now, okay I go on...

Finally Rachel stopped sobbing and came closer to kiss me, and that's when I saw how beautiful she was, she was thirty-nine years old then, but she looked more like twenty-nine, she was so gorgeous and so well made-up...

When she lifted her veil to look at me, I admired her big black eyes with long curved eyelashes that almost touched her eyebrows, later after she went back to her hotel, the other aunts said that Rachel's eyelashes were false, personally I couldn't care less if her eyelashes were real or false, I thought she was magnificent, especially when her face came close to mine to kiss me and I smelled her perfume, she smelled so good, her perfume was so strong it made me dizzy, her black mascara had trickled down her cheek when she cried, but that black stain under her eyes made her look even more beautiful and exotic, her lipstick was so red and shiny it looked like blood, she had a marvelous mouth with thick sensual lips, when she kissed me I felt the softness and wetness of her lips on my face...

I tell you, I had never seen such an incredibly beautiful woman, so well made-up, so elegant, except in the movies, I could not believe she was my aunt...

I was overwhelmed, but I didn't have much time to reflect on her beauty because all of a sudden she put her arms around me and clasped me so hard to her heart it almost knocked the wind out of me, I could feel her body against mine while her red mouth kissed my face, leaving lipstick marks all over, she was so affectionate, so tender, I was filled with emotion...

You see, I think my Aunt Rachel hugged me so tight for several reasons, first because I am the son of her favorite sister with whom she suffered so much in the orphanage, but also because of all her brothers and sisters my mother was the only one who wasn't there, the only one who had been exterminated, so when Rachel took me in her arms it was like she was also embracing my mother, and at that moment I was like her sister, a substitute for her absent sister, so when my Aunt Rachel squeezed me in her arms I became the equivalent of three people, the nephew she was seeing for the first time, the son of the sister she had loved so much, and her sister since she saw in me the image of my mother, I was the nephew-son-sister of my aunt, you see what I mean...

No, of course not, I was not her lover, it's not because we kissed and hugged like lovers that you can jump to that conclusion, you really have a filthy mind, aunts that screw with their nephews, that only happens in novels, not in real life...

Naturally, I got excited, what do you think, I'm not a saint, I've got feelings, when a sexy woman puts her arms around you, even if it's your aunt and even if you're only fifteen, it still affects you, but in spite of the emotion I felt being inside her fur, literally inside, because you see when she grabbed me to kiss me, her coat half-opened and suddenly I found myself inside her fur, so to speak, and that's when I noticed, despite the emotion the softness of her coat caused me, that my aunt was rather short, like her sisters, and she had to get on tiptoes to kiss my face, and I also noticed, well, I should say, felt her generous breasts against my chest, big and firm, I was so surprised and moved by this burst of affection, I couldn't help myself, I put my arms around her and squeezed her tight against me, I'm telling you it was just like love at first sight, except that she was my aunt, so maybe I shouldn't tell you this, but right there on the sidewalk, holding my aunt's fur coat in my arms with my aunt inside the coat, I suddenly remembered Tata Rachel's black pubic hair of my childhood dreams, and I started feeling something bulge inside my pants...

I don't think she noticed, but when she took a step back to look at me, and told me again how much I looked like my mother, she saw my flushed face and said, as she tenderly pinched my cheek, the poor darling he's shy, so tell me sweetie how do you like your aunt from Africa, isn't she gorgeous, here give us another kiss...

I didn't answer, but it's true that I blushed, so to hide my embarrassment I bent down to pick up my blanket which had fallen to the ground when I embraced her, and I put it back around my shoulders holding it tight around my waist to hide my emotional eruption, meanwhile Rachel was staring at me, it's amazing how he looks so much like his mother, the spitting image, he has her eyes, the same sad eyes, ah your poor mother, if only you knew how much she cried in that orphanage, how she sacrificed herself for me and for your Uncle Maurice, your mother was a saint, you know, a real saint...

When Maurice hears this he throws his arms around me and kisses me, but his kiss is not soft and sensuous like Rachel's because he hasn't shaved and his beard is prickling my face, and then he bursts into tears like a kid and once again I feel confused...

Alright, enough sentimentality, if you don't mind I'm going to skip the rest of this scene because it became unbearable when all the aunts started to cry and moan at the same time, repeating over and over like a litany, poooor Margot, poooor Margot, if only she could be here with us to see her sister again, if only she could see all of us together...

I'll skip that pathetic moment, I don't want to bore you with their lamentable wailing, instead let's go up to Marie's apartment where after the kissing and the crying on the sidewalk everybody went for a snack...

So here we are in Marie's flat, I can't even begin to describe my aunts' befuddled faces when Rachel took off her coat, hat and gloves, and they saw the elegant suit and the expensive jewelry she was wearing...

There she stood in front of us, like a doll, with her perfect make-up, lots of pink on her cheeks, black eyeliner on her eyes, crimson red lipstick, and her hair so black and so curly it looked like a wig, her sky-blue tailored suit was sharply cut, with a very short skirt revealing most of her exquisite legs in black stockings, around her neck she had a long pearl necklace, she wore large gold earrings, and on her fingers silver rings, or maybe they were platinum, I don't know much about precious metals, in any case she had rings with huge diamonds on every finger, I'm telling you Aunt Rachel was like a walking jewelry store, she was as glittery as a shooting star...

Marie had set the table and prepared tea with cakes, everybody hurried to sit around the table, Léon insisted that Rachel sit next to him, the pervert, he was probably planning on pawing her thighs under the table, my little brats of cousins were pushing each other to sit next to Rachel, especially Giselle who had already put her lacy ass on the chair next to Tata Rachel, as she kept calling her, but Rachel said, be a dearie, ma petite cocotte, go and sit over there, and grabbing me by the arm Rachel pulled me to the chair, sit here mon chéri next to your aunt, and don't be shy, he's so bashful that boy, and when I sat down she leaned over and gave me a big kiss on the cheek, a handsome young man like you shouldn't be shy, she said, come give your aunt a kiss right here on the cheek, and she offered me her lovely cheek...

Not knowing how to react, since I was so charmed, I gave her a big smile and a timid peck on the cheek, her deliciously perfumed cheek, she put her arm around my shoulders and squeezed me tight, look how strong my adorable nephew is, she said feeling my biceps, wow is he muscular...

It's true that although I was skinny, the hard work I did on the farm had developed my muscles, so for a boy my age I was rather strong and well-built, okay I was no Marcel Cerdan, but still...

I'm not bragging, look at me, I'm in great shape, that's because in America I do a lot of sports, I play tennis and golf, it's not because I'm always broke that I can't play tennis or golf, in America you can do anything you want, it's cheap, besides it's never me who pays, it's Susan...

Susan's rich Boston family belongs to a country club, so when she was a kid she learned to play golf and tennis in her parents' fancy club, when we became lovers she decided that I too should learn how to play those bourgeois games so we could have fun together, Susan is a fanatic of tennis and golf, so to keep up with her I learned, and now I play a damn good game of tennis, and at golf, I have a six handicap, yes six...

I see you don't know a damn thing about golf either, you don't have the faintest notion of what I mean when I say I have a six handicap, no it doesn't mean that I'm physically handicapped, on the contrary, in golf the lower your handicap the better you are...

Well, no need to waste time explaining golf to you since you'll probably never learn to play, here in France only les snobs riches play golf, the rest of the population plays pétanque...

Anyway, what I was trying to tell you with this detour into golf and tennis, is that my Aunt Rachel thought I was strong and handsome, and that made me happy because nobody before had ever said that to me...

But let's go back to the gathering chez Marie, so here we are all seated around the dining-room table, we were kind of crowded because there wasn't enough room for everybody, usually for the Sunday lunch the children ate in the kitchen, but on that special day Marie made an exception, that's why we were so cramped, I could feel my aunt's thigh against mine under the table, and again I got all worked up...

Look, I'm not going to relate the whole conversation, I only want to say that after the aunts and uncles complained about how much they had suffered during the war, and how they were so poor now because they had lost everything, they started asking questions about Rachel's whereabouts during those twenty-five years, and so she explained that she had traveled all over the world, but without really saying what she had been doing exactly, and just before the war started, because of a lucky turn of events, she settled in Senegal where she now owns two big hotels in Dakar...

Imagine, my Aunt Rachel owner of two big hotels in Dakar, you should have seen the look on the faces around the table when she described her hotels, they sounded like palaces, of course later, after she left, Léon said, two hotels, my ass, brothels rather, did you see how Madame Rachel dresses, with that skirt up her ass, and all that fancy shiny jewelry, she looks like a high class whore...

Well, that's about all there is to tell of my first encounter with my Aunt Rachel, what an unforgettable day, one of the most important moments of my life, and you know what, two months later, when she was ready to go back to Senegal she wanted me to go with her, she kept saying, you'll see I'll put you up in my hotels and you'll be happy, you won't have anything to do, I'll take care of you, you won't have to worry about your future, and when she said that, I pictured myself wearing a dashing white linen suit, a colonial hat, with a cigarette casually hanging at the corner of my mouth, swaying my shoulders like a tough guy in my aunt's hotels, I looked like Humphrey Bogart in Casablanca, yes just like him, but instead of going to Africa, I decided to go to America, maybe it was a mistake, Senegal could have been interesting, but America seemed more romantic to me then, more intriguing, it was like leaving for a great adventure, how dumb can one be...

You want to know something, I bet if I had gone to Senegal with my Aunt Rachel, today I would be a millionaire instead of an unrecognized, misunderstood starving American writer...

Who knows, maybe if I had gone to Senegal I would not be here telling you my stories, I would be dead already, because in Africa all kinds of deadly things can happen to you, you can get bitten by a scorpion, or a venomous snake, or a tsetse fly, you can catch yellow fever, malaria, AIDS, and also there are savages there who eat white people, finally I think I made the right decision even though America turned out to be for the birds, a catastrophe, and I almost committed suicide there...

I suppose it was plain stupid to go to America and starve instead of going to Africa and become rich, but one doesn't always make the right decision in life, sometimes you take the wrong road, life is full of crossroads, but that's why life is worth living, otherwise it would be boring to always go in the same direction and never entertain other hopes...

Well, enough deep thoughts, you wanted to know what my aunt did after her stay in Paris, she went back to

Senegal alone, but did she spend money during those two months...

I saw her almost every day because we became kind of ... how shall I say, I was not just her nephew, but her escort in a way...

No, not her gigolo, really you disgust me with your perverted mind, I was more like her friend, like her son even, together we were like a mother and a son who adore each other, that's how it was with my Aunt Rachel, we loved each other, and she was so nice to me, and so generous...

First she bought me clothes, because, as you know, I didn't have a thing to wear, so she took me to a good tailor Boulevard Sébastopol who made me two superchouette suits to measure, a grey one and a navy blue one, Léon was so pissed when he saw my two suits, he erupted with rage because another tailor made the suits, he said to Rachel, how come you didn't ask me to make him suits, after all I'm the tailor in this family, but Rachel retorted, so why didn't you make your nephew a suit before I came so he could have something to wear besides a torn blanket, you couldn't make him a suit before, or even a pair of trousers...

That sure put that miser in his proper place...

In addition to the suits, she bought me silk ties, shirts, underwear, socks, fancy Italian shoes, everything I needed to be presentable, because during her stay in Paris we went out together almost every night to expensive restaurants, night clubs, cabarets, dance halls, my aunt even taught me how to dance the tango, the rumba, the paso-doble, she was a wonderful dancer, you should have seen how she wiggled her hips when she was dancing the rumba, almost every night we went to the Lido, Mimi Pinson, Le Monocle, or le dancing de la Coupole...

What are you talking about, I wasn't too young to go dancing in night clubs, anyway I was precocious for my age, I didn't look like a young puceau, you see, even though I wasn't sixteen yet I looked older than my age, more mature, maybe because of the suffering I endured during the war, that's why I could go dancing in night clubs with my aunt until late at night, and around three or four in the morning I would take her back to her hotel in a taxi...

Yes in a taxi, and it was me who paid, well, with the money my aunt gave me of course, she must have been loaded because let me tell you money was flowing freely in all directions, she never counted, whenever she saw something she liked in the window of a store, she just went inside and bought it, and if I happened to look at something in a window shop, she would say, do you like it darling, let's go in and buy it, and that's how I got my first wrist watch, a gold Swiss watch with a lizard skin band we bought in a ritzy jewelry store Boulevard des Italiens...

Look, I won't deny it, I was like her boyfriend, so what, there are lots of wealthy aunts like my aunt who take care of their nephews, doesn't mean they sleep together, that kind of stuff only happens in cheap novels, or porno movies, my aunt and me we were just buddies, platonic lovers...

So late at night, I took her back to her hotel, do you know the Ritz, place Vendôme, that's where she was staying for two months, I'm not kidding, do you have an idea how much a room costs for one night in that hotel, certainly more than you make in one year listening to stories, she stayed two months in that fabulous hotel, must have cost her a fortune...

Everybody at the Ritz knew me, the porter, the concierge, the elevator boy, the chambermaids, the receptionist, they all knew I was the orphaned nephew of Madame Rachel du Sénégal, I was like a celebrity, and sometimes when I came to pick her up to go eat in a restaurant or to go dancing, the clerk at the reception would say, Monsieur, yes all the employees at the Ritz always called me Monsieur, Monsieur, the receptionist would say with a polite smile, your aunt told me to inform you that she's not ready yet and to please join her in her suite...

I was always a little hesitant about going up to her room because often when I came in she was wearing her pink satin robe and it was always half open exposing her thighs, or else she was half naked wearing only sexy panties and a bra, and she would say, oh excuse me mon chéri, I'm running late, we danced so much last night I was tired and fell asleep this afternoon, I'll be ready in a minute, have a seat, have a glass of champagne, so I settled in one of the deep luxurious armchairs, style Empire, and just admired her while she put on her makeup, or decided which dress to wear, while she hummed a tune as if I wasn't there, then she would sit on the edge of the bed crossing one leg on top of the other to slip on her silk stockings, she would slowly roll them up to her thighs and hook them to her garter-belt, after that she would bend down to put on her shoes, and I would stare à son derrière acceuillant, and I would fantasize...

Did I enjoy the sight, what a question, well let's put it this way, je barbotais derechef, je flippais beau hors-bite, that's the only way I can put it...

Tante Rachel was very laid-back, cool and relaxed, as they say in America, she didn't give a damn about anything, nothing bothered her, she was totally carefree, I suppose when you're rich it's normal to act like that, you don't care what people think of you, and if they don't like what they see well you just show them your ass, and my Aunt Rachel she had one hell of a nice ass, that much I can tell you because when I went up to her room I got to see it often, my Aunt Rachel's superb ass, it was so generous and welcoming, you felt like burying your head in it, but it wasn't just her ass, Tante Rachel had a stunning body, a sensational body for a woman her age, with a pair of boobs so large they looked like they overlapped on top of each other...

She also had some strange habits, for instance when I came into her room she always asked me to take off my shoes and even my socks, she told me that you should always go barefoot in a house, a habit she picked up when she lived in the Orient, also she used to tell me that nudity is the most beautiful thing in life, and so I always took off my shoes and socks as soon as I entered her room, and sometimes Rachel did weird stuff to me, to my feet especially, she loved to kiss my feet, yes my feet, she'd take them both in her hands while I was lying on the bed resting a bit before going out, or relaxing in one of the armchairs, and she'd kneel before me and cover my feet with little kisses, or she licked them, it felt so good, but when she licked the sole of my feet it tickled and I would burst into laughter, one day I asked her, Tata Rachel why do you do that to me all the time, and she answered, ah if only you knew, my love, if you knew, don't ask, don't ask anything, it's a long story, so I didn't insist, and to tell you the truth I kind of liked what she did to my feet, but it doesn't mean that ... that...

You of course must think that ... well you're wrong ... she just made me feel good and that's all, and I suppose it made her feel good too...

Rachel enjoyed nudity, and once when I entered her room I saw her lying on top of the bed completely naked drinking a glass of champagne, I stared at her, but she didn't move, she didn't even try to cover herself, she simply told me to come and sit next to her on the edge of the bed, and offered me a sip of her champagne, then she caressed my face saying, ah you're such a handsome young man, you know, mon chéri, you'll be quite a heartbreaker when you become a man...

Nobody before had ever told me I was handsome...

Oh you think my nose is too big, like Cyrano's, well what about my beautiful black hair, and my malicious dark eyes full of passion, don't you think that counts...

Well, in any case that's what my Aunt Rachel used to tell me, that I was handsome and charming and sexy, and I believed her...

That day when I found her naked in bed, we stayed there next to each other for a while drinking champagne, then she said to me, come here mon petit chou, lie down next to me, take a rest before we go out, we'll go dancing later, so I lay down close to her and I put my head in the hollow of her shoulder while she gently stroked my hair, while whispering, sleep my darling, go to sleep, fais dodo, and I closed my eyes and pretty soon I fell asleep...

You sonofabitch, you'd like to know if I screwed my aunt, well I won't tell you, there are things you just cannot tell, it wouldn't be correct to say that I slept with my aunt, besides I was still a virgin at the time, well, I think I was, since on the farm, as I told you, I never got to mount the farmer's wife...

In any case, nobody will ever know what happened with my aunt in our intimacy, that's my secret...

Okay, now I'll finish Aunt Rachel's story, one day she announced that she had to go back to Senegal to take care of her hotels, and she asked me again if I wanted to come with her, I told her that I had already made a request for a visa at the American Embassy, so she said, too bad, we're so happy together, don't get your hopes too high darling, you know it might be hard for you over there, America isn't a dream country, I never went there but I heard a lot about it from girlfriends who tried to make their fortune there, anyway listen, if it doesn't work for you in America don't worry, just come to Dakar, I'll send you a plane ticket, I'll take care of you...

That's it, end of Rachel's story...

I never went to Africa, besides while I was in America, my aunt was forced to sell her hotels when Senegal became a free country, after that she settled in Paris in a deluxe apartment near Pigalle, and that's why she was there when I went to have lunch chez Marie after I came back from America...

I did tell you she was there with the others at the windows of the second floor when I entered the courtyard Rue Louis Rolland and Marco shouted, it's Rémond, l'Amerloque...

Yes Rachel was there too, but let me tell you, she was no longer the gorgeous Jewess from Senegal, unbelievable how she had aged while I was struggling in America, it had been twelve years since our nights of dancing in the night clubs, but now at the second-floor window with the others, she looked like an old aunt, even though her hair was dyed and she was well made-up, after all she was past fifty now, I don't know if it was because of the kind of life she led in Paris or because she was with her brothers and sisters again, they all looked old, wrinkled, used, in any event that's how I always saw them, like old people, and Aunt Rachel looked just like the rest of them now...

Ah that Sunday lunch, what a disaster, what a fight I had with them, and let me tell you, I didn't weigh my words, especially about the reparation money they stole from me, how they abandoned us, and all the rest...

I'll have to recount all that, but not right now, it's getting late, besides I already told you too much today, I can't tell everything at once, when you tell a story you have to know where to start and when to stop, so enough for today, what time is it...

Nine o'clock, I'll be darned, I've been talking for more than eight hours, you must be exhausted, I'm sorry, I forgot the time, shit my British girl is going to kill me, we were supposed to meet at eight, wow is she going to be pissed...

Well that's all for today, I've got to go, I'll see you tomorrow, same place, same time, and tomorrow I tell you about the lunch chez Marie, I'll even add a little something about my British girl, after all I'll have to talk about her too eventually, you'll see she's not bad for a Britisher, tomorrow is going to be a great storytelling day, you'll see, I can feel it, okay bye, I'm out of here, take care...

——

AN UNEXPECTED EVENT
INTERRUPTS THE STORY
TEMPORARILY...

OH YOU WANT TO KNOW WHY
I DIDN'T SHOW UP YESTERDAY...

Yesterday was Wednesday, the day I had my appointment with the lady from Les Éditions de l'Amour Fou,
you remember, the sexy Chief Editor with the friendly
ass whom I sweet talked chez Laplume, well, that's why
I didn't show up...

So yesterday ... wait, let me first flashback to what happened right after the Laplume lunch...

The following morning, I'm still half asleep in my shitty
hotel room when I receive a message from la Directrice
asking that I drop off my manuscript at the reception
desk of Les Éditions de l'Amour Fou as soon as possible
so it can be read before our meeting next Wednesday...

Well, well, I thought, the woman is serious, she's interested in my noodles, so I rushed to Rue de l'Ancienne-
Comédie where La Maison de l'Amour Fou is located,
number 138 to be exact, and left my package of noodles
with the receptionist, a fat, spectacled brunette who tells
me with a smile full of teeth, oh yes, of course, Madame

Trucmuche, that must be her name, informed me that someone was going to deliver a manuscript today, thank you very much Monsieur for your delivery...

I got a little irritated when that fat nana said *thank you Sir for your delivery*, as if my masterpiece was just a package of meat from some butcher's shop, my noodle novel has nothing to do with hamburgers, it's literature, the four-eyed blob could at least have said, thank you for leaving your manuscript, or thank you for giving us a chance to read your work, but to throw the word *delivery* at my face, that really bugged me, even though she didn't know who I am, she could have shown a little respect, serious writers should not be treated like butchers...

I was so nervous after leaving my manuscript, you see the most difficult moment for a writer is when his work is being scrutinized and judged by those who are going to decide its fate, it's even more painful and anguishing than the writing itself...

Didn't you notice how tense and nervous I was these past few days, can't you tell people's feelings by the way they speak or act, what kind of professional listener are you anyway, all you care about is the story, you don't give a shit about the frame of mind of the storyteller...

It's true, I'm not the kind of guy who reveals his emotions on his face, still knowing that my manuscript was being dissected at Les Éditions de l'Amour Fou troubled me all week long, even if you didn't notice, but let me put aside my anxieties and tell you what happened yesterday...

You may recall that my appointment was for ten o'clock, but I was so nervous, impatient like a wild mustang, excited like a virgin in heat, saying to myself this is it, today is the big day, today I'm going to be discovered, I'm going to be offered a huge advance for my book, sign a contract, and tonight I'm going on a hell of a binge, so, seething with impatience, I was already pacing up and down Rue de l'Ancienne-Comédie at eight o'clock in the morning after four cups of coffee and four croissants at the corner bistro Rue de l'Odéon, and at ten sharp I enter La Maison de l'Amour Fou...

Oui Monsieur, how may I help you, the fat four-eyed receptionist asks from behind her desk, the bitch doesn't recognize me, so trying to look relaxed, calm, and cool, I tell her I'm the writer who deposited a manuscript last week, I have an appointment today with Madame Trucmuche to discuss a contract...

I should mention that I was wearing my navy blue blazer, remember the one I wore the day I went to see the family, and also my silk tie, I wanted to look my best, create a good impression and show that charming lady that although I'm still an unrecognized avant-garde novelist, I am a gentleman...

So I tell the rotund receptionist that I have an appointment, and she answers, oh I'm terribly sorry Sir, but Madame la Directrice isn't here today, she had to go out of town on an urgent matter...

Patatras, crash, plouff, I tumble back into the obscurity of my unrecognized condition of a screwed-up unpublished unread writer, I knew it, I knew it, never fails, you meet a charming lady editor, she flirts with you, she tells you she's dying to read your masterpiece, but when you show up to discuss the book, nobody's home, Madame is out of town...

That bitch, she toyed with me, suddenly I feel a ferocious rush of rage through my body, I'm ready to explode, the fucking broad, she read my stuff, she didn't like it, she may even have been offended by it, but she didn't have the guts to tell me to my face what she thought, she didn't have the courage to tell me in person that she couldn't publish my noodles, screw her...

I agree, it's disgusting to act this way, but it's always like that with publishers, especially French publishers, they always tell you they can't receive you at this time even though you have an appointment, always the same excuse, because Monsieur le Directeur or Madame la Directrice had to leave unexpectedly for the province on some urgent matter, it never fails, and then you hear them snicker behind your back when you leave, your tail between your legs, your soiled manuscript under your arm...

I was so enraged, I almost leaped on top of the receptionist's desk to make her swallow her teeth with a punch in the mouth, but then she said with her ultra-bright smile, oh you're the gentleman who wrote that funny book full of noodles, we all laughed so much, yes it's you, the author of the noodle novel...

The bastards, they all read my novel and laughed at my expense, even that stupid receptionist wallowed in my noodles, I didn't know if I was supposed to be happy or angry that everybody in that crummy joint had fondled my book with their filthy paws, but before I could decide where to direct my furor the chick says to me, Madame Trucmuche asks that you excuse her for not being able to discuss your book with you today, but her assistant, Monsieur Gaston, is going to do it for her, so if you don't mind waiting a moment, I'll inform Monsieur Gaston that you are here, and he'll see you in his office in the basement as soon as he gets off the phone...

Suddenly I feel better, at least Monsieur Gaston read my novel, and we are going to discuss it, personally, I don't care if I sign the contract with the sexy Directrice on the main floor, or with Gaston in the basement, it's all the same to me, kif-kif, I don't give a damn as long as my noodles are well taken care of and I make a nice bundle of dough...

Still, the lady editor could have informed me herself that she couldn't see me, instead of leaving me in Monsieur Gaston's hands, besides, as I told you, I thought she was rather attractive, and who knows, maybe the sexy passages in my novel got her excited, things like that happen you know, well I hope my noodles didn't give Gaston some weird ideas...

That's what I am pondering while waiting for Gaston to get off the phone when a young man appears before me, I swallow hard when I see him, he looks like a little twerp in his wrinkled grey suit and his sad tie full of food stains, what the hell is that, five feet four at most, no more than twenty-two years old, this is the assistant who is going to discuss my book with me, this skinny red-head with freckles all over his face and thick glasses on his nose is going to decide the future of my novel...

The near-sighted midget holds out his hand, I shake it without enthusiasm...

First impression rather negative, not only is the myopic twerp's hand limp but humid like a wet rag, it feels as if I'm squeezing a dead fish, shit, an ugly sticky spongy guy like that, with a fishy handshake, probably didn't react too favorably to my novel, I'm sure he didn't get the symbolic subtlety of the noodles, a guy that short-sighted must be short-minded too...

So here we are now in his office, a tiny messy hole with yellowed newspapers and magazines all over the floor, books covered with dust, apparently never read, piled up on shelves, bits of manuscripts all over, and an awful smell of rotten paper in this tomb-like office without windows, that's promising, obviously Gaston is not at the top of the editorial committee of this publishing house, just a mediocre worthless unimaginative myopic reader who blindly clears away the loads of manuscripts on his desk, a second-rate editor who goes through all the pseudo-literary bullshit waiting in line in front of his office door, a miserable manuscript-sweeper, and my great noodle novel instead of gently landing on Madame Trucmuche's desk ended up in this little piece of shit's shoddy office, well that's one hell of a start, suddenly I have a dark presentiment that my noodles may not have been as welcome as I thought, oh well, it's going to be quite a scene when Monsieur Gaston starts explaining why Les Éditions de l'Amour Fou cannot publish my book...

She sure fucked me over the charming Directrice, she dumped me in the basement with this miserable half-blind reader, well it doesn't matter because I'm going to give her assistant a little working over, make him understand what laughterature is, how it laughs at all the constipated assholes of the world...

Please, have a seat Monsieur, says Gaston interrupting my interior monologue with a self-congratulatory smile that reveals rotten yellow teeth, as he leans back in his chair to appear important, taking the pose of someone who has the power to decide your fate in two minutes...

I don't say anything, I just sit on the rickety chair in front of his desk and cross my legs...

A moment of silence while Gaston casually flips over pages of my manuscript on his desk as if rehearsing what he's is about to say, while glancing at the pages, he takes a pack of cigarettes out of the inside pocket of his jacket, Marlboros, and offers me one...

Poor jerk, he's trying to impress me with his American cigarettes, I say no, thank you, and take out my pack of Gauloises and light one, I only smoke Gauloises sans filtre, I tell him, I smoke real cigarettes, blond tobacco is for fairies...

Gaston doesn't react, but I hope he got the message, if he got weird ideas reading my book he can shove them up his ass...

Another moment of silence, finally Gaston says, tipping his chair back on two legs, and letting the cigarette smoke out of his nose, trying to look tough and professional, well, Monsieur, I read your novel with great interest, I must say that it is very amusing, yes very funny, but...

Ah, here comes the **but**, I knew it...

I was going to ask Gaston if the fact that he found my book amusing meant something positive or negative, if it was good news or bad news, but instead I give him a twisted smile and let him go on, I plant myself firmly in the wobbly chair, light another Gauloise, and wait for his monumental critique...

Gaston takes off his glasses and starts sucking one of the side tips, as if mulling over what he is going to say, he's trying to look editorial, I notice that his eyes are tiny and oval like cock-holes...

T'as les yeux en trou-de-bite, Jacques Ehrmann used to say to me in the morning after a bad night, or even a good night, of literary creation or fucking, same thing, he always said that to me, well looking at Gaston's tiny oval eyes I almost felt like telling him that he had cock's eyes...

Excuse me for getting off the subject and talking about my old friend Jacques Ehrmann, whenever I see eyes like those of Gaston, I think of Ehrmann who died at the age of forty-one, it was so sad, he was such a great guy, so smart, a genius, we met in Los Angeles, he was a displaced frog like me, an experimental writer, too bad he changed tense too soon and didn't get a chance to finish his work, I would have loved for him to read my noodle novel, at least he would have told me the truth about it...

But back to Gaston's **but**...

The story you are recounting, he begins while putting his glasses back on his nose, the story of that young French Jew, survivor of what you call *The Unforgivable Enormity*, a rather interesting expression to refer to ... well you know what I mean ... yes the story of that young man who goes to America to become a jazz musician is certainly interesting and worth telling, but it is the way you tell it that presents a problem, you see, all those reflections about the creative process become irritating after a while, all those digressions, and that, that ... how shall I put it ... that triviality of the novelist who locks himself in a room and eats only noodles for an entire year in order to write the book we are reading, well this is not very convincing, nor plausible, or to put it more succinctly, your work is too ... if I may borrow an American term now in vogue, too *self-reflexive*...

I don't say anything, I let him talk, but inside my guts I feel that all hell is about to break loose, things are going to get hot in a moment, especially when he gives me his *self-reflexive* shit to impress me with his knowledge of the English language, just wait little Gaston, there's going be a heck of a storm in a moment, I feel it coming...

Scratching himself behind the ear, Gaston continues his rehearsed speech, telling me now that my novel is basically an autobiography, a barely disguised autobiography, the little asshole really wants to reduce me to nothing, I'm starting to boil inside, your novel, he goes on with an effeminate giggle, to put it differently is simply a somewhat narcissistic self-portrait done with some humor but lacking a coherent story-line, a plot...

That does it, I cannot contain myself any longer, plots are for dead people, I say to the myopic twit as I stand up and lean over his desk to stare into his pint-sized oval eyes, and then, hitting his desk with my fist I shout, **AUTO...BIO...GRAPHIC my novel**, but tell me Monsieur Gaston what do you know about my life to say that my novel is autobiographical...

I sit back in the chair, and slowly, calmly, I hissss, *a-narcccisssssissssstic-sssself-portrait*, hey monsieur l'éditeur de mes deux, don't you understand that one must have the courage of one's narcissism if one wants to be a writer, but that's not the point, no, the point is, what the fuck do you know about my life, you little piece of shit, to conclude that what I'm writing is the story of my life, I can assure you that everything you read was pure invention, I made it up word by word, it's all improvised...

Gaston looks shocked at my reaction to his prepared rejection speech, I don't suppose too many writers come to his office and call him a little shit...

He opens his mouth to say something, but I cut him off, don't you know that everything that is written is fictitious, you see my Dear Gaston, I think you confuse life with writing, writing is not, I insist, the mere repetition of life, imagine how boring it would be to write the pathetic story of your life, it would be impossible to find words to match its mediocrity...

It's not because I followed a road somewhat parallel to that of my protagonist that what I write is a photocopy of my life, no, my dear little man, I do not write to say what I was, nobody gives a shit about what I was, **on s'en fout de ce que je fus,** I suddenly burst out to that morpion, I write to find out what I should have written, or if you prefer, the little I know about myself I invented it because writing is not what you remember but what you have forgotten, so Gaston you better think twice before throwing your narcissistic self-portrait imbecility in my face, also think in that little bird-mind of yours what a self-portrait is, because you see a portrait, self or not-self, that shifts from the visible to the invisible, that detaches itself from life to become written symbols, that portrait always transforms itself into something else, because writing the self inevitably leads to the great ambiguity of self-transformation, do you understand what I'm saying, or is it too complicated for you...

I stand up again, walk around his desk, put my hands on his shoulders, and as I push him back in his chair, and switching to the familiar *tu,* I say, tu vois Gaston, it's obvious that you didn't comprehend a damn thing when you read my book, you must understand, you little cretin, that when the writer makes the transition from the visible to the invisible, as he plunges into the invisibility of language, he confronts the incapacity of seizing the subject who writes, because no matter how hard one tries, the subject who writes will never be able to seize himself in what he writes, he will seize only the writing itself, which by definition excludes him, and so, Gaston, in that sense, maybe my novel is an autobiography, but a failed autobiography, since it fails to seize the subject who writes, me, Moinous, you know what you should have said, your book is an obscene **Auto-bio-graffiti**...

That's what you should have said, but if this is too self-reflexive for you, that shows that you are in the wrong business, and that you don't understand a damn thing about literature, and that you should be doing something else than deciding the fate of manuscripts, personally I think you would make a fine plumber, you have a plumber's hands, I tell Gaston pointing to his sweaty hands, but an editor, no way, or maybe you could try the meat business, I can see you as a butcher, or a charcutier...

I swear, that's exactly what I told him, and poor Gaston just sat there, completely flabbergasted, looking at me as if I was some kind of maniac, a runaway lunatic, or else he must have thought I was a genius, but wait that's not all, wait till you hear the rest of what I said to that myope when suddenly he said, as if he hadn't heard me, as if everything I told him had passed above his head, because all he wanted was to finish his prepared speech, as if he absolutely had to recite the catechism of rejection he had learned by heart on his knees before the Saintly Chief Editor, it was obvious that he was merely repeating what she had told him to say in order to get rid of me, before she took off...

This is what that dimwit tells me next...

You see, despite all its good aspects, we think that your novel...

I immediately notice the **we**, it's clear that Assistant Gaston is only mouthing word for word what the bitch whispered to him about my novel, ah la pouffiasse, and she was so pleasant during that lunch, so attentive, she even rubbed her knee against mine a couple times, what a hypocrite, and then she reads my stuff, finds it shocking and disgusting, and decides to throw my noodles into the trash, wait till I run into that charming lady on the street one of these days, it's not my cock in her ass she'll get, it's my foot...

While I mentally settle the score with Madame la Directrice, Gaston keeps on reciting his bullshit...

You see, we find your novel too postmodern, we believe that our readers will not be able to follow your postmodern detours and circumvolutions, of course this doesn't mean your work is bad or has no literary value, but it's too complicated, too cerebral for our readers, as such it has no commercial value, that's the problem with the postmodern novel today, it's not accessible to the general public, the reader who reads for fun cannot follow what is going on, he wants to be told a straight story, or else he becomes frustrated...

I shake my head, I let him continue his bookseller's speech, I decide to let him conclude before finishing him off...

While he's talking I play the soliloquy battle with myself, it's true that for years I've been stuck in digressiveness, wandering endlessly in narrative detours, tumbling again and again into self-reflexiveness, and these old habits, so dear to the storyteller enamored of the interior mirrors of his recitation, will indubitably prevent that wonderful book from being published here in France, that book which caused me so many sleepless nights, but that's the way it is, I'm addicted to self-reflexiveness, I cannot write if I don't watch myself writing, to step out of my writing, to close my eyes on the writing process would reduce it to pathetic realism or romantic agony...

While I am self-reflecting, Gaston is going on spouting his absurdities of a publisher in search of bestsellers, clearing his throat, he now explains, it is your reluctance to let the story be told that prevents your novel from being what it should be, a *Bildungsroman*...

Oh, very nice Gaston, Bildungsroman, did you hear that, unbelievable...

The twerp now wants to impress me with his Bildungsroman, once again I stand up, I lean towards him, both hands resting on his desk, my big nose almost touching his and I sputter in his face, in other words, if I understand correctly, you and your Saintly Directrice find my novel too intelligent for your readers, in your opinion one should write dumb stories to please the dumb general public, one should tell them the same old stories that they already know, otherwise they don't understand anything, but you idiot, don't you know that it's in the nothing that great stories take place, the truth hides in the nothing, behind the words, in the depth of words, in the white space between the words, in the vanishing point where trivial details become irrelevant, in the silences inside the story...

I pause a moment, and then as if talking to myself, it is in the shadow of the story, in that imperceptible moment when the story collapses into its own form beyond the lies of the fable that the truth is revealed, when the writing like fire delights in its own form, its own dance...

I go back to the chair, light another Gauloise, blow a puff of smoke towards Gaston, and continue...

Or better yet, imagine yourself in the reverse of farness beyond the artifice of a painting, inside the paint, where the geometry and coherence of the work of art is hidden...

I was so worked up I was throwing all kinds of wordshit at him, saying whatever came to mind, but Gaston is stubborn and ignores my beautiful tirade...

Well, there is also the problem of your style, your sentences, your syntax...

My sentences, my syntax, I don't allow him go on, I know what he's going to say...

Gaston you understand absolutely nothing, listen carefully I'm going to explain my style and syntax to you...

I pick up one of the pages of my manuscript and shove it in front of his face, you see there are people who speak and write in sentences, correct complete sentences punctuated according to the rules, and in neat paragraphs with the obligatory indentation at the beginning of each, well, look at this page, and what do you see, you see words that go in all directions, like macaroni inside a box, because, Gaston, I do not write normal regular syntax, I write crooked paginal syntax, I let the words wander on the page, I do not tell them where to go, I just write the words, I go from one word to the next, I word-word, or if you prefer, I do linguistic wordage using only the comma to shape my writing, get it, and that's my style, Take It or Leave It...

You know what, Buffon was wrong when he proclaimed, *le style est l'homme même*, bullshit, style is not the man himself, style is a manipulation of syntax that brings the monstrosity and aberration out of language, that's what my style is, an error of nature...

Satisfied with my explanation, I sit down again and light another Gauloise to calm myself, those damn French cigarettes are going to kill...

This time poor Gaston looks stupefied, crushed, he puts his head down on top of my noodle pack trying to pull himself together, I think this time he is convinced that the noodler is a genius...

But I'm not done, I have to put him in his place regarding the postmodern question, exterminate him once and for all, there is no way I'm going to let his postmodern remark go by without a rebuke...

So you find my noodle novel too postmodern, wrong again Gaston, you've arrived too late, we are already beyond postmodernism, it's dead, dead and gone, don't you know, it's been buried, where have you been, and that's precisely the problem for literature today, now that postmodernism is dead, writers don't know how to replace it, the disappearance of postmodernism was devastating for the writers, but it was not surprising, it was expected to happen for sometime, the last gasp happened the day Samuel Beckett changed tense and joined the angels, I can give you the exact date if you want to, postmodernism died because Godot never came...

Gaston looks as if he is on the verge of tears...

In a way my novel circulates the death certificate of postmodernism, it warns those who are still stuck in the postmodern sack to get out before the banks repossess the houses and the cars and the washing machines they bought on credit because their books didn't make the best-seller list...

Gaston tries to say something, but I tell him to shut-up and listen, I'm not finished...

It was sad to see postmodernism disappear before we could explain it, I kind of liked postmodernism, I was happy in the postmodern condition, as happy if not happier than in the previous condition, I don't remember what that was called but I was glad to get out of it, and now here we are again faced with a dilemma, what shall we call the new thing towards which we are going, this

245

new thing I haven't seen yet, did you see it Gaston, what can we call it, postpostmodernism seems a bit too clumsy, and popomomo not serious enough, I thought of calling this new condition The People's Revolution Number Four, or The New Pot Revolution, but I'm afraid that Gallimard or some other big bookseller already has these names under copyright, in any case I think the name of this new condition that's about to descend upon us should have the word *new* in it, what do you think, Gaston...

Gaston doesn't answer, he stares at me with a look of panic on his face, his mouth is half-open and his tiny oval eyes keep blinking hopelessly...

How about The New Novelty, I say to reassure him, or maybe The Postnovelty, or better yet The New Post-future, somebody suggested Avant-Pop, I find that too familiar, you see the difficulty, if we must name that beast looming in front of us, I say pointing to my pack of noodles on his desk, we better hurry, otherwise it'll be too late and we'll already have reached the next new post-condition, the one that will follow what we are unable to name...

Hey, maybe you have a suggestion, after all you're an editor, it's your job to name literary novelties, but you better think fast, Gaston, before that new thing disappears...

Gaston seems totally lost, he has closed his eyes, but suddenly he grabs his head and says with a pitiful look on his face, does that mean that the novel is dead, that there isn't any hope for the novel...

Of course not, you imbecile, it's not because the postmodern is dead that the novel is also dead, don't worry you're not going to lose your job, there still are loads of guys out there who write novels without paying attention to where and when they are, and have no idea why they do it, although, as Roland Barthes once put it, the novel is always a death, it's a death because it transforms life into a destiny, and memories into useless sentences, so you see, the one who writes his life is in fact writing his death, in that sense neither life nor writing are primary, neither of them can provide an understanding of why we are on this planet because neither of them are entities unto themselves, that's more or less what Roland Barthes wrote regarding the futility of writing novels...

Don't you think it was smart of me to quote Roland Barthes, but of course Gaston didn't understand that I had made that detour in order to return full circle to his remark about my novel being nothing but a barely disguised autobiography, he didn't understand what I was trying to tell him, that between life and fiction there is no difference, that when life is at the center, fiction is at the circumference, and vice versa...

So to close the seminar, I said taking on a professorial tone of voice, you see GasCON, if you really want to go on with your publisher's job, you have to understand once and for all that not all those who write or pretend to write are writers, and not everything that is written echoes life...

To write is to create a new model that helps us better understand our life before dying...

In that case, Gaston says bouncing his ass up and down on his chair, are we right in saying that all writing is finally autobiographical, and so it goes for your novel...

You're finally starting to understand, good for you, I tell him holding out my hand to congratulate him, it's so simple when you think of it, your life is not the story you write, the story you write is your life, got it...

But Gaston isn't finished, he wants more, he is tenacious, suddenly he asks, but tell me, Sir, why don't you write in French, after all it is your mother tongue, the tongue in which you lived most of your life...

The noodle novel, of course, is written in English, did I forget to mention that, I always say that the title is **Le Temps des Nouilles**, but in fact it's **A Time for Noodles**, and naturally Gaston had read it in English, hence the reason for his question...

It's true, I answer him, it is true that it's in the French language that I suffered the most in my life, perhaps that's why I write mostly in English, to escape my suffering, and now I'm part of that notable exception of multi-linguists, those **lingoverts**, as my buddy Peter Wortsman calls us, what a smart guy Wortsman, he has a gift for inventing new words, **lingoverts**, great word to define all the uprooted writers who bring chaos into borrowed languages, yes I belong to what Wortsman calls, that literary foreign legion made of runaway aristocrats, political deportees, indigent adventurers, travelers without luggage, soldiers of fortune, roving intellectuals, refugees of all sorts, survivors, who leap-frog the linguistic and geopolitical boundaries to create an alternative tradition, a literature of the elsewhere...

You see Gaston, I'm a writer from elsewhere, I leap-frogged across the Atlantic, that's why they call me a frog over there, but you know what, it takes a lot of courage and daring to write in another language, it's easy to write in your own mother tongue, it comes to you ready-made, as if you learned it by heart, it even tells you how to write it, but when you write in a tongue other than yours, you have to invent it word for word, it takes arrogance to write in a foreign language, what you write in that language eventually becomes a pile of old rags you can throw away after it's written since it doesn't really belong to you, well, one could say that I am a ragman of fiction...

Gaston obviously worn out couldn't take it anymore, he didn't even react to that last harangue, he just sat there crushed, but he did manage to mumble, Sir, if you would agree to write for us in a straight-forward fashion the story of the young French Jew who goes to America to seek his fortune, and leave out all the rest, well...

I didn't let him finish, all the little jerk wants is a story, the story of my life, he might even offer me a couple of thousand bucks for the story of my life, he's not interested in my novel improvised in sad laughter, no, he wants real life, well, how sad...

I had enough of that assistant, besides it was obvious that I was in the wrong place, the wrong publishing bordello, and that Gaston and Madame Trucmuche would never understand that for me a novel is less the writing of an adventure than the adventure of writing...

So I took my manuscript from his desk, but before leaving his cave I said, you want me to tell you something Gaston, even if you and your Directrice aux belles fesses offered me twenty grand for my novel right here and right now, I wouldn't give it to you, because you're nothing but fucked-up editors who don't know how to read, you might do better selling cheese in a grocery store than getting mixed up in the literature...

That's what I told him, and I added, people like you suffer from intellectual atrophy, you're lost in the mercantile stampede, you're conditioned by false writing, cute writing, dumb writing, boring writing, non-writing, l'écrit faux, l'écrit emmerdant, l'écrit con, l'écrit chiant, *L'ÉCRITURE*, I shouted as I slammed the door behind me...

But then through the door I hollered, Gaston you've just been rejected as an editor, and I laughed, for once it was not me who was rejected, I rejected the publisher...

That's how I finished him off...

In any case, I hope Gaston understood that even though postmodernism is dead it doesn't mean that literature is done for, literature won't end that way, it would be too easy, too much to hope for, it would be a fine death, the kind of death that keeps on going and going, as Sam used to say, no, literature is tough, it'll die only when we humans disappear from this planet...

The fat receptionist, who was probably listening to the discussion behind the door, tells me with a sneer on her face, goodbye Monsieur, I hope we'll see you again...

When I heard that I stared at her and said, hey you chubby, you want to know something, instead of sitting on your fat ass all day, you should try to hustle on the sidewalk of Rue Saint-Denis, that way you'd lose weight fast, and I'm sure you'll make a better living than in this joint...

Out in the street, I took a deep breath, and burst into laughter...

Well, that's what happened yesterday, so you understand now why I couldn't come, but let's forget about those assholes, someday that cunt will be sorry she didn't grab my noodles...

Enough of that, what do you want to hear now...

You want me to tell you more about the farmer's wife, or how about...

Oh you can't stay, you have to leave early today, where are you going, you got a date with your girlfriend...

Don't tell me you're going to listen to another story, are you cheating on me with another storyteller, I would really be disappointed, I thought you were more faithful than that, you could at least wait until I'm finished...

No that's not it, phew, I got scared, for a second there I thought you were going to abandon me in the middle of my story...

Tomorrow then, same place, same time, okay...

Hey don't stay out too late tonight, go to bed early so you can be in good shape to listen tomorrow...

Tomorrow, it's going to be fantastic, don't be late...

▬

THERE IS BAD NEWS & GOOD NEWS...

The bad news, looks like I won't be able to tell you the end of the story...

The good news, tomorrow I'm going back to America, Susan can't come, she just sent another telegram saying that for family reasons she cannot join me, she's really sorry, forgive me Darling Moinous, I implore you to come back to me, I can't stand another day without you my love, I swear I'll die if you don't come back, that's what she says in her telegram...

How can I resist, I've already packed my stuff...

She can't come because of family reasons, she says, but no details, maybe another one of her rich Boston aunts died and left her another million dollars, I wouldn't be surprised, money always attracts money...

Anyway, she sent a plane ticket, prepaid, it's waiting for me at Orly, so that's it, I'm going back to America, tomorrow Nouillorque here I come, and this time, who knows, maybe Susan will let me marry her, and I'll be rich, I won't have to worry about my next meal, every-thing will be perfect, I'll be loved, happy, well fed, I'll have clean underwear all the time, and I'll be able to write my stories in peace and tranquillity, because here in Paris, I just can't work...

In this stinking city I waste my time talking, blabbering, that's all I do, tell stories, and my words get lost in the wind, everything I say vanishes into thin air, that's not writing, I mean writing according to the rules, solid writing, you know what I mean...

That does not mean that everything I told was wasted, but still only the written withstands time, so enough of this verbal shit, America here I come again...

It's too bad you won't get to hear the end of my story, or maybe it's better this way because, to tell you the truth, I really don't know what the end would have been, when you improvise you have no idea where it will lead you, but it's okay because I'm happy to get out of here, I've had it with the pomposity of France and the arrogance of the French people, there's nothing left for me here, only sad memories and humiliation...

I know it's unfair to leave you like this, in suspense, with an unfinished story, but that's how it is, I have to think of my future...

Look, why don't you give me your address, and if some day I ever return here, I promise I'll tell you the rest, I hate to leave my stories unfinished...

You know what, all things considered I don't think I'm made for France, or let's say, France isn't made for me, we just can't put up with each other, France is too rot-ten, and I'm too angry for what she did to us...

You see France refuses to accept the fact that it got kicked in the ass by the Germans, so it pretends that nothing really happened, that in fact even during the Occupation the French were in charge, oh yeah, they were in charge of shipping out the Jews that Hitler didn't even want, take the children too, they said, so how could I be happy living here, me an orphan of The Unforgivable Enormity, and yet deep inside I still feel so French, if only you knew how often, during those ten miserable years in America, I dreamt of my glorious return to France, I kept imagining myself landing at Orly, *rich & famous*, photographers and journalists waiting for the return of the prodigal writer, and look at me...

Ah la France, Take It or Leave It, well, I can't take it any more, I'm going back to America for good, I prefer America's mediocrity to France's hypocrisy...

You're upset again because I'm criticizing your country, my country too you know, and I'm not the only Frenchman who holds a grudge against France, who's ashamed of the country where he was born and raised, ashamed especially of its disgraceful recent history...

Here, let me recount a conversation I had the other day with an old war veteran, a World War One poilu, a Frenchman who witnessed all the filth in which France has been floundering these past fifty years...

Remember the café on that beautiful infamous Place des Vosges where I dragged you the other day to show you where it all ended for the unwanted Jews on July 16, 1942, well, after you left to see your girlfriend, this old geezer who was sitting at the table next to ours, I don't know if you noticed him, approached me and apologized for having listened to what I was telling you...

That was the day I was telling you how La Belle France acted like the whore she is and couldn't wait to get fucked in the ass by Hitler, well after you left, I sat there for a while thinking about my problems, about the family, my British girlfriend, Susan, my novel, my next meal, and all the rest, and that's when that old guy spoke to me...

Do you want to hear what he had to say...

First, I tell him, no need to apologize, Sir, we all enjoy listening to other people's stories, we all love a good story, and do you know what he tells me, it's part of his job, so I ask him if he's also a professional listener like you, but he says no, he is not a listener but a storyteller, and he understands the problems of the profession...

How you like that, so I thought he wanted to talk about what he called our profession, but I wasn't in a mood to discuss storytelling, and I was going to excuse myself and leave when he tells me that's not what he wants to talk about, he wants to discuss what I said about France...

I got interested, so I asked him to join me for a drink, hoping, of course, that he would pay...

Well, let me tell you the whole conversation, it was a revelation, I never thought a Frenchman would speak like this about his country...

Monsieur, he begins as he sits next to me and orders two Pernods...

Oh, by the way, I should mention that when he walked over to my table I noticed that he was limping, he had a peg leg, you know, a wooden leg...

Monsieur, he says shaking his head, I share your opinion of France and your indignation towards her, when you say Take It or Leave It, I entirely approve the sense of that expression, that slogan reflects perfectly the obtuse narrow-mindedness of a country that proclaims itself eternal, ah La France Éternelle, and so I must reflect on the meaning of those words, and I speak now as someone who has witnessed much of the sordid history of this century...

That's how this guy spoke, with an elegance of expression, I liked him immediately, so I told him to go on and tell me about his thoughts since I had an evening to kill and no place to go...

This slogan, Take it or Leave It, he went on, has been, alas, mine for such a long time that I must give you an explanation of the sense it has for me...

Suddenly this old man, whom at first I found somewhat strange, perhaps nutty or senile, began to interest me...

A votre santé, I said raising my glass to his, please go on...

He took a sip of Pernod, and then, as if telling a story, he began with sadness in his voice...

It started on the 30th of September 1938, the day the Munich accords were signed, that day I saw my father cry, I was fifty-four then, he was eighty, we were far beyond youthfulness, and that day I remembered how I lost my leg in the trenches of Verdun, for France, and I cried with my father, who said to me, I am ashamed, I am ashamed to be French...

I interrupt the old guy to tell him that me too, although much younger than him, just a little boy in 1937, I remember how my father cried in frustration and anger when he was told that he could not go to Spain to fight against Franco's Fascists because he was tubercular...

The old guy nods in a gesture of sympathy and understanding, and goes on with his story...

It reached another plateau of shame in June 1940, during the exodus, when the Germans invaded France by trotting arrogantly around the Maginot line, ah *La Grande Illusion Maginot*...

Ah yes, L'Exode de juin 1940, I interrupt, isn't it amazing how nobody talks about it anymore, as though it never happened, how the shameful debacle of the French army has been swept under the carpet of history, I suppose it's because of what Le Grand General de Gaulle said about the Vichy Government when he returned gloriously, do you remember, *nul et non advenu*, he proclaimed, just like that, as if Pétain's disgraceful government never existed, and with these words he made us believe that France had won the war, and the exodus, the defeat of 1940, the deportation of the Jews, les Maquisards Communistes who were executed during the occupation, and all the other ignominious things that happened between 1940 and 1945, were erased from the books...

But like you, Sir, I have not forgotten that terrifying moment, the exodus...

We left Paris, my parents, sisters and I, in June 1940, first by train, but not very far, the train stopped, just like that, in the middle of nowhere, and so we continued on foot to Normandy with thousands of other people, there were abandoned cars all along the roads, cars and army trucks that ran out of gas, the people were carrying all kinds of stuff, on their backs, on bicycles, on little buggies, my mother was lugging two huge suitcases because my father was too weak to carry them, eventually we reached Argentan, exhausted, starved, frightened...

You probably know that beautiful city in Normandy, it had a splendid Gothic cathedral that was destroyed by the bombardments...

Oh they have rebuilt it, I didn't know, maybe someday I'll go look at it, just to remember, I love those old churches where people go to give themselves the lie...

Anyway, the irony is that when we arrived in Argentan, the Germans were already there, they greeted us with Prussian sneers on their faces, they shouted at us, Achtung, Achtung, as they gathered us on the main square, we thought they were going to shoot us, but instead they gave us some food, I will never forget how impressed I was by their splendid uniforms, they looked so sharp, so military those fucking Germans, especially the officers with their fancy kepis, their boots, and their riding pants, but forgive me for having interrupted you, please go on, you were saying that during the exodus...

During the exodus, the old man begins again while lighting the pipe he took out of his pocket, I saw German and Italian airplanes drop bombs on columns of refugees...

Yes, that's true, I saw that too, I was only a boy then, I was horrified, it was alongside a little road in Normandy that I saw dead people for the first time, real dead people, not fake ones like in the movies, there was blood all over the pavement, I almost fainted, it always happens to me when I see blood, especially my own, I pass out immediately, my mother told me not to look, but I couldn't stop staring at these torn bodies strewn all over the road...

Oh, you saw that too, the old man says banging his fist on the table, so you probably saw how French soldiers, even officers, were pushing refugees out of the way, into

259

the ditches, in order to escape faster, and that day I felt so ashamed, I was fifty-six years old, I'm now seventy-four, but this ugly vision will remain engraved in my memory until my final breath...

Seventy-four, I would have given you sixty-five at most, you're in great shape for your age, in spite of your ... your infirmity...

Thank you, young man, you're too kind, but I'm just an old war cripple, and believe me, I carry these seventy-four years on my shoulders with a lot of shame, even though at one time I was proud of that wound, he said hitting the floor with his wooden leg...

I know how you feel, I said, you would have liked my father, he too was ashamed to live in this country, you should have seen how the French treated him, just because he was a foreigner and a Communist, and you should see how they are treating me, I won't tell you what happened yesterday in this publishing house, I was so angry, me a future world-famous author...

The old man didn't seem to be listening to me as he continued, I cannot recount an entire life of shame, it would be too long and too painful, besides I'm sure your young life is as full of shame as mine...

You can say that again, and you overheard only a small part of my story, maybe someday you'll get to hear the rest, or read it in a book if it ever gets finished and published...

By now the old man was all worked up, but he paused a moment to order a second round of Pernods...

I started to worry about who was going to pay for the drinks...

In any case, he went on, up to the dirty ugly Algerian War and the Vietnam fiasco, not to mention the on-going corruptions, I have not stopped being ashamed of this country that wallows in political turpitude...

Political turpitude, well said, Sir, I totally agree with you, France is riddled with corruption, but you know, it's the same everywhere in the world, I know, I travel a lot...

It's true, the French are arrogant, provincial, cowardly, xenophobic, they hate foreigners, they hate the Jews, the British, the Americans, they hate BBQ sauce, ketchup, they think they are superior, and yet here in France you have delicious fromages, paté de fois gras, French fries, French kisses, free love, rationalism, Notre Dame, the Eiffel Tower, and so much more, where else can you find all that...

The old man didn't seem to pay much attention to what I had just said to bring a little comic relief into the conversation, he continued, they say this is the country of Montaigne, Racine, Voltaire, Balzac, Zola, Proust, Sartre, Camus, Ségalen, it's true, but alas it is also the country of Daladier, Laval, Gamelin, Raynaud, Weygand, Pétain, Touvier, Le Pen, and all those decorated with la Francisque, I am ashamed to have the same nationality as these people, and I'm afraid, yes I'm afraid that...

Well, I interrupted him again, do as I did, leave this stinking country, go to America, not that it's better over there, in America we have McCarthy, Nixon, Agnew, Oli North, Rush Limbaugh, not to mention the Ku Klux Klan, the bigots and the racists, but what can you do, there are people like that everywhere, political clowns and religious fanatics...

Yes I know, the whole world is rotten, so where can one go...

Do you know what the slogan of the politicians was in America during the Vietnam war, Love It or Leave It, well I used to say, Take It or Leave It, and someday I'll write a novel by that title...

Well, that goes for me too, Take It or Leave it, I don't like France anymore, she's not my motherland, she's cruel and perverse...

I couldn't agree more, so do as I did, become a citizen of another country, better yet, become a citizen of the world...

It's not as easy as you think, for years and years, I've been wanting to leave France, but I cannot resolve myself to do so, I admire you for having had the courage to go into exile, whatever your reasons were, do you know that I consulted lawyers to find out if I could renounce my French nationality, and you know what, I learned that in the country of human rights, the country of freedom, equality, fraternity, you don't have the right to renounce your nationality...

That's right, I know, because you see, even I who became an American citizen, for economic reasons, I still have my French nationality, that's why I feel I have the right to criticize, and even insult my native country without the least embarrassment...

In order to become a citizen of another country, I would need to adopt another nationality, but which one, only Iraq or Libya would accept me...

Don't do that, don't get mixed up with Arabs, believe me, I know what I'm talking about, they're all liars, cheaters, quibblers...

It may be so, but these are the only two countries where I could be naturalized, and where I would lose my French nationality, but I cannot bring myself to do this, and for such a dumb reason, these countries have very hot climates, and you see, I suffer from a heart condition, I had open-heart surgery, and I cannot endure heat...

Oh, I'm so sorry, personally I love the heat, I love the desert, that's where I feel the most free...

In any case, young man, please give me another slogan to write on the walls of Verdun, even though I am an old man, I still feel young enough to protest and express my shame, believe me, as a writer you know as well as I do that words don't always have the same meaning, when I say Take It or Leave It, it is not the slogan of shopkeeper or fanatic nationalists, I say it because for me it is the only solution, I do hope you understand what I mean, and suddenly the old man got up, finished his drink in one gulp, shook my hand and left the café dragging his wooden leg behind him...

As I sat there in front of my drink puzzled by his last words, and wondering how the hell I was going to pay for the drinks, I watched him go out the door, and I called out after him, but too late, he was already in the street, Monsieur, Monsieur, there's no cure for shame, believe me, I know...

Well, that's the conversation I had with that old cripple, it was quite a revelation to hear what that outraged Frenchman, that old disabled veteran, had to say about his country...

So now you see why I can't wait to get the hell out of here, and why I can't finish telling you my story...

What...

Oh you want to know what became of my Aunt Rachel...

Well, as I told you yesterday, after Senegal became a free country, she returned to France for good, she lived on the Riviera for a while with a gigolo, I think he was Egyptian, or maybe Pakistani, he smoked oval-shaped cigarettes and always wore a silk scarf around his neck, he must have been a good twenty years younger than my aunt, they spent most of their time in the casinos, I heard that my aunt was quite lucky at the roulette, eventually she moved to Paris, into a fancy apartment near Pigalle, and that's all...

One day she will die, like everyone else, and so will the rest of my aunts and uncles, and do you know what she'll do, I'm speculating here, but knowing her as I knew her, I wouldn't be surprised if she did that, I mean to whom she'll leave her fortune...

No, not to me, nor to my cousins, not even to her brothers and sisters since they'll probably be dead from old age and avarice before Rachel dies, no, she'll leave her entire fortune to the orphanage where she and my mother suffered so much, yes that's exactly what she will do, leave her inheritance to the orphanage, in my mother's memory...

That will be such a beautiful gesture, don't you think, and what a great ending for the novel I will write some day about my Aunt Rachel, what a touching ending it will be...

So that's it, now you know everything, and today is our last time together, but before we part could you tell me your name, who knows, perhaps I will need you again in the future to listen to another one of my stories, so tell me, what's your name, I mean your real name...

No, really, your name is Féderman, I'll be damned, what a coincidence, I know a guy in America with the same name, Federman, but he spells it without the accent, he's quite a character, a gambler, everything he does is a gamble, he is a Jew who survived the Unforgivable Enormity, maybe the two of you are related...

Are you Jewish...

Oh you're not sure, with a name like Féderman, even with the accent, you must be Jewish, well, doesn't matter since you're not a survivor...

The Federman I know in America always says that being a survivor is a joy, an occasion to celebrate, that it should never make you sad, that on the contrary this excess of life relieves you from all responsibilities, personally I don't agree with him, once I even explained to him that my role as a survivor here or over there, in the cities, the countries, in the books I write or will write, my responsibility is to give back some dignity to what has been humiliated by the Unforgivable Enormity...

Well, that's all I have to say, goodbye then, but before we part, I want to ask you something, tell me, should I pay you for having told you my story, or is it you who should pay me for having listened to it...

What, it's free, nobody has to pay, that's great, my stories are free, that's terrific, here, let me embrace you before I go, you've been such a good patient listener...

Goodbye, my friend, take it easy, and as we say in America when starting a new life, **wish me luck...**

ADDENDA

Names of Fictitious People [Invented or Borrowed] in Order of Appearance in the Story

The I of the Storyteller
The Professional Listener
Susan/Sucette [American girlfriend of storyteller]
Darling Moinous [Susan's endearing name for storyteller]
Waiters [passim]
The Multi-Multi-Millionaire Athletes
The Great Fucker Basketball Player
The Masturbator Crap Shooter
The British Girl [temporary girlfriend of storyteller]
Le Neveu de Rameau
Aunt Rachel
Namredef/The Noodler [author of noodle novel]
The Yid/Youpin/Brudny Żyd
The Pollacks
Oedipus
The Mother & Father [of storyteller]
Suzanne/Susannah
Judith/Judy of Detroit
Jacques le Fataliste
Rémond Namredef [storyteller's full name]
The Jews [passim]
Uncle Léon
Aunt Marie
Cousin Marco
Schimele-Bubke-Zinn [another name of storyteller]
Schimele-Bubke [another name of storyteller's father]
The Grandmother
The Grandfather
Moinous [storyteller's best friend]
The Tzar of Russia

Michel Strogoff
Uncle Maurice
Uncle Jean
Aunt Fanny
Aunt Léa
Aunt Sarah
Marguerite [storyteller's mother]
Sarah [storyteller's older sister]
Papa/Tate [storyteller's father]
The Great-grandfather
Fils-de-Tubard [another name of storyteller]
The Communists
The Trotskyists
The Fascists
Jean-Louis Laplume [famous French writer]
Madame la Directrice [Les Éditions de l'Amour Fou]
Madame Trucmuche [Les Éditions de l'Amour Fou]
Monsieur Bouquin [publisher]
Madame Laplume
Ramon Hombre della Pluma [distinguished professor]
Robert Laurent/Robbie [the taxi driver]
Madame Lalouche [the teacher]
Gugusse & Mimile [childhood friends of storyteller]
The Parents of Taxi Driver
Jacqueline [storyteller's younger sister]
Les Amerloques
Les Russkoffs
Josette [wife of taxi driver/childhood friend of storyteller]
Machinchouette [unknown person]
Madame Machinchouette [unknown writer]
Coco [another name of storyteller]
Privat/Privot/Pridevot/Pinot/Pinard [televison host]
Julien Sorel
Fabrice del Dongo
Les Sidis [North Africans]
Adolphe [barman in La Nausée]
Roquentin
Godot

La Comtesse de Montrouge *[Fernandel's mistress]*
Fernandel's Chauffeur
The Christian Martyrs
Les Pétainistes
Les Étrangers
Les Maquisards
Margot *[storyteller's mother]*
Les Malabars
The Pimps
The Gangsters
The Rich Arabs
The White Virgins
The Pashas
Bubbe *[the grandmother]*
Tante Nénette
Le Bon Dieu
Jule & Juliette
Uncle Nathan
The Cousins
The Jewish Beauties from the Old Testament
The Sexless Zombies
The American G.I.s
The Farmer's Wife
The Farmer's Wife's Father-in-law
The Farmer's Wife's Kid
The Husband *[of the farmer's wife]*
The Priest/Le Curé *[Monflanquin]*
The Germans/Krauts/Boches/Doryphores/The
    Mütter-Fuckers
The Displaced Children
The General Public
Bigleux *[the dog on the farm]*
The Black Prince
The Farmers/Hicks/Culs-Terreux
Pétain's Militia
The Légionnaire in the Dream
Marius *[owner of bistro in Montrouge]*
The Gestapo

The French Police
The Schleps
Marius' Brother-in-Law
The Collaborators
The Burglars
The Cops/Les Flics
The Rich Fat Jews
Cousin Giselle
The Rich Snobs
The Concierge of the Ritz
The Elevator Boy of the Ritz
The Chambermaids of the Ritz
The Night Porter of the Ritz
Cyrano
The Receptionist [Les Éditions de l'Amour Fou]
Monsieur Gaston [assistant of Madame la Directrice]
The Disabled French War Veteran/Poilu
The Ku Klux Klan
The Bigots
The Racists
The Political Clowns
The Religious Fanatics
Féderman [the professional listener's name]
Federman [friend of storyteller in America]

Names of Real People [Dead or Alive]
Mentioned in the Story

Walt Disney
Rimbaud
Georges Simenon
Baudrillard
Jean-Paul Sartre
Simone de Beauvoir
Boris Vian
Céline
Hitler
Serge Doubrovsky
Christian Prigent
Diderot
Georges Michel
Voltaire
Michel Serres
Descartes
Jules Verne
Montaigne
Zola
Tommy Flanagan
Kenny Burell
Frank Foster
Charlie Parker/Yardbird
Francis Ponge
Shakespeare
Gilles Deleuze
André Gide
Gaston Gallimard
Marcus Aurelius
Louis-René des Forêts
Charlie Chaplin
Mallarmé
Samuel Beckett/Sam
Flaubert

Boileau
René Char
Racine
La Fontaine
Molière
Corneille
Didier Anzieu
Freud
J.P. Privat
Maurice Blanchot
Stendhal
Sergio Leone
Fernandel
Yeats
Casanova
Rockefeller
Victor Hugo
Paul Célan
Pierre Laval
Maréchal Pétain/Pète-Un
Courbet
Max Jacob
Paul Valéry
Derrida
Lautréamont
Rembrandt
Rubens
Cranach
Picasso
Modigliani
Gauguin
Fragonnard
Signorelli
Ingres
Tintoretto
Poussin
Maillol
Moore

Renoir
Dubuffet
Van Gogh
Holbein
Brueghel
Chassériau
Bellmer
Matisse
Toulouse-Lautrec
Giacometti
Schiele
Magritte
Salvador Dali
Lipschitz
Arp
El Greco
Motherwell
Pissaro
De Koonig
Copley
Tissot
General de Gaulle
Cecil B. De Mille
Fellini
Marcel Cerdan
Johannes Gootfried Herder
Humphrey Bogart
Jacques Ehrmann
Buffon
Gallimard
Peter Worstman
Roland Barthes
Franco
Balzac
Proust
Camus
Ségalen
Daladier

Gamelin
Raynaud
Waygand
Touvier
Le Pen
Senator McCarthy
Nixon
Agnew
Oli North
Rush Limbaugh

Literary Works or Others Mentioned
or Quoted in the Story

A Time of Noodles [novel — Namredef]
Amer Eldorado [novel — Namredef]
The Melting Pot [poetic list — Anonymous]
La Comédie Humaine [novels — Balzac]
Le Neveu de Rameau [novel — Diderot]
Entretiens avec le Professeur Y [novel — Céline]
Bagatelles pour un Massacre [anti-Semitic pamphlet]
L'École des Cadavres [anti-Semitic pamphlet — Céline]
La Question Juive [essay — Sartre]
Les Bancs [novel — Georges Michel]
Tarzan [comics]
Mandrake le Magician [comics]
Les Pieds-Nickelés [comics]
Tintin [comics]
Michel Strogoff [novel — Jules Verne]
Jacques le Fataliste [novel — Diderot]
Ramona [abandoned novel — Namredef]
Before That [poem — Namredef]
Take It or Leave It [novel — Namredef]
Remembering Charlie Parker / or How to Get It Out of
     Your System [fiction — Namredef]
Les Faux-Monnayeurs [novel en abîme — Gide]
Le Bavard [novel — Jean-Louis des Forêts]
Modern Time [film — Charlie Chaplin]
Le Vierge le Vivace et le Bel Aujourd'hui [poem —
     Mallarmé]
Le Monde [newspaper]
La Quinzaine Littéraire [literary magazine]
Le Figaro [newspaper]
Les Lettres Françaises [literary magazine]
Le Cid [quotation — Corneille]
Mémoires en Miettes [prose poem — Namredef]
Le Livre à Venir [criticism — Blanchot]
Le Rouge et le Noir [novel — Stendhal]

La Chartreuse de Parme *[novel — Stendhal]*
Duck You Sucker *[movie — Sergio Leone]*
La Nausée *[novel — Sartre]*
Les Misérables *[novel — Victor Hugo]*
The Bible
The Old Testament
Waiting for Godot *[play — Beckett]*
Maître Pathelin *[medieval farce — Anonymous]*
The Origin of the World *[painting — Courbet]*
A Day of Rare Intensity *[poem — Namredef]*
Le Cimetière Marin *[poem — Valéry]*
TXT *[avant-garde literary magazine]*
Ass *[poetic list — Anonymous]*
Le Cul *[poetic list — Anonymous]*
The Museum of Imaginary Asses *[poem — Namredef]*
The Apocrypha
La Marseillaise *[song — Rouget de Lisle]*
Casablanca *[movie]*
Le Temps des Nouilles *[novel — Namredef]*

Real or Imaginary Places Mentioned in the Story

France
Paris
The Bronx
Boston
Nouillorque [New York City]
Brooklyn
U.S.A.
Parisian Cafés
Las Vegas
Hollywood
Detroit
North Carolina
Montparnasse [artist neighborhood in Paris]
Rue Delambre [Montparnasse]
La Coupole [café in Montparnasse]
La Belle France
Olympic Stadium [Berlin]
Manchester [England]
Westend Avenue [New York City]
Riverside Drive [New York City]
Susan's Apartment [New York City]
England
Oklahoma
Kentucky
Liverpool [England]
Central Park [New York City]
Trifouillis-la-Tirelire [elsewhere]
Sans-Sous [elsewhere]
Motown/Shitcity [Detroit]
Shoe Store [Detroit]
Judy's Apartment [Detroit]
Le Métro [Paris]
La Boulangerie [Montrouge]
University of New York [elsewhere]
Montrouge [suburb of Paris]

Marie's Apartment [*second floor, 4 Rue Louis Rolland*]
Porte D'Orléans [*Paris*]
The Storyteller's Apartment [*New York City*]
The Courtyard [*of building, 4 Rue Louis Rolland*]
The Storyteller's Apartment [*third floor — 4 Rue Louis Rolland*]
The W.C. in the Courtyard
The Clinic/Le Dispensaire de Montrouge
The Ghettos of Detroit
Parc Montsouris [*Paris*]
The Atlantic Ocean
The New World
The Far East
Korea
Chrysler Factory [*Detroit*]
The Blue Bird [*jazz club — Detroit*]
Shimbashi [*Tokyo*]
La Sorbonne [*Paris*]
Columbia University [*New York City*]
Manhattan
The Hudson River
Rue des Belles-Feuilles [*Paris*]
16ème Arrondissement [*Paris*]
Chicago
San Francisco
Los Angeles
Europe
Far West
East Coast
West Coast
Place Denfert Rochereau [*Paris*]
Avenue D'Orléans [*Paris*]
Chez Marius [*bistro in Montrouge*]
Orly Airport [*Paris*]
L'Autoroute du Sud
Vanves [*suburb of Paris*]
Avenue du Général Leclerc [*Paris*]
Jean-Louis Laplume's Apartment

Place d'Italie *[Paris]*
Apostrophe *[ORTF studio in Paris]*
Aunt Marie's Dining Room
Rue de Bagneux *[Montrouge]*
La Zone/The Slums *[Paris]*
Les Champs-Élysées *[Paris]*
North Africa
Le Périphérique *[highway around Paris]*
Le Rendez-Vous des Cheminots *[La Nausée]*
The Staircase *[4 Rue Louis Rolland]*
La Seine
Ancient Rome
La Maison Rothschild *[orphanage]*
Marseilles
Rue Vercingetorix
Le14ème Arrondissement *[Paris]*
Poland
Calcutta/Quel-Cul-Ta
Singapore
Bangkok
Manila
Tokyo
Hong Kong
The Ocean Liner
La Zone Libre/The Free Zone
The Farm in Southern France
Lot-et-Garonne *[French Province]*
Villeneuve-sur-Lot
Montflanquin
Germany/Vaterland
German Factories
The Montflanquin Church
The Farmhouse
The Barn
The Fields/Woods
The Shit-House
The Farm Kitchen
The Loft

The Staircase to the Loft
Le Bordel [rue St.-Denis]
La Bastille
Chez Jule & Juliette [restaurant]
Provence
Le Château de Bandol [Provence]
Le Cimetière de Bagneux
Le Vel d'Hiv [stadium in Paris]
The Gas Chambers
Le Cinéma [Place de la République—Montrouge]
Dakar [Senegal]
The French Colonies
The Sidewalk in Front of Building [4 Rue Louis Rolland]
Aunt Rachel's Hotels [Dakar]
Boulevard Sébastopol [Paris]
Le Lido [night club in Paris]
Mimi Pinson [night club in Paris]
Le Monocle [cabaret in Paris]
Le Dancing de la Coupole [Paris]
The Ritz Hotel [Paris]
Place Vendôme [Paris]
Aunt Rachel's Suite [Ritz Hotel]
The Orient
The American Embassy [Paris]
Rue de l'Ancienne-Comédie [Paris]
Rue de l'Odéon [Paris]
The Office of Monsieur Gaston
Place des Vosges [Paris]
Munich [Germany]
The Maginot Line
Argentan [Normandy]
The Roads of Normandy
Iraq
Libya
Cannes
Pigalle
America

CHRONOLOGY OF THE STORY